Lucy took a step toward him and pointed a finger at his chest. "This isn't over, Flynn, not by a long shot." To Mrs. Duncan, she said, "There's got to be a way out of this mess and I promise I'll find it." With that, she blew out of the room with the screen door banging and her threats echoing through the rafters of the old log structure.

Ian angled his head to watch her storm down the path among the pine trees. Her feet were moving so fast that she was sending up tiny clouds of dust in her wake. Her ponytail danced in syncopation over the part of her back exposed by the tank top, and her cute little behind pumped nicely over the long, tanned legs protruding from navy shorts.

Interesting woman, for someone with nothing better to do than swim with children all day. Obviously, she needed adult attention.

Once the dust settled, Mrs. Duncan returned to her chair. "Oh my, I was afraid of that. Lucy, and God knows I love her, has quite the temper."

A grin spread over Ian's features. That had been refreshing. She'd called him pompous. Self-serving. Well, maybe, but Lucy Mitchell didn't pose a threat to him or to Northland Progression in the least. Of course, it would be interesting if she tried. This place might not be such a bore after all.

Moonlight Bay

by

Tess Morrison

*To Herri –
one of my
newest fans –
Tess Morrison*

This is a work of fiction. Names, characters, places, and incidents are either the product of the author's imagination or are used fictitiously, and any resemblance to actual persons living or dead, business establishments, events, or locales, is entirely coincidental.

Moonlight Bay

COPYRIGHT © 2007 by Tess Morrison

All rights reserved. No part of this book may be used or reproduced in any manner whatsoever without written permission of the author or The Wild Rose Press except in the case of brief quotations embodied in critical articles or reviews.
Contact Information: info@thewildrosepress.com

Cover Art by *Tamra Westberry*

The Wild Rose Press
PO Box 708
Adams Basin, NY 14410-0706
Visit us at www.thewildrosepress.com

Publishing History
First Champagne Rose Edition, 2008
Print ISBN 1-60154-020-5

Published in the United States of America

Dedication

For Tom

Chapter One

An annoying prick to his right arm sent Ian Flynn's tolerance level dangerously high. He slapped at the mosquito drawing its noontime libation and missed, of course. The annoying little speck flew off, buzzing a satisfied, lazy tune on the golden ray of afternoon sun that struggled through a disgustingly streaked window. Damn it all, he'd forgotten how many blasted mosquitoes lived in this godforsaken part of Wisconsin. And damn it all again, was Mrs. Duncan ever going to resurface?

One hour. That was all he had before a telephone conference with his colleagues, and he was at the mercy of some disorganized old crone. All he'd wanted was another walk through the property to assess his plans to redirect the driveway. Instead, the old woman had pulled him into the lodge office under the guise of "something important" to show him.

Old people and kids. He avoided them whenever possible, and now he was smack in the middle of both. Normally he was a man to stand his ground, never to be deterred from his path to success. But at the moment he found himself squelching the surge of anxious energy that made him want to bolt.

He'd assumed Mrs. Duncan would have whatever that "something important" thing was at her fingertips. He'd assumed wrong. It amazed him that this child-infested camp had not been on the auction block long before he took notice of it, considering the sorry state of the books.

From the adjacent room, the shuffling of papers resounded in a cacophony of disorganization. From the disheveled appearance of the lodge office, he wasn't holding much hope for the recovery of the papers she sought. Her battered oak desk was a heap of paperwork and—what the hell—pinecones. Even the large photograph of, he could only guess, Mr. Duncan was askew on the log-hewn wall. With a speculative eye he studied the black-and-white likeness of the camp's founder. Henry Duncan's face was one of calm and reserve, and his eyes held an infinite patience. Must have been how he dealt with his wife, poor guy.

Ian swung his head in the direction of the noise. "You all right?"

A high-pitched warble answered, "Yes, yes, yes, I'm just fine. Left my brain somewhere down the track, I'm afraid. I'll be right there." More shuffling noises, the slamming of a metal drawer, and, unbelievably, more shuffling.

Ian shook his head as he massaged the bridge of his nose. Patience had never been a virtue for him, nor an even temper when it was tested as Mrs. Duncan was managing.

He unclenched his jaw and asked, "Are you sure you don't need some assistance?"

"Oh, goodness, no." Her chortle sent Ian's blood pressure up a point or two.

Breathe, just breathe. She could still change her mind and blow the whole deal.

He stopped massaging and turned his attention to the dirty window and the lake beyond. Lacy birch branches and massive evergreens framed the azure-jeweled lake in the afternoon sun. Even through his momentary anxiety he could see the beauty this setting offered, not to mention the tranquility, once the kids were shipped off. The money this sale would bring Northland Progression almost caused him to chuckle out loud. That is, if he wasn't so annoyed and his head hadn't begun to pound.

This deal could be one of the crowning achievements of his development firm. He dug his hands into the back pockets of his Dockers and, in an attempt to keep from bursting into the adjacent room to rifle through the files himself, allowed his imagination free rein as dreams of what could be played out before him. Cedar-sided condos, tennis courts, racquetball, and a spa. Plans for a golf course were well under way. The earning potential was mind-boggling.

Two small heads flashed under the window, causing

Ian a start, just as another mosquito bounced off his nose. He swiped at it, missed again, and hit his hand on the metal filing cabinet next to the window.

"Damn!" He grimaced and checked to make sure he still had skin on his knuckles, which he did. He waved the injured hand to chase away the pain and bit back an expletive.

"You say something, Mr. Flynn?" Lida Mae Duncan's chubby face and spectacled eyes, crowned by a silvery froth of curls, peered around the doorway, then disappeared again.

"Did you find what you were looking for? Need I remind you of the meeting I have in less than an hour?" He checked his watch for dramatic affect, although she wasn't watching, nor did she appear to care.

A snow globe was perched atop a stack of papers on the corner of her desk. It was one of those cheap plastic ones. An angel cradling a young child sat amid the water on the inside. Ian hadn't seen one of those in years. He tipped it on its top and watched as the snowflakes gathered in the bottom. He set it down atop a paper mountain and watched as the snowflakes wafted in swirls about the figures. He'd given his sister one of these once, a lifetime ago.

"At the risk of sounding redundant, I repeat, my meeting is in less than an hour, and I have to—"

"I know you're in a rush and I apologize, but I think I've found what I've been looking for." More shuffling. "Oh, yes, I did. Right here in front of my big nose all the time." A metal drawer slammed shut, and she came waddling out from behind the door, reminding him of a California Raisin in her purple sweatsuit. She pushed dark-rimmed glasses up her pug nose, aimed her backside at the wooden chair behind the desk, and squeezed into it. In her hands she cradled a large, leather-bound book about the size of a photo album. Photographs? She'd wasted his time for a walk down memory lane?

She waved him forward with a chubby hand. "Come here, come."

Ian rolled his eyes and stood before the desk.

Mrs. Duncan pulled her glasses down on her nose and spied him over the rims. "Now, Mr. Flynn, humor me,

I'm old."

A weary sigh escaped him. "I'm not going to fit in that walk-through of the property, am I?"

Her face expanded in a smile adorned by the twinkling in her eyes. "Probably not."

Why had he stopped here? He could have simply bypassed the office and trekked the property on his own.

"I want to show you something." She gingerly patted the worn cover of the album. "This is our history, and I think it's important you understand what you're getting."

"Is this really necessary?" He sucked in a breath and felt his hands fist.

"Yes, it is. This is my prerequisite for signing the final papers. Like I said, humor me." Something in her eyes told him he'd better do just that.

The screen door banged, and two ragtag boys exploded into the room, followed by a furry mass resembling a mangy English sheepdog with a twisted red rag tied around its neck. This was not a good sign.

"Mrs. Duncan, Mrs. Duncan," the boys shouted in unison, shoving each other at the same time. The taller of the two looked to be Hispanic and had a bashful air about him. The shorter had freckles, unruly sandy hair, and "scrapper" written all over his wiry frame. The dog nearly bowled the two over as he plowed his way into the room.

"What's going on?" Mrs. Duncan's expression was one of concern while she replaced the cover of the album and Ian felt the muscles in his shoulders tighten.

This was unbelievable. He drew a hand over his face and groaned.

Mrs. Duncan relieved her nose of the glasses, her small eyes narrowed on the boys. "What is the big to-do here?"

The taller of the two spoke first. "The soda machine is busted again, Mrs. Duncan. All us kids wants ta try the new orange kind, but we can't get the machine to take any coins."

The shorter boy elbowed in front of his companion. "Yeah, my quarter just slid on through. Pissed me off, it did. This is the second time this week. My dad would crap if he knew he was payin' big bucks for this place, and we can't even get us a damn can of soda."

Ian did his best to stifle a grin and turned his attention to the view beyond the window. Oh, what the hell, this was entertaining. He turned from the window to the two ruffians.

Mrs. Duncan appeared absolutely poleaxed. She regained her wits, set the album aside, and planted her hands on the desk. "Jonah Bates, is that any way to talk? You watch your mouth, young man," she said, shaking with indignation. "This is a good Christian camp, and we don't allow such talk. My goodness, where do you learn that kind of language?" She shook her head. "Never mind, I don't want to know."

Jonah Bates jammed his hands into his baggy shorts, rolled his eyes, and turned his freckled nose away from them.

The taller boy looked apologetic, although he'd been completely innocent. He slunk toward the door. "Sorry, Mrs. Duncan."

"That's all right, Carlos. You did nothing wrong." The glasses returned to her nose, and she lowered a reprimanding glare on Jonah as she moved around the desk.

He met her gaze and shrugged, then raised his chin in Ian's direction. "That your car out there? The red one?"

"Yes, the car is mine." *Little urchin better keep his hands off it if he knows what's good for him.*

"You wanna take me for a ride?" The kid gave him a deadpan stare.

"Not particularly." Ian had to admire the kid's guts. Something in the recalcitrant boy's no-nonsense delivery beckoned to a memory of the child he'd once been. A child he'd left behind, never to be dredged out of hiding. The revelation caused a prickle of anxiety he swiftly tucked away.

"Figures." The boy flashed him a disgusted look, and Ian felt thoroughly admonished. "Hey, Mrs. Duncan, what about the soda machine? You gonna fix it or not?"

Mrs. Duncan eyed the clock on the wall. "It's not even noon yet. You boys shouldn't be drinking soda this early anyway. It's against camp rules. I'd gander a guess that the machine is unplugged to discourage anyone getting soda before snack-time at three." She waggled a finger at them.

Jonah's shoulders slumped in defeat. "Oh, all right." To Carlos, he said, "Come on, let's get outta here. Damn, stupid rules."

Mrs. Duncan gasped. "Jonah." She was completely ignored.

The screen door banged behind the two boys. As they sauntered away, Ian was amused to hear Carlos say, "Well, Jonah, ya shouldn't a put that slug in there. You're gonna break that machine yet." And they were gone. Only the dog remained, panting, his tongue hanging out. His gaze darted between his owner and Ian.

"Now, Gabe," Mrs. Duncan addressed the mutt, "you be a good dog and sit in the corner until we're done, and then we'll go for that walk." She peered over her glasses at Ian. "Actually, Gabe walks me, but I pretend I'm in control." She chuckled and patted the dog's shaggy head before returning to her desk.

Patience, Ian, patience. He thought of Jonah Bates and smiled. Then he thought of his meeting, and anxiety washed over him once again.

"Now, where was I? Oh yes, the album." She picked up a bunch of papers and shuffled them into a neat stack. Gabe padded over to Ian and stood before him with hopeful eyes, ears pricked.

Ian leveled a gaze on him. "What?" The dumb thing kept grinning its doggy grin up at him. "Don't you have a corner you could occupy?"

"You say something, Mr. Flynn?"

"No, just talking to the dog." The dog came closer. Ian stepped back to avoid a tongue-wash.

"Oh, that's nice of you. Gabe certainly likes to make new friends. You know"—she peered at Ian over her glasses—"I think he likes you. He must sense something in you. Dogs do that."

Ian looked down into big doggy eyes. "Not gonna happen, buddy. I'm not a dog lover."

"Oh, everyone's a dog lover. Do you have children, Mr. Flynn?" She pulled the cumbersome, leather-bound book before her and opened the cover.

"No." *Hell no.*

"Too bad." The older woman tsk-tsked. *Why did old*

women feel the need to do that? "Maybe you should reconsider."

Just then, the screen door banged again, and a tall, slender female strode in. "Have you seen Jonah and Carlos?" She stood before them, hands on hips. "Those two little bandits have run off on me for the last time." She blew out a huff of frustration.

What the hell. Was this some damn conspiracy? Ian realized he was clenching his jaw so tightly that his teeth were getting sore. This tall, gangly thing in front of him didn't have a clue how to politely knock. No, she barged right in. At least the urchins before her had the excuse of immaturity. This woman, well, she needed to learn a thing or two.

Mrs. Duncan closed the cover of the book again and Ian clenched his jaw, again. Blood pumped through his temples. His eyes narrowed on the intruder as though she were a clay pigeon. She wasn't only gangly, she was plain as well. Her hair was tied severely into a ponytail at the back of her head and her face a bit too long. Not a lot to offer as far as curves go, either. She did appear to be athletic. That was something in her favor.

"Why yes, we have. They were in here only a moment ago complaining about the soda machine not working. I reminded them that it was not time for snacks just yet, and then they ran off again." Mrs. Duncan gave a wave of her hand toward the screen door. "As you can imagine, Jonah was not very happy."

"Ooh, those two wear my patience to the max." The young woman brought a slender hand to her forehead and massaged lightly.

"I'll bet if you hurry, you can catch them. They went in the direction of the lake," Ian interjected from his corner, hoping she'd take the bait. The young woman's chestnut ponytail swung as she turned in his direction. "Really, miss, maybe you should scurry along before they cross the county line."

The woman's sable eyes narrowed on him, and for a moment he had the feeling she was going to vault over the desk and wring his neck. The change that anger made in her features was definitely interesting. Fire flashed in her eyes, veins pulsed in her slender neck, and her jaw set in a hard line. She would definitely be a handful for the poor sap stuck with her.

"Ah, Lucy." Mrs. Duncan appeared to be squirming in her seat. "Honey, this is Ian Flynn." Her eyes shifted nervously to Ian. "Ian, this is Lucy Mitchell. Lucy's our swim instructor, among other things. She's very talented with the children, and they just love her." Her gaze shifted between the two.

It was obvious that Mrs. Duncan was attempting to calm the waters in advance, but why? The business he had was with her, and no one else.

A brief silence ensued while Ms. Mitchell's face softened ever so slightly. Then she surprised him. She stepped forward and thrust a hand in his direction.

"Mr. Flynn." Her gaze was direct, self-assured.

Ian took her hand in his and noted the firm handshake she offered. "Miss Mitchell, nice to meet you." Unfortunately, his voice couldn't disguise his annoyance. It wasn't nice to meet her. It was a thorn in his impatient side.

Lucy returned her hands to her hips and shifted her weight to one leg, looking him up and down. "Sorry to have interrupted. Are you a friend of Lida's?"

Before he could answer, Mrs. Duncan quickly jumped from her chair. "Nooo, no, he's not." She flashed him a brief smile. "Well, he is now. Lucy, honey, there's something you need to know." The woman was clearly nervous. Hell, she was nearly shaking.

Ian had the feeling she was about to drop a bombshell on this latest intruder, and, personally, he'd love to see the reaction, but there simply wasn't time for unscheduled drama at the moment.

"Maybe you should grab yourself a chair. We have something to discuss." Mrs. Duncan's hands patted the air as though she were attempting to calm the situation. Lucy Mitchell, on the other hand, continued to stand before them, with distrusting eyes.

"I *really* don't have time for this," he said, hopeful she'd leave.

Lida Duncan ignored him. She slowly lowered herself into her chair, continuing to keep her eyes on Lucy as one would a storm-threatening cloud. "There's an empty chair against the wall behind you." Her voice hitched. "Go ahead, have a seat."

Lucy crossed her arms over her chest and concern knit her brows. "No thanks. What's going on?" Her eyes questioned Ian. He had the distinct impression the next few minutes were not going to be pretty at all.

"Well..." Mrs. Duncan avoided eye contact with Lucy. "You know we've been having a hard time making ends meet lately."

"Yes, I know," Lucy answered in a measured, guarded tone.

"The food distributor has raised his rates, the taxes have gone up, and most of the cabins need work. You know that. Why, Willow and Bear are in bad need of roofing, and I don't know where the money will come from. It's so hard to find counselors to work for the little we can pay. It's...it's just getting to be too much."

The woman did indeed look pitiful, but this was business and no place for emotion. In another setting, Ian just might feel a bit sorry for her.

"Mr. Flynn, here, is going to help us out of this mess."

Lucy raised her eyes to him once again. "Are you a banker? I don't believe I've seen you at any of the local banks. Or maybe from the state? We must be eligible for a grant from the state or the fed, or possibly a small business loan."

Ian opened his mouth to answer, but Mrs. Duncan broke in. "No, he owns a development company out of Madison." She delivered the words and then shrunk back in her chair.

"Development company? What? I don't understand." Lucy angled her head to one side, her eyes piercing Ian. The daggers she was sending told him she had at last begun to comprehend the situation.

"Honey, his company is going to buy the camp." Lida recoiled further into the chair, if that was even possible.

"Buy the camp? Buy the camp." She said the words slowly, deliberately, as though she were deciphering the meaning, nodding her head as she did so. The air crackled with tension. "Buy...the...camp." She blew out a breath, swung her eyes from Ian's to Lida's, and angled her body toward the woman behind the desk. Her face seemed to soften, although the veins sticking out in her neck spoke otherwise.

"Lida, this place was the dream you and Henry built together. How can you let that go? I knew times were tight, but I didn't realize it was that bad. There must be something we can do. You can't give it up so easily."

"I didn't want to burden you with all this, but we're in a bad state of affairs. Henry was the one who took care of the business side of this. I was in love with the children and didn't concern myself with the rest. Since we didn't have any children of our own, they were our family, you all were. Still are. But I've no head for the business end, and I'm getting too old to worry about it anymore. I simply can't do it."

Ian glanced at his watch for dramatic effect. Again, no one cared.

"Lida, you can't," Lucy said. "Listen to me, you've just bitten off too much. We'll get you some help. You're trying to take on too much. You've been doing all the cooking like you always have, with all of Henry's duties piled on you now, as well. We can hire a cook or an office manager. I know there's a solution. You simply can't sell the camp."

"Yes, dear, I can. I have to." Mrs. Duncan sniffled. She began to rummage through her drawers, pulled out a tissue, and dabbed under her glasses. "This has been an awful decision to make. I know I've let you down, but I have to do this. I have to."

"Look, I'll buy the camp." Lucy stuck an indignant chin out before her and straightened her stick of a body, hands on her hips. Ian pressed his lips together to stifle the guffaw that nearly escaped at her ridiculous bravado.

"Oh, honey"—Mrs. Duncan attempted a smile—"you're a schoolteacher. How could you possibly buy the camp? I can't afford to give it away, but if I could, you'd be the one I'd give it to. No, this is what I have to do."

This was all so touching. Ian crossed his arms and blew out a weary breath. Lucy's body remained in place. It was clearly evident this woman was not going to give in easily, but it didn't matter. This was a done deal.

"There has to be a solution. There has to be." He watched a creeping blush work its way up Lucy's long neck as she swung her gaze in his direction. Sparked by the fire of anger, her eyes flared to a deep bronze. To her credit, she kept her mouth shut. Good thing.

Lida cleared her throat. "There is, honey, and that's where Mr. Flynn here fits in."

Ian couldn't hide his amusement. This Lucy woman was a real character. The daggers she was sending his way were almost comical. He returned her glare with as close to an expression of pure innocence as he could muster, which was a stretch for him to begin with, but produced the desired effect. She was infuriated all the more.

She turned to the screen door, her back to Ian and Mrs. Duncan. "Lida, what will you do? Where will you go? This is your home."

Mrs. Duncan honked into the tissue. "I'm going to go live with my sister, Thelma, in Alabama. She's got a room all ready for me." She honked again, and Ian winced at the sound. "It'll be good for me. I'm so sorry."

This melodrama was costing him precious time. He was tempted to give Ms. Mitchell a helpful shove through the screen door and be on his way.

Lucy swung back toward them, her gaze slicing through Ian as though he was the devil incarnate before it softened and settled on Mrs. Duncan. "Is there anything I can do to make you change your mind?"

"No, there's not." She tossed the tissue and took out another to pat her reddened cheeks. "Please tell Ellie for me. You two mean so much to me."

Ian decided it was high time he expedite this conversation. "The paperwork is all but signed, sealed, and delivered, Miss Mitchell. My company, Northland Progression, will assume ownership at the end of the season. We won't touch a thing until that time, so you've got the rest of the summer to wrap things up and honor those who've paid for time here. I think that's more than fair."

Lucy crossed her arms again. All softness in her features vanished when she angled her head to one side to consider his words. "Somehow, I can't see some big corporation running a summer camp for kids. Excuse me, but you don't strike me as a kid-oriented type of guy, *Mr. Flynn.*" She nearly spat his name back at him.

"That's because, *Miss Mitchell*, we plan to level the camp and build condominiums here. Lots of them, a golf course too, tennis courts perhaps." Okay, that was a rather severe way of putting it, but he honestly didn't feel the need to justify the company's plans to her or anyone else. He watched the fire glowing in her eyes take on a new intensity.

"Condos?" She looked as though he'd somehow sucked the air from the room.

He shifted his weight and crossed his arms over his chest. "Yes, condos. It'll mean quite a boon to this area as far as tourist dollars go." The veins on her neck were popping quite nicely now, and the bronze fire that lit her eyes was nearly a spectacular shade of auburn. Of course, neither compared to the nipples rising through her tank top.

"You mean to tell me you're going to rip up this beautiful piece of lake property and cover it with condominiums." She shook her head as though she didn't believe him. "That's the most ridiculous thing I've ever heard. This camp is important to the economy of this area as well. People from all over the Midwest bring their children here. Why, we even have a boy from New Jersey and a girl from Kentucky this year. To bulldoze this down in the way of progress and tourist dollars is nothing but the wealthy trying to feather their pockets. You can't do this. I won't let you."

Her eyes moved to the window, and she drew a ragged breath and brought a hand to her mouth as though she was attempting to calm the emotion threatening to spill forth. The hand at her mouth clenched into a fist and her eyes returned to him with an expression of new purpose.

"I've spent the past fifteen years of my life here—first as a camper and then as a counselor. I've seen this camp grow and thrive in ways you could never understand. Henry Duncan's death was a blow, but we can survive. I know we can." She pointed a finger in his direction. "This cannot happen. The kids rely on having this camp as a refuge, a safe haven, every summer. We cannot give up so easily."

"Don't you mean *you* rely on this camp every

summer? Maybe it's time you get a life."

The accusatory finger pointed his way again. "Why, you pompous, self-serving jerk. How dare you insinuate anything about *my* life? You don't know a thing about me, and you don't know a thing about what a place like this means to a child. I'll fight you every step of the way on this, and don't think I won't." Flames of indignation shot from her eyes.

Ian didn't for a moment doubt that he'd have a fight on his hands with Lucy Mitchell although, at this point, there was nothing to fight about. The deal was done for all intents and purposes. Of course, the final papers hadn't been officially signed, but he didn't expect any trouble whatsoever. The firm offered Mrs. Duncan what she regarded as a generous price for the property, one that would take care of her sufficiently in her retirement.

Mrs. Duncan stood at her desk once again and put her hands out. "Now, let's not get so upset. Lucy, I know this is a shock to you. I had every intention of telling you this very week, but, well, you have stumbled into it, and I know it'll take some adjustment. I can't do this anymore, and Mr. Flynn's company is willing to take the burden from me."

Lucy took a step toward him and pointed a finger at his chest. "This isn't over, Flynn, not by a long shot." To Mrs. Duncan, she said, "There's got to be a way out of this mess and I promise I'll find it." With that she blew out of the room with the screen door banging and her threats echoing through the rafters of the old log structure.

Ian angled his head to watch her storm down the path among the pine trees. Her feet were moving so fast that she was sending up tiny clouds of dust in her wake. Her ponytail danced in syncopation over the part of her back exposed by the tank top, and her cute little behind pumped nicely over long, tanned legs protruding from navy shorts.

Interesting woman, for someone with nothing better to do than swim with children all day. Obviously, she needed adult attention.

Once the dust settled, Mrs. Duncan returned to her chair. "Oh my, I was afraid of that. Lucy, and God knows I love her, has quite the temper."

A grin spread over Ian's features. That had been refreshing. She'd called him pompous. Self-serving. Well, maybe, but Lucy Mitchell didn't pose a threat to him or to Northland Progression in the least. Of course, it would be interesting if she tried. This place might not be such a bore after all.

Chapter Two

"Ooh, the nerve." Lucy stormed along the path that followed the shoreline of Balsam Lake. Her feet could barely carry her fast enough. Anger propelled her more powerfully than a tank of rocket fuel. "He thinks I need a life...city...ass. I'll show him."

She left the path and cut through a stand of birch trees, each footfall creating a depression in the soft princess pine moss carpeting the forest floor. She climbed the slant of land from the lakeside toward Otter Cabin, which rested at the top of the hill and faced the water.

As she approached, Jule Sutherland bounced down the steps of the cabin, the screen door slamming behind her. When she saw Lucy heading in her direction, she stopped abruptly.

"Hey, Luce, where you been?" She flicked a blond strand from her youthful freckled face, her blue eyes wide, as though she sensed trouble.

Smart girl.

"Didn't I tell you I was going to the office? I know I did. I really wish people around here would listen to me." Lucy was seething inside and dying to rip someone's head off. Unfortunately, Jule didn't deserve to be the recipient, but oh well, someone had to be. Lucy buttoned her lip and rushed by Jule as she climbed the seven wooden steps toward the screened-in porch.

"No, you didn't," Jule answered, her brow furrowed. She hopped to the edge of the steps to clear Lucy's path. "You said you were taking the kids over to the nature walk to search for frogs for the frog-jumping contest tonight."

"The frog search was a bust. Jonah and Carlos took off on me, so we had to stop to look for those two little snots." She pulled on the handle of the screen door only to have it come off in her hand. "Damn." She threw the unfortunate knob into the forest.

"Whoa." Jule's eyes grew large.

Lucy blew out a puff of air and attempted to rub away the raging in her brain. She sucked in a slow, steady breath of pine-scented air. "I'm sorry, Jule. There's some stuff happening at the moment that has me a bit rattled."

"Anything I can do?" Jule came up two steps. The perfect innocence usually adorning her face replaced with concern.

"Nope, I'm fine. Thanks for asking after I railed at you like that." She stopped rubbing; it wasn't going to work. She sat on the top step, resting her elbows on her knees. Jule sat alongside her. "Have you seen our two partners in crime?" she asked after a moment to focus her thoughts on the task at hand.

"They came back to the cabin a few minutes ago, and I took them over to join the others at the lodge for crafts. You can imagine how excited they were about that. Pouted all the way. Anyway, I just got back myself." She waved a fly away from her face.

"Thanks, I owe you one." Lucy's eyes scanned the perimeter of the lake before them. She tried to picture the serenity cluttered with boxy condos, her precious pine trees viciously uprooted, the rolling hillsides hideously gutted, the deer, squirrels and chipmunks run from the property, the ferns and wildflowers plowed under. Her stomach lurched at the thought.

"You don't owe me anything. That's what I'm here for. You sure you're okay? You look like you could slay a dragon right now, or have a good cry." Jule nudged her knee to knee.

Lucy offered a half-hearted smile. A dragon, you could say that. A dragon by the name of Ian Flynn, and slaying his plans was exactly what she had in mind. She could still feel his steely blue eyes upon her. All she needed was a good plan and a chance to get over the shock of Lida's bombshell.

"That obvious, huh?" Damn if she didn't feel her chin quiver just a bit. Just nerves, anger, rage. That's all. She clenched her jaw to gain control.

"Like, yeah." Jule bobbed her head in confirmation, her blond bangs swinging from side to side. "Very obvious."

Just then the revving of a sports car captured their attention, and the two turned their heads in the direction of the road just as a flash of red sliced through the birch trees and disappeared over the rise in the forest. Lucy felt her heart rate increase another ten points. There was only one person the car could belong to.

"Who was that?" Jule asked. "You don't see many cars like that around here. Oooo, I bet it was that piece of eye candy I saw down at the lodge earlier."

"Eye candy?" Sometimes she had to remind herself that Jule was only twenty-one years old. At twenty-nine, Lucy felt more like her parent at times.

"Lida was waving this guy into her office. I gotta tell you, he was one hot property. Kind of old though. I'd guess somewhere in his mid-thirties."

"I don't know who it could have been," Lucy lied. Hot property, eye candy. If she had to hear one more word about him, she was going to puke. "Anyway, are you going to be running down to the office at all?"

"Yep. I have to refill my first-aid kit. I seem to have some accident-prone kids this year. Heidi cut her big toe on a clam and used the last of the antibiotic cream."

"That little girl is one trauma after another. Anyway, please let Lida know I'm going into town and will be back later, in case she's looking for me. Smokey the Bear's visit cancelled my two o'clock class, but I'll be back for the four, so make sure you tell her."

"Don't worry, she'll get the message." Jule was thoughtful for a moment. "Is everything okay with Lida?"

"Lida? Why do you ask?" Lucy was feeling a bit foolish that Jule seemed to know something was in the air when she had not. Lida was planning to sell this place and never bothered to mention a word to her. It stung. The woman certainly didn't need Lucy's approval, but this camp had been her refuge for nearly as long as she could remember. Lucy, at times, thought of Moonlight Bay as her second home. With feelings akin to shame, she wondered how could she have been so blind to what was happening around her.

"Well, she seems a bit distracted," Jule said. "Not her old chipper self, you know? I really think something is wrong."

"She's just got things on her mind, that's all. Nothing that can't be fixed." *Or slayed.* There had to be a solution out there somewhere.

"I hope you're right. I heard Kimmy and Brian say they're worried too."

Lucy placed a hand on Jule's knee and gave a squeeze. "Everything is fine, trust me. I think she's missing Henry more than normal. Tell Kimmy and Brian and all the other counselors not to worry. Everything will be fine."

"We'll have to think of something to cheer her up." Leave it to Jule. Ever the little cheerleader. "But now I'm worried about you as well. You look like you could use a break." Jule's face showed genuine concern.

"More than you know." Lucy stared off in the direction of the lake. "You have no idea." Jule studied her for a moment. A long, uncomfortable moment. "I'm fine, Jule, really."

Jule's face brightened. "Get out of here for a while. Go into town and see your sister. I'll make sure Lida knows you've left."

"Thanks. Like I said, I'll be back for the four and then the frog-jumping contest. I promised I'd help." A trip into town was just what she needed. If anyone would understand, it would be Ellie. Lucy needed to vent, to clear her head, devise a plan to deal with the dragon, and if she had to slay him, so be it.

****

Ian clicked his cell phone shut, tossed it onto the bed among his papers, and eased his body into the low-backed, dismal-brown motel room chair. He crossed his ankles on the corner of the bed and cradled the back of his head in his hands. Closing his eyes, he allowed a self-satisfied grin to spread across his face. The phone conference had gone as well as he had anticipated.

His cell phone buzzed and he stretched to retrieve it.

"Yes, Zelda." Finally, a sane person to talk to.

"Well, hello to you too. Did you forget how to check your messages? I was beginning to wonder if you've been abducted or left for dead somewhere. You know, you do have a business to run and people who care about you, although I don't know why."

Just the sound of her voice made him smile. Zelda Vargas had been his secretary for nearly seven years now. She was professional, classy, and more than willing to bust his chops when he needed it. That's why he liked her.

When she had walked into his office looking for a chance, he'd been impressed with her calm, her manners, and the stylish way she dressed. She'd worked her way out of the projects and through school all on her own. Not an easy task for a single black woman with a young son to care for. Ian admired that. Zelda was more than capable and ready with a wide, generous smile, but guarded his business like a rabid bulldog.

"Anything new?" he asked. Hearing her voice chased the tension from his shoulders and eased the pounding in his head.

"We received the wire transfer from the Riley Group, and the Petroskis are waiting to set up a meeting to discuss another hotel in Lake Geneva. Do you want me to set a date?"

He could hear her penciling notes, always the multitasker. The two of them were a good match. "No, I don't want to set anything up until I get back."

"Well, that's just wonderful," she said sarcastically. "I don't know what you expect me to tell them. You've been stonewalling them for a month, and I haven't for the life of me figured out why, but that's your business. I don't mind telling you you've been distracted lately. Very unlike you." She blew out an exasperated sigh. "How did your conference go this morning?"

Ian appreciated her not pressing him about the meeting. "About as expected. This project should come off without a hitch. Sam Compton's handling the legalities, and we should be ready to start in just over two month's time. I have to coordinate the contractors and sign the final papers and that's that." He stroked his chin as visions of his plan played out before him.

"Ian, just what are you doing up there? If I didn't know what a workaholic fool you are, I'd think you were in hiding. From who or what, that I couldn't say, but something is different with you lately. Is this some kind of middle-age-crazy kind of thing coming on you a little early?"

"I'm not middle-aged yet. I'm working on the purchase of a children's camp, you know that." He also knew how ridiculous that sounded coming from someone who avoided kids like the plague.

Zelda chuckled into the phone, causing Ian to ask, "What's so funny?"

"The thought of you at a camp for kids. You've got to admit, that's funny stuff."

He pictured her smiling into the phone. "Glad I could brighten your day."

"I don't mean to question your vision. You have an impeccable knack for finding properties you can reshape and revitalize, and, Lord knows, you always make money."

"Hmm, yes I do." Ian pulled his long legs from their perch on the corner of the bed and took the yellow legal pad from under a stack of papers. He'd drawn a map of changes to his original plan and studied them while he continued. "You should see this community, Zelda. Most of the buildings have retained the same appearance since, I'd guess, the fifties. These people don't know what they have here. If we could generate a tourist crowd around these lakes and encourage an environment conducive to local artisans, the possibilities are endless."

"Sounds quaint. People from around here would pay buckets for a vacation in a place like that. Interesting, isn't it, that someone who doesn't know how to take a vacation himself would have a clue what other people would enjoy," Zelda said in a condescending tone. "You've got oodles of money, why not spend some of it enjoying life?"

"Are you trying in some weird psychoanalysis way to tell me you need a raise?"

"Of course I'm not. Would I do that to you?"

"Sure you would." Ian puffed out a sigh. "You can ride me about anything else, but my personal life is off limits.

"What personal life? Oh, sorry. Anyway, I think you're on to something."

"I am." There was a brief pause before Ian gave a satisfied chuckle.

"Now let me ask *you* what's so funny?"

"One of the counselors became quite agitated when she learned of the sale. Although agitated isn't quite the word, enraged is more appropriate. No, maybe livid. Actually I thought her head was going to pop off her skinny body. She's threatening to find a way to block it."

"Is this a serious threat? Need I remind you after the Belling deal we've learned to take every threat seriously."

"No way. She's upset at loosing her summertime distraction and thinks I'm taking the old woman for a ride. Which I'm not. Mrs. Duncan will make out quite handsomely when all is said and done. You should have heard this woman. She whined on and on about my taking the experience away from the children. Well, I'm not wasting one precious moment of my time worrying about the displacement of spoiled little rich kids. It's nothing more than a glorified babysitting service. You'd have thought the sky was falling by the way Lucy acted."

"Lucy?"

"Lucy Mitchell. She was quite entertaining."

"Well, sorry I missed the showdown, but I've got work to do. I've got an absent boss, you see, and piles of paperwork to organize into neat little stacks in wait of his triumphant return."

"That's what I like about you, Zelda, always cracking the whip. See you soon. I promise."

"I'll hold you to that."

He sat for a moment and studied his yellow notepad, unseeing but for the plans taking shape in his mind. He began to scribble. The area that now claimed Otter and Beaver cabins would make a fine area for a tennis court. Perched upon the hill, the view would be perfect for a garden area as well, a place to relax after a rousing game. Filling in the area around the lodge was going to cost him, but raising the land would give the condos a spectacular view of the lake.

Setting the pad aside, he angled out of the uncomfortable chair and pushed back the thick, beige curtains covering the solitary window to view the village beyond. From this vantage point he had a clear view of Main Street and the quaint business district.

He had to admit that his heart tugged a bit at the anguish Mrs. Duncan expressed after that thundercloud of a counselor slammed out of the office. She'd get over it as soon as she had check in hand and was on her way to Alabama.

Thankfully, Mrs. Duncan appeared too drained after Lucy blew out of the office to continue torturing him with the photo album. She'd said it was a prerequisite to the sale. She couldn't be serious. He didn't have the time or the inclination to appease her, unless she pressed the point.

Ian turned from the window, hands on his hips. Lucy Mitchell thought she could take on Northland Progression and Ian Flynn, did she? Well, too bad for her, there wasn't a blessed thing she could do about it. He had to admit, she was actually kind of cute when she was near to spitting nails. It wasn't possible to fear a creature with as delicious a derriere as the one she presented when she'd sailed out of the office. And those legs, damn, they were spectacular. Tanned and athletic, yet totally feminine. Those were the kind of legs a guy would love to have wrapped around him. And nearly as captivating as the heat smoldering in those gorgeous sable eyes and that wicked mouth of hers. For a brief, fleeting moment he'd thought she was going to smack him for suggesting she "get a life." Lucy and her tirade were nothing if not amusing.

With a finger, he drew the curtains back again, allowing a slash of light to pierce the shadows of his mundane room. It had turned into a beautiful afternoon, and this depressing excuse for a motel room was feeling stuffy.

At present he was stuck in this town for another few days, so he may as well make the best of it. Small towns generally bored him to death, but he was beginning to see the earning potential of these forgotten little villages with the tourist trend turning to the charming, quaint escape from city life.

It was time to mingle with the locals, see what he could learn about the town of Butternut Creek and see what interesting tidbits were tucked among the woodsy hills of northeastern Wisconsin. Who knows, there may be more areas awaiting his expertise. He'd lay money on it.

****

Lucy was still fuming when she parked in front of Ellie's Pantry and entered through the lace-covered French door of the coffeehouse and gift shop. In long, purposeful strides she crossed the hardwood floor toward her sister, who was scribbling on a legal pad behind the glass counter.

"You wouldn't believe the day I've had, and it's not even three. I'd have been better off to have stayed in bed." Lucy swung her large shoulder bag onto the counter and laid her keys next to it. Her body vibrated with so much pent-up frustration that she could explode at any moment. She noted one customer with his head buried in a newspaper, in a booth at the back. She'd have to keep her temper in check.

"On such a beautiful day? This must be bad." Ellen Mitchell Barlow's usual sunny smile slid from her round face. She set the pad and pen aside, tucked blond curls behind her ears and with hands on hips, gave her full attention to her younger sister. "Okay, tell me all about it. But first, do you want a cup of coffee? I've got your favorite, Southern Pecan with buttercream creamer. It's the daily special and bound to fix nearly any bad day. I'm also trying out a gingerbread latte I want to introduce for the Christmas season this year."

"No, thanks. The last thing I need is a caffeine buzz. I'm as keyed up as I care to be." Lucy pulled out a chair at one of the bistro tables, sat down, and then stood up again. Her anger couldn't contain itself to one position.

Ellie picked up a rag, swiped at a spot under the cappuccino machine, and once again gave her full attention to Lucy. "Okay, tell me all."

Suddenly, Lucy didn't quite know how to begin. The camp had meant so much to her, and, she knew, to Ellie as well. The girls had spent nearly every summer there since they'd been in fifth grade. Ellie had given up working at the camp when she opened her shop, but continued to volunteer when needed.

Lucy tucked an errant strand of hair behind her ear and placed both hands to either side of her face to massage her temples with her fingertips.

"Honestly, El, I don't even know where to begin. I need a minute to calm myself down a bit," she said with a slight tremble in her voice.

Ellen leaned her elbows on the counter. "Oookay, although you're scaring me a bit. Before you get started, I just got off the phone with Mom about an hour ago."

Lucy stopped massaging her throbbing temples and turned to her sister. "Really? Everything all right?" Something had to be amiss for Corrine Mitchell Callan to disrupt her busy vacation schedule for a phone call to her daughters.

"Everything is wonderful. Alaska is spectacular in June, and she and Steve are loving every minute. They're meeting new friends and doing a little fishing. The weather's been perfect." Ellie gave a wistful sigh. "It's so good to see her happy after all those years alone."

"Yeah, great."

Ellie leveled an older-sister glare upon her. "Lucy..."

"Okay, okay, it's time to move on." Sometimes ancient history just didn't feel so ancient.

"Anyway, they've bought a place in Anchorage to use for future trips. She said she'd email some pictures of it. Here, I wrote down the name." Ellie handed her a piece of scratch paper.

"Mountain View Condominiums." A frustrated sigh escaped Lucy's lips, and she balled her hands into fists in an attempt to contain her anger. "Uhh, condos. If I hear one more word about condos, I'll scream."

"Okay, spill. What's fouled your mood so, and what in the world could it have to do with condos?"

Lucy arched her eyebrows for dramatic effect. "Well, for starters, Mrs. Duncan is thinking of selling the camp and moving to her sister's in Alabama."

Ellie stared at her a moment, eyebrows knit together, appearing to not quite understand. As Lucy's words seemed to filter through, her shoulders slumped, and her face registered the shock. "No, she can't." She raised a hand to cover her mouth.

Lucy bobbed her head. "She is, and get this, she wants to sell it to some cutthroat development company that wants to demolish it for condominiums along the lake." Lucy was feeling the full force of her anger, becoming more animated with every word. "You should have seen this egotistical snob the company sent to try and swindle Lida from the very thing she and Henry spent their lives building. This guy was the most self-centered ass I've seen in a long time."

Ellen took the hand from her mouth and placed in on her forehead. "I can't believe this." She moved from behind to counter to stand alongside Lucy. "I've so looked forward to the day I could send Abby there."

"Oh, I know. If I hadn't stumbled in on the meeting, I wouldn't have believed it myself. Poor Lida had tears in her eyes as she was telling me what this jerk was trying to get her to do, and he stood right there with this smug look on his face. He couldn't have cared less. The man is robbing Lida of her life's work."

"What did you say to her? Did you try to talk her out of this?"

"I was in shock. I pleaded with her to hold on to it, but she said the camp is doing so poorly financially that she has to." Lucy leaned both hands on the countertop and hung her head. "Oh, Ellie, if she'd have only told me, I'm sure we could have tried to find a way to get her back on her feet." The women were silent for a moment. Then Lucy raised her head with a defiant look in her eyes. "I'll find a way, and I don't care what it takes. That'll be the day when I let Lida sell out to that arrogant piece-of-work. Do you know, when I became upset about this, he told me to get a life? He actually said that to me. *Get a life*. I repeat—what an ass."

Ellie's eyes widened. "How incredibly rude. Oh, poor Lida. She must be so upset."

Suddenly, the sound of someone clearing his throat came from the far corner of the coffee shop. The two women turned their heads in the direction of the noise and the sight that met Lucy's eyes rendered her speechless. In one of the booths by the window, Ian Flynn held his coffee cup aloft with an insolent smirk upon his face before he leveled a piercing glare upon Lucy.

"Excuse me, ladies, but could this arrogant piece-of-work, this jerk, this two-time ass, get another cup of coffee?"

Lucy felt the floor beneath her had become quicksand and was threatening, promising, to swallow her whole.

"You," she said.

Ellie's eyes darted between the two.

"Yes, Miss Mitchell, it's me, the snob." A steely expression frosted over Ian's chiseled features as he angled his long form out from the booth and stood with coffee cup in hand. Somehow he seemed taller than she'd remembered.

Lucy watched him stalk toward her. Every footfall echoed off the floor below him, causing her temperature to rise another degree. Ellie stepped back to the safety of the cash register as Lucy steeled her emotions for the eventual onslaught.

"On second thought," he said, his eyes capturing hers, "forget about the coffee." He smacked the cup on the glass with a crack. Ellie checked the condition of her countertop. He stood as close to Lucy as convention would allow and lowered a glacial blue gaze on her. "For one thing, I am not trying to swindle Mrs. Duncan as you suggest. For another, she had contacted a local realtor, who in turn notified us of a possible sale. So, you see, Miss Mitchell, it's a done deal. And those tears you saw in Mrs. Duncan's eyes were tears of *relief* for what we are doing for her. She wasn't upset at all until you came in and threw a hissy fit."

He pointed a finger, stopping just short of touching her. "Until you came bursting in, she was grateful to my company for the offer we gave her. If anyone is causing her upset, *Ms. Mitchell*, it is you, and you alone. You might want to offer her support rather than condemnation."

Lucy regained her composure enough to fire back at him. "That's crap and you know it. I care very deeply about her and the camp. She knows that."

"Hey, guys, let's talk about this calmly." Ellie's attempt to break in fell on deaf ears.

Lucy pushed his hand aside and placed her hands on her hips. "You're taking advantage of an old lady who's vulnerable. She'd never have so easily given up the camp she and her husband had devoted their lives to. It's bad enough that she's lost him and has no children of her own to comfort her. Now she's going to lose the very thing that's remained constant for her throughout all of this."

Ian leaned over her, causing her to tip her head back

slightly to keep eye contact. "Well, you're wrong. She's made up her mind, and you would be better off to respect her decision and butt out. It's none of your concern."

Lucy wasn't about to be intimidated. "It certainly is my concern. Lida is a dear friend of mine, and I care about her welfare as well as the welfare of the camp and those kids out there. I can't stand to see a lifetime of work swept under the carpet, or should I say bulldozed into nothing but rubble, all for the profit of some big development company that doesn't give a hoot about people. I'll bet all you do is ride around in your fancy, shmancy car and pick out all the nice pieces of property you can find and figure out how you can annihilate them to line your pockets."

"Now I can say, you don't know a thing about me."

"You're right, and I don't want to know anything about you or your company. Why don't you just pack up your little briefcase and run off to pillage some other town. This one doesn't need you."

"This one needs me more than you know." Ian pulled his wallet from his pants pocket, pulled out a five-dollar bill, and threw it on the counter. "This should cover the coffee. Keep the change."

Ellie carefully picked up the bill and set it on the cash register. "Thanks, I think."

He moved around Lucy and strode toward the door as she called after him, "Why don't you stop by the nursing home? You could send those old people packing, take a wrecking ball to it and build an airport to shuttle in all your rich friends. Who needs nursing homes or camps for kids anyway?"

Ian shoved the door open so hard that the hinges creaked. The two women watched him stomp down the sidewalk and around the corner.

Chapter Three

Ellie raised her eyebrows. "Wow, you told him."

Lucy blew out the breath she hadn't been aware she'd been holding and bit her lower lip. "Yeah, I did, didn't I?" She forced down the lump in her throat. "Do you think telling him to knock off the nursing home was a bit too much?"

"Hmm, you may have pushed the envelope a little too far with that one." Ellie swung her gaze from the door to Lucy and chuckled. "Clean out the nursing home for an airport? Lucy, where do you get this stuff?"

Lucy tore her gaze from the now Ian Flynn-free sidewalk and met that of her sister and the two women burst into laughter.

"You know..." Lucy ran a finger under each eye. "This isn't funny in the least. It really isn't."

"I know, but I don't think I've heard you pounce on someone like that since you fought the school board for new playground equipment." Ellie pulled out tissues from a box under the counter, handed one to Lucy, and they dabbed at their eyes. "It is a serious situation, and I am shocked Lida would accept their offer because of what this company plans to do with the camp. I suppose it was unrealistic to think she'd be able to hang on to it forever. But how could she possibly allow this to take place? I don't get it."

"I have to find a way to help Lida out of this mess. There must be something I can do." She held a palm up as though hoping to pluck the perfect solution from the air.

"Lucy, you don't have to champion every cause that comes along. It sounds like the sale has already been completed. If that's the case, there's nothing you can do. Lida must have very good reasons for doing this or else she wouldn't."

"There's got to be something I can do. I'll find a way. Do you think Randy would help? He'd know something about real estate sales and how to get out of one."

Ellie tipped her blond head to one side. "I'm sure he'd love to help, although I don't know what an accountant can do. I do think you're going to need all the help you can get. Especially since you've royally ticked off one of the principal players in this game."

"Thanks for reminding me." The memory of Ian Flynn's tall frame glowering down upon her caused a shiver to shimmy down her spine.

Ellie leaned her elbows on the counter and laced her fingers together before her. "And to think only fifteen short minutes ago I was thinking of calling you to tell you about the great looking guy that came in here for coffee today."

"Save your breath. I know all I care to regarding Ian Flynn." Lucy's cheeks still burned with indignation over the heated confrontation. "Isn't he the most arrogant man you've ever seen? I hate men like that."

Ellie nodded in agreement, until a smile brought forth the dimples Lucy always admired. "You know what they say, 'there's a fine line between love and hate.'"

Lucy narrowed her gaze on her sister and pursed her lips. "I'm going to forget you said that." She threw her balled tissue at Ellie, who scooped it up just before it landed on the floor. "I will take you up on the offer of that cup of coffee. I'll get it myself." Lucy went to the thermos and pumped a generous cup of the aromatic brew.

Just then the door opened and a sprite of a girl entered. With arms crossed over her little chest and her lower lip jutting out in all her pouting glory, she marched toward them like a little soldier with flaxen braids flapping behind her.

Lucy grinned, set her cup down, and held her arms open wide. "There's my favorite niece." The tiny thundercloud marched on past her and stood before her mother.

"What's the matter, Abby?" Ellie knelt in front of her daughter and placed loving hands on her shoulders.

"I'm mad." The child spoke with such authority that Lucy fought to keep a straight face. She stamped a sandaled foot to dramatize the depth of her anger.

"Who are you angry with?" Ellie's tone was

concerned, yet calm.

Abby Barlow jabbed her thumb in the direction of the door. "Him." As if on cue, Randy, Ellie's husband and Abby's father, entered the shop. Lucy'd always thought he had yuppie written across his tanned forehead, although she could forgive him that. He was blond, handsome and thoroughly self-assured. Now, his shirt was loosened at the neck, his tie missing-in-action, car keys dangling from his fingers.

"Luce, how's she hangin'?" With a wink, Randy strode past her.

Lucy chuckled. "Better than most."

Randy nodded in her direction, a playful grin on his face. "Great, glad to hear it." He stopped in front of his wife and daughter, bent and brushed Ellie's cheek with a kiss, and patted Abby's head. "I brought Abby a little early. I have a business dinner tonight."

Abby stomped her little foot in protest and tightened her arms about her chest. Her lower lip couldn't have hung any lower.

Ellie stood before him, obviously disappointed. "What? When did that come up? We planned a picnic for tonight. Randy, we discussed it just this morning."

"That's why I'm mad." Abby stomped feet adorned with tiny blue-painted toenails. "I want to have a picnic. You promised."

Ellie smiled down at her. "We will, honey." To Randy she said, "Are you sure you can't change your plans? This is the second time you've done this in a week."

Randy took a gingerbread pretzel off a sample plate on the counter, sniffed it, and popped it into his mouth. "You know I've been working with these clients for some time now. They're in town, and I've got to entertain them. It's my job."

"But..." Ellie seemed at a loss for words, and Lucy suddenly felt like an intruder.

"I want a picnic," Abby shouted between them.

"These people are important to our future, El. I can't back out. I knew you'd understand." He slung an arm over Ellie's shoulders, gave her a squeeze. "I'll make it up to you both, I promise."

"I want a picnic." Abby tugged on her father's pant

leg.

Ellie looked up at him with hopeful eyes. "But we've hardly spent any time as a family lately. I was counting on tonight."

Abby tugged at his arm. "I want a picnic. Daddy, you promised. You said we'd cook out and then go swimming. We haven't been swimming in a long time."

Randy placed a hand on the top of Abby's head. "Not tonight, Sweetstuff. We'll find another time." To Ellie he said, "I have to be there in an hour and a half and I've got some paperwork to wrap up first." He kissed her cheek and whispered something in her ear. Ellie blushed and smiled at him, although a reluctant concession. Randy turned and popped another gingerbread pretzel into his mouth.

"Abby and I will have a picnic anyway. It'll be just us girls." She looked to her daughter, who still refused to meet the eyes of her parents, then to Lucy. "You busy tonight? Come with us."

"I'd love to, but we've got frog-jumping contests tonight, and I said I'd help out. Hey, why don't you two come out after your picnic? It'll be fun." Lucy knelt before the little girl. Tears were beginning to threaten Abby's stubborn facade.

"I don't wanna see dumb frogs." Abby jostled her body away from Lucy. Ellie sent a weak smile Lucy's way.

"They're pretty funny the way they jump all over creation, and the kids cheer and laugh. You'd have fun, I guarantee it." Abby just shook her head, sending her braids flapping, and looked so cute that Lucy just wanted to gather the little girl in her arms. But she knew better. Abigail Lucinda Barlow held a grudge much like her Auntie Lucy.

"Will you be late?" Ellie asked Randy. Lucy noted that Ellie was putting on her "little trooper" face, but her eyes belied a genuine disappointment.

"No telling, but I'll try to be home early." He bent and with a hand on his daughter's back placed a kiss on her cheek. "Sorry, Sweetstuff, we'll do it another night. I promise." Abby turned her back to him. Lucy watched as Randy and Ellie's eyes shared an unspoken thought. "You ladies have a good time tonight. Love you, guys. You too,

Luce." He winked at Lucy, ever the charmer, and left the shop, taking the same route as...

As Ian Flynn. Lucy couldn't help but compare Ian's stiff gait to Randy's easy saunter. She quickly pushed aside the memory and returned her attention to her sister and her niece.

Abby rushed to her mother and hugged her waist. Ellie held her and looked to Lucy with eyes that said "I give up." "We'll have fun, honey, you'll see."

"I want my daddy there." Tiny tears trickled down her face, and Lucy's heart swelled with love.

Ellie wiped her daughter's face with her palms. "Ab, that's not possible. You heard what Daddy said. He has a meeting, so we'll have to make fun on our own."

"He always does this."

"No, he doesn't. Daddy works hard for us." Ellie sent a pleading look Lucy's way.

Lucy knelt down next to Abby. "You're right, Ab. I'd be mad at him too, if I were you." Abby immediately stopped her tears and looked at Lucy with curious eyes while her mother registered a look that clearly said 'shut up.'

"Luuucccyyy, thanks, but..." A strained look passed Ellie's face.

Lucy shrugged. "No, really, I'd be mad too. He made a promise and he broke it."

"He didn't mean to." Abby seemed infused with maturity beyond her years.

Lucy reached for her hand. "Oh, I'm sure he didn't, but he promised your mommy, too, and she's disappointed as well. So why don't you take her on that picnic since Daddy can't, and make sure she has a great time."

Abby shrugged. "Okay, but I'm still mad at him. Auntie Luce, you wanna come over tomorrow? I've got Chutes and Ladders now, and we could play."

Lucy rose and placed a hand under her little chin and drew her face upward. "I'd love to, but how about Saturday? I don't have to work, and we can spend the day together." She smiled down into Abby's face with all the love she had in her heart.

Smiling, Ellie shook her head at her sister. "You really should have babies of your own, you know, as long as you're mentoring and teaching everyone else's. I know..." She held her hands up in surrender. "You're tired of me preaching at you, but you'd be a great mother."

"Hmm, maybe someday." Honestly, the idea was beginning to nudge her from time to time.

"Seriously, Luce, you're almost thirty, and you'd make a wonderful mother. You're not only a gifted teacher, you're someone the students look up to. Anyone can see they love you."

"I appreciate the support, but you're forgetting one important part of the quotient."

"And that is?" Ellie popped a pretzel into her mouth.

"I can't do it on my own. I won't. A man would be a welcome addition." Even before the last word left her mouth, she knew what Ellie's response would be.

"What about Shooter?" *Bingo.* "It's not like the two of you haven't been practicing at it for years."

Lucy blew out a bedraggled sigh. "Shooter and I, well, we keep each other company. That's kind of about it. It's been on and off with him so long that it almost feels like a marriage. You have the only decent guy left in this town."

Ellie looked toward the door her husband had exited and pumped a shoulder in a half-hearted shrug. "Yeah." A very unconvincing affirmation if Lucy every heard one.

"Trouble in paradise?" Lucy watched her sister closely.

Ellie's gaze suddenly cut to Lucy. "Not at all. Anyway, back to our hashing over of your life." To which Lucy groaned before Ellie continued. "Oh, quit. If you put the time and energy into a life outside of Abby, the camp, and your students, you'd have a family by now. Don't get me wrong. You are an asset to this community, but maybe you should stop throwing yourself into work at the camp and coaching volleyball and all the other programs you're involved in and take some time for you. Maybe it's time to make a commitment to Shooter and get on with life."

Lucy was thoughtful a moment. "You have this perfect life with your wonderful husband, beautiful home, successful business, and the cutest little girl in the county." She reached down and pinched Abby's cheek and was promptly brushed away. "There's only so much of that to go around."

Ellie pointed a finger in her direction. "That's bull, and you know it."

"Look at Mom. Perfect example. Dad left her with two little kids to raise on her own. She went through years of wallowing in self-pity and trying to find comfort from her barfly friends." Lucy sent her sister an all-knowing glance.

"Yes, look at Mom. She found Steve and she's never been happier."

"Yeah, now." Lucy waggled her head for effect. "It took her a long time to find him and look at what we all went through until she did."

"Yeah, well, when Dad left, Mom got a little off track. We don't need to revisit that again. Oh, before I forget, Dad called yesterday."

Lucy held up a hand. "Don't start. We're not discussing him."

Ellie rolled her eyes. "Yeah, yeah, okay. People change. Anyway, my point is, although our parents weren't good examples, there's someone out there looking for you as well. By the way, my life isn't all that perfect, although we're not discussing it."

"Well, let's face it, El, from what I've seen until just now, you've got it pretty good."

"Don't make something out of nothing, and yeah, I can't complain." Ellie's face broke into a wide smile. "Where's Shooter been hiding out lately? He used to stop in for a cup of coffee every now and then. It's been a while."

"Good question. I haven't seen him either." A hint of worry gnawed at her. Shooter had been elusive lately.

"Hey," Abby interrupted, "I want my picnic."

****

The walk back to the Northern Lights Motel was a blur. Ian's feet pounded the ground the entire trek. Who the hell appointed Lucy Mitchell judge and jury to what he was trying to accomplish in this forgotten village? The clientele this project would attract would be an economic boon as it was. Why did he care what Lucy or anyone thought? He'd finish his business here and be gone. He certainly had enough on his mind without having been thrown in the path of Hurricane Lucy.

Ian entered the motel room and threw his key on the dresser with a clang. He plopped his weary form into the chair in front of the window again, but was unable to relax. He was restless, malcontent. But why? This room was suffocating, confining. He hadn't turned on the air conditioning, and the sun streaming through the window made the room absolutely steamy. The humidity had risen to an oppressive level. He needed a release. He'd noticed a sign for the city beach on his walk into the business district, such as it was. A swim and a run just may be the thing to calm his nerves. And take his mind off Lucy Mitchell.

The muffled ring of the cell phone in his pocket broke through his thoughts. It had to be one of his colleagues, because no one else ever called him. Not bothering to check the caller ID, Ian answered.

"Flynn, here."

The gravely voice of an older woman answered him. "Ian?"

Silence followed. A long, burning silence that nearly tore Ian in two.

"Ian, this is your mother. Are you there?"

Ian closed his eyes and slid a hand over his face. "Yeah, I'm here." His voice was in no way welcoming, and he wasn't the least bit sorry.

"I hope you don't mind my calling you. Your office gave me this number." *Zelda, we're going to have to have a talk about this.*

"What do you need?" What a stupid question. They needed money. Ian could feel the muscles in his jaw tighten and cold, hard steel clamp his heart.

"I've left you messages, but you must not be getting them. You haven't been home in forever and, well, I have something to tell you."

This couldn't be good. It never was. They either needed money or legal advice, or both. She certainly wasn't calling to say that she loved him or missed her only son. He waited, in silence, for her to continue. Far be it from him to make this easy on the woman who'd given him life, just as she'd never lifted a finger to ease his existence.

"Are you still there?" The question was followed by a

raspy cough.

Ian puffed out an impatient sigh. "Of course I am."

The voice of Gladdy Flynn quavered. "It's Dad."

Ian remained unfazed. "What's Mike's problem this time? Let me guess. He forgot to pay the electric bill, or is on his fifth drunk driving ticket, or, let's see, he fell off his bar stool and hurt his back and wants to sue."

"The doctors say he has cancer, and it's real bad." Gladdy sniffled.

Ian caught his breath for a moment as her words slammed through his brain. He could have easily spewed more insults at his father via his mother, but he didn't have the patience for it today. "What kind of cancer? How bad?" He plopped on the edge of the bed.

"It started in his stomach, but now it's all over. There's nothing they can do." Now Gladdy began to cry into the phone. "The doctor says it's a matter of a few weeks. What am I going to do?"

Ian's heart failed to soften. "What do you want from me? Somehow I don't think Mike would appreciate my sitting at his bedside pretending to be the grieving son. As for you, you've got all your friends down at Slickey's Bar. Ah, I get it. There'll be medical bills to pay. Now I see where I fit into this."

"Well...yes, there's bills to pay. But I...I just thought you'd want to know. He is your father after all." Another cough.

"Is that what he was? A father? I'm sorry, I guess I failed to realize that."

"Don't be mean, Ian. He did the best he could."

"If that was his best, it doesn't say much for him, does it?" Ian wanted this conversation to be done and now. "Look, I have to go. I'll get you a check when I get back into town."

"I'll let you know how much we need. I'm sorry I bothered you, Ian."

"So am I."

The phone clicked, and then nothing. He sat there, not sure if he wanted to cry or kick a hole in the wall. He threw a pen at the pottery lamp on the table. It missed and clanged off the air conditioner under the window, finally coming to rest under the bed. In the silence of his room he sat with steely eyes focused on the cold, hard lessons learned by a child no one wanted.

****

Lucy eased the screen door open just enough to crane her head into the office to see Lida Duncan sitting behind the desk, pencil poised in her puffy hand, her round face fraught with worry. Today was green sweat-suit day. At least the color suited her better than the glaring purple of yesterday. Or the yellow before that.

"Lida, you have a minute?" Lucy tried to sound as upbeat and nonconfrontational as possible. Years of experience told her that Lida wouldn't respond well to a heated discussion. She'd always deferred that kind of discomfiture to Henry whose quiet demeanor gracefully diffused every debate.

Lida raised her eyes over the crescent-shaped lenses perched on her pug nose. "Thank the Lord, I need a respite from this bookwork. Come right in, honey. I've been expecting you." She gestured toward the wooden chair in the corner next to the file cabinet.

"Great." Lucy pulled the chair from the corner and placed herself directly in front of Lida's desk. "Lida, we need to talk about your plans for the camp."

"Lucy, honey, you're like my family. I suppose that's why I didn't say anything to you before. I just couldn't bear to let you down." Lida looked at her with tired eyes.

"I shouldn't have gotten so angry. I'm sorry." Lucy began to feel her resolve crumble. Straightening her shoulders, she fought the emotion that could easily overtake reason. She wanted to use good, solid argument to sway Lida's decision. "Lida, I have a bad feeling about this Mr., ah, Mr. Flimflam or whatever his name is ..." She flailed a dismissive hand through the air.

"It's Flynn, dear." Lida sniffed once and peered over her glasses.

"Flynn, okay, but my point is, he rubs me the wrong way. How do you know you can trust him? I mean, Lida, he could be planning to swindle you for all we know. Just looking at him, with those dark, sinister eyes, gave me chills. How could you do business with him?" Thinking of Ian Flynn brought a strange heat to the pit of her stomach.

"I suppose I should have told you Mr. Flynn was coming here and why. You've always been so passionate about the camp. But, frankly, I knew you'd be angry, and I needed to make this decision on my own. I need to do what's best for me." She reached across the desk for Lucy's hand and clasped it in her own. "I hope you can understand that. And I do feel I can trust him. My attorney has reviewed the paperwork and can't find a single thing that's out of line."

"I think we need to look at all the options here. There must be some way you can get by without selling. I do have a few ideas, if you'd like to hear them." Lucy took a cleansing breath to steady her thoughts before pleading her case.

Lida sat back in her chair. "I really don't think so. I want to be with my sister." Lida's eyes became glassy with tears at the ready to be shed. She reached for a tissue and dabbed under her glasses. "Thelma will be seventy-five in November, and I want to spend time with her while she and I can go places and do things."

"I understand, but can't you find a buyer that will take over the camp rather than obliterate it from the face of the Earth? Lida, he's going to bulldoze the place." *Okay, that was a little strong, Lucy.* She opened her mouth to apologize and then changed her mind. "We could open the lodge year 'round for meetings or seminars or as a dining establishment. Think of it, Lida. Butternut Creek doesn't have anyplace for meetings except the high school auditorium or Hadley's restaurant out on County A."

"Lucy, I tried all winter long to find a buyer. No one was interested. I prayed that someone would come along, and the next thing I knew, Mr. Flynn called. No one will ever offer me what this company has. The camp hasn't pulled in the money it once did. Insurance is outrageous; taxes have gone up along with the food bill; the cabins need maintenance. Oh, I could go on and on. Kids don't go to summer camps like they used to, and I need the money. I just don't have the head for it since Henry's gone." Lida's eyes clouded over as she looked to the screen door as though imagining her husband walking through the door, a child or two filling his shadow.

Lucy blew out a breath and held her hands up as

though to slow time. "Okay, let's think about this calmly. Is there a chance we could market the camp more aggressively and hold out for another buyer? Perhaps put in a stipulation that they have to keep the camp in business. The internet is a wonderful source. We could advertise there. This doesn't have to be such a hasty decision, does it?"

"I have a good feeling about Mr. Flynn." She waggled a weary finger in Lucy's direction. "Just give him time. I think he came my way for a reason."

"With all due respect, Ian Flynn does not instill in me anything but hatred. I know that's a strong word, but I think you're wrong about him."

Lida blew into a tissue, and suddenly seemed frighteningly breakable. "Don't you see, this isn't exactly a booming area and buyers aren't knocking down my door? Oh, Lucy..." A sob escaped her trembling lips, and she covered her mouth with the tissue. Lucy came around the desk and squeezed her shoulders, feeling guilty for being so harsh.

"There, there, Lida. It'll work out. It'll be okay." How lame she sounded, but they were the only words she could utter without completely losing her composure as well. "Is there something more going on here than you've told me, because, frankly, this just isn't like you?"

"It's not my sister's health I'm worried about...it's mine." She blew into the tissue again, then dabbed at the corners of her eyes.

"Your health?" A mixture of confusion and fear gripped Lucy. She angled her head to meet Lida's watery eyes.

"Yes, Dr. Murphy, a doctor I saw in Alabama last winter, sent me to a specialist before I came back in March, and I've been diagnosed with Parkinson's. I'm on medication that will hold off the major symptoms for a while, but it will catch up with me sooner or later. I can't possibly think about the camp now, and I'm so worried about the medical bills and the cost of the medication. I just don't know what will become of me." Lida's rounded shoulders shook with sobs as she buried her face in what was left of the tissue.

"I don't...this..." Lida's words swam through Lucy's

head, but she wouldn't allow them to take full meaning. She closed her eyes and fought the desire to dissolve into the maelstrom of emotion swimming through her. Lucy sank to her knees alongside this woman who meant so much to her and gripped the arm of the chair. "Oh, Lida..."

"The symptoms started over the winter when I was visiting Thelma. Thank God she made me go to the doctor. I honestly thought it was a nervous twitch due to stress and tipsiness from age. I was wrong." The pleading look in Lida's tired eyes nearly tore Lucy's heart from her chest.

She gathered one of Lida's hands in both of her own. "No, Lida," she breathed, and the tears fell freely in rivers down her cheeks and dripped onto her knees. "I'm sorry if I made you feel guilty about selling the camp. I didn't mean to."

"You see, Lucy, I really need the money for my medical care. I want to enjoy this summer with the children as my last, and then go to my sisters' and live out what time I have left with the only family I have and in warmer weather. She'll take care of me until I have to go to the nursing home." Lida patted Lucy's hands. "I'm not afraid. I've lived a good life, and my faith will see me through this. My Henry will be by my side and waiting for me at the end." The tears had stopped and, somehow, Lida seemed almost at peace.

In stark contrast, outside the screen door, children splashed in the lake, their laughter echoed through the pines and danced upon the morning air.

"There," Lida whispered, "hear that? That sweet sound will fill my heart and carry me home to Henry." The two women clung together, eyes focused on the children, hearts aching, hearts breaking.

Hope for Lucy's cause had vanished on the wind that sighed through the pines. It was impossible to argue against the plea she'd just heard. Her heart sank with the sadness and realization that her friend and the camp would no longer be a part of her life. Ian Flynn had won.

Well, maybe.

Chapter Four

Ian drove in as far as the first cabin and parked along the shoulder of a wooded crest. He saw a path separating the ferns just below the hill and decided to follow. Perhaps fresh air would serve as a balm for the angst he felt after his mother's call. The last time he'd walked the property had been in March when the last of the snow was still puddle beneath the pines. The forest appealed to him as much now as it had then, offering peace, solace, in contrast to the bustle of Madison and the demands of business.

The walk was a short distance through the lacy green canopy of birch and maple to one of the cabins. He wasn't sure which one. The weight of the mighty logs used in construction years ago had begun to sink into the earth, as was the case with old log structures. Despite that, the cabin seemed sound, although the roof was capped with a mossy blanket and some of the shakes were gone. A small wooden sign marked the cabin's name, Beaver, in well-worn red.

Walking around the front, Ian noted a rusted screen door and a small window, both trimmed in green paint, what paint was left. He stopped and took in the neglected appearance. He'd thought about keeping one cabin for the caretaker. It certainly wouldn't be this one.

On the lake side of the cabin, a dilapidated screen porch hung out over the hillside. It made the entire structure appear in jeopardy of toppling over and rolling down the hill to land in the lake below. He shook his head in disgust and continued to the rocky edge of the lake.

An island rose just off-center, thickly populated with pines and maple and a lonely loon bobbed on the surface, dipped its head, and then released a haunting call that echoed through the trees. Caramel colored water lapped in steady rhythm along the shoreline while the reflection of puffy clouds ghosted the surface.

He breathed in the sweet scents of evergreen and grass and water and a strange sensation washed through him. He found himself lulled further into the serenity of this place. For the first time in a long time, he felt his muscles and his mind release. When was the last time he'd truly felt that?

Inexplicably his bliss was suddenly and violently shattered. A foreign object whacked his head from behind. The force, along with the stinging pain in the back of his head, knocked him to his knees.

"Shit." He'd definitely been hit with something, but what? Fearing he may have to defend himself, he grabbed a large stick and, still crouched on his knees, waved it about as his eyes frantically searched the forest for the unknown assailant. Overhead pine branches danced as though something large had taken flight. That couldn't be it. The attack came from behind, not on top of him, and no bird, to his knowledge, could throw something that hard. Swinging his eyes to the ground around him, he saw nothing that could have been used as a weapon other than a single acorn in the dirt by his knee.

Damn, that hurt. While keeping who or whatever at bay with the stick, he used his free hand to massage the burning lump taking shape. Ian angled his head from side to side to assuage his muscles as the pain began to radiate down his neck.

The sound of rustling leaves gave him a start, and he twisted around to see a boy move from behind the massive trunk of a maple tree.

"Sorry, Mister, didn't see ya there." The boy came toward him, a slingshot dangling from one hand. "You can get up now." It was the boy who'd interrupted them in Lida's office the day before. The one with the nasty mouth.

Ian, suddenly embarrassed at having been brought down by a child, stood and angrily tossed the stick into the brush. "What the hell were you thinking? Do you know you could have taken an eye out?" Angrily, he brushed his pants clean. "Didn't anyone ever tell you to look before you do something like that? It makes no difference if you're in the middle of nowhere. You never know when someone could be in your line of fire."

"I wasn't aimin' for ya. I tripped just as I let 'er fly and my aim was off." The little brat didn't look sorry in the least.

"That's an understatement. I ought to run you right down to the lodge and turn you in. I'm assuming you aren't supposed to be here in the first place." *Damn, that hurt.* He reached up to feel the lump again. "Just what were you aiming for anyway?"

"Well, that big, old bald eagle sittin' just over your head."

"What bald eagle?"

"Geez, Mister, how could you miss it?" The boy pointed a dirty finger skyward. "It was sittin' right up there. Practically on top of ya."

Ian raised his eyes into the tree where he's just seen the branches moving. "Guess I missed it. Still," he narrowed his gaze on the youngster, "you could have caused some real damage. And for Christ sake, it's illegal to attack a bald eagle. That's the stupidest thing I've ever heard." The little shit grinned at him. And it was a dirty, freckly grin at that. *Someone needs to give this kid a spanking.* "You know you're not going to get anywhere in life by being a troublemaker, Jeffy."

"The name's Jonah and yeah, I've heard it before so save your breath. What'd you care anyway?" The defiance in the boy's eyes was a bit unsettling for someone who looked to be only ten years old. This kid had either stunted his growth somehow or he was ten going on thirty.

"That's a good question. I *don't* care." Okay, that was mean. But he was just a kid, and kids get over things like adults that are mean and uncaring. "Aren't you supposed to be taking part in some camp activity?"

"Yeah, Jule's got us making pictures with glue and leaves and sticks and stuff. It's not my kinda thing. I snuck out. 'Course I s'pose it's time for swimmin' by now. Lucy's probably lookin' for me so I can do the dog paddle or somethin' stupid like that."

Ian felt his anger melting, although he didn't want Jonah to know this. He crossed his arms over his chest and looked down his nose at the boy. "Is she going to be angry with you?" The thought of Lucy Mitchell having something to rant and rave about other than the sale of Moonlight Bay Camp pleased him to no end. "I'd think twice before making Lucy angry. She looks rather mean."

"Well, I figure I ain't gonna spend my time putzing around with crap like that. I got better things to do. 'Sides she's pretty nice and lot's of fun. Kinda good-lookin', too, for an older girl." Jonah sauntered to the shoreline, squatted, and began moving rocks. "I thought I saw a pine snake here the other day."

Ian felt a grin escape across his face as he watched the boy. He had to agree, Lucy was kind of good-looking, now that he thought about it, for an older girl, that is. And then the strangest thing came out of his mouth. "You need help finding that snake?"

Jesse glanced over his shoulder and shrugged. "Do whatever ya want."

Ian squatted over the rocks, moved a few stones. "How long are you here for, Jonah?"

"As long as my mom and dad can get them to keep me, I s'pose."

Ian stopped, dropped the rock in his hand, and studied the boy next to him. Suddenly, he could relate to this boy in a way he hadn't related to anyone in a long time.

"Do you like being here?"

Jonah shrugged a skinny shoulder. "Heck, yeah. I have fun here, and the people are nice. The cooks make the best sloppy joes I ever had. Sometimes we camp out at night and sit around the campfire. They all sing these dumb songs. I don't. I just roast hot dogs and marshmallows. It's nice. And if you keep shovelin' food in your mouth, ya don't have to sing such dumb stuff like 'Kumbaya.'" Jonah wrinkled his nose in disgust as he kept up the search for the snake. "That song sucks ass."

Ian studied the boy for a moment. "You really need to clean up your language a bit. Do your parents talk like that?"

"Hell, I mean, heck no. My dad's a preacher."

With that, Ian threw his head back and laughed a booming laugh that seemed to come from his inner most self. The sound of it echoed off the water and ricocheted through the trees. He hadn't laughed like that in, well, forever. To think this little urchin was the spawn of a man of the cloth was too much.

Jonah stopped looking for the snake and leveled serious eyes on Ian. "What's so funny?"

"Nothing, nothing at all." He stood and brushed his hands together. "Well, Jonah, I have to go down to the office to see Mrs. Duncan. Sorry we didn't find that snake."

Jonah stood as well. "I'll keep lookin'. At least until Lucy finds me again. She always finds me."

"Good luck, you're going to need it." Ian started to turn away when Jonah stopped him.

"Hey, you're not going to tell anyone I said it's nice here, are ya? Cuz, ya know, I got a rep to think about."

"No, I'll keep it a secret."

"Thanks." Jonah's usually serious freckled face broke into a brief grin that, for only a moment, seemed to light the forest around him. "And don't tell anyone I'm here."

Ian raised a hand and winked, then turned and strode back up the hill to where he'd left his car, grinning all the way. What summer sun pierced through the trees felt good on his shoulders, and a light breeze whispered through the forest around him as the leaves sighed overhead.

Aside from the unwanted phone call from his mother, it was turning into an ideal afternoon. That is, until he crested the hill and saw Lucy Mitchell heading his way. So much for a beautiful, tranquil summer's day.

"You, again. Well, you've won, you know. For now." Lucy's foul mood sank a few degrees further toward the abyss of pure, unadulterated self-pity. She was still reeling from her meeting with Lida. Poor Lida. And now she had to deal with this Flynn person again. Seeing him standing there by the side of the road sent her blood to boil. She was sad and angry and needed someone to blame. Lo and behold, that someone appeared in the form of Ian Flynn, and blame him, she did.

"Hello, Miss Mitchell. Good to see you again." Flynn flashed his perfect teeth her way, and her temper soared to the surface. She had no doubt that he understood completely how upsetting the sale of the camp was to her. He was the very embodiment of that threat and he had the nerve to stand there smiling at her, hands on his hips, tall, confident, arrogant. In other circumstances she might find him quite appealing, sexy even. But not now, not ever. She stopped before him, at a complete loss for words, civil words.

He looked at her quizzically. "I won? Well, it's time you admit that. Looking for something?"

"If I was, I wouldn't need your help; that is, if you're offering. You've done plenty around here as it is." How she wanted to slap that smug look into the next county.

"Me? Why, I haven't even gotten started."

Ooh, she was gritting her teeth so hard that she was afraid they'd crack under the pressure.

She pointed a finger at his chin. "Is that a threat, Flynn? Because if it is, you'll be sorry you came up against me, against all of Butternut Creek for that matter. I'll make your name mud in this town. You can count on it."

Before she could retreat, he engulfed her hand in his own. The massive size of his hand swallowed hers, only allowing the tip of the accusatory finger to stick out the opposite side. The amused expression on his face angered and oddly thrilled her at the same time. Their eyes locked and an electrical jolt sizzled up her arm. Her heart pounded in her chest; her breathing quickened. She pulled once, then again, but he refused to free her hand.

"Now, now Ms. Mitchell, you don't worry me in the least." His voice was smooth, condescending. "There's nothing you can do to stop what's going to happen here. If you want a fight on your hands, you've got one, and I'll win because, like it or not, I have the resources to win. Namely, Lida Duncan. So maybe it's time you butt out, continue on whatever quest you're on at the moment, and go play with the children. They need you, I don't."

"You can go straight to hell." She yanked her captive hand once again, but he held her fast.

She pulled again, and he released her before she'd fully completed the movement. When she stumbled, he caught her in the strength of his arms and brought her back to him as her feet fumbled to regain a solid stance. He could have laughed at her, but he didn't. Good thing, because she'd have to slap him then for sure, not that it wasn't tempting anyway. Instead he held her against him and as he did so, a queer churning began in her stomach. He encircled her in his arms a moment more than was necessary in her opinion.

"Let go!" She roughly pushed her body away from his.

"Just trying to help a, well, a lady." He seemed to be enjoying this far too much.

Lucy recovered and stood before him, hands on hips, and steeled herself for one ugly confrontation. He deserved the worst tongue-lashing she could muster, but the words eluded her. Never had such anger and frustration and confusion stifled her. She filled her lungs with air as words spun in her brain and she fought to harness her temper-driven tongue to reason with him, rather than spew insults. She was certain the veins on her neck must be bulging by now, and that was not a good sign. The face of dear, sweet Lida loomed before her, and she realized that her anger was not winning her this battle. She released a puff of air, bowed her head, and closed her eyes, searching for reason and clarity.

She raised her face to his. "You know, I would butt out, but I care," she said evenly. "On one score, you've won. I see I won't be able to stop the sale of the camp, but I still believe that something can be done to try to save this place. It would be a tragedy for you to take this away from the children."

Finally, Flynn's expression sobered, and he held his hands out to either side. "Ms. Mitchell, do I look like a camp director to you? Do I look like I could lead a bunch of kids in making pictures with glue and leaves, or on a nature hike, or singing dumb songs like 'Kumbaya'?" She was impressed he actually knew the song. Somewhere, under that cold, urbanite exterior, he had once been a child who sang "Kumbaya."

"No, you certainly do not. For once we agree on something. My point is, you are not the right buyer for this property and your plans are all wrong. If I can't deter you from buying, maybe there's another option out there to continue the camp."

"I highly doubt that. I have very clear, concise plans for this property."

She studied him a moment. It was evident to Lucy

that she could stand here all day and trade barbs with him, and it wasn't going to accomplish one blessed thing. She needed a new tactic, a new way to deal with the indomitable Mr. Flynn. A change of direction, perhaps. It was true enough; Lida did need to sell. Lucy was willing to accept that now, but there still could be a chance she could convince him to keep the camp going once he became the owner.

Lucy crossed her arms over her chest and considered him for a moment. "Would you care to have dinner with me tonight?" The words almost shocked her as much as they obviously shocked him. Of course, she wasn't about to let him know that.

"Dinner...with you. Do I need to worry that you'll poison my food?"

"Maybe." *Oh, boy, what have I gotten myself into?*

Ian grinned and butterflies gripped her. "What the hell, a little danger with dinner sounds intriguing."

"Good, you might just get it. Meet me at Harper's Landing at seven. Do you know where that is?" The situation seemed absurd to her, but she couldn't take the words back now. Harper's Landing was out of the way enough that they could discuss the situation fairly privately, within the safe confines of a public restaurant.

"That's out on County W, isn't it? I'll see you there, Lucy. Looking forward to it." He winked at her and grinned. She hated guys who winked at girls, and now she was having dinner with one of them. *Ish.*

Lucy gave a quick nod in acknowledgement, then turned her back to him and continued her trek along the road, feeling his eyes burning into the back of her head. What was it she had been looking for? Oh well, it would come to her as soon as she calmed down, and a walk would certainly help that. Or not.

****

Lucy was in the process of rifling through her closet in search of just the perfect outfit for her dinner meeting with Flynn. The outfit had to be stylish, to refute his opinion of her as just another hick from the sticks, and also convey the seriousness of the agenda she planned to present. An agenda Ian Flynn was so certain would go his way.

He didn't know Lucy Mitchell.

Responding to the chime of her cell phone, Lucy noted her sister's shop number and answered.

"Hey, El, you aren't going to believe what I've gotten myself into."

"I can't imagine."

"I invited Flynn to a dinner meeting at Harper's tonight. You should come over and help me pick out an outfit." She continued to look through the closet.

"I can't."

"Why not? I trust your judgment. Besides, you're the only one I can count on to tell me if I look stupid or not."

When Ellie failed to answer, Lucy stopped what she was doing. "Is something wrong?"

"Oh, I just need a sounding board."

"Okay, spill." Lucy sat on the edge of the bed.

"Remember when you were in the coffee shop and asked if everything was all right between Randy and me?" Ellie's voice hitched as she said his name.

"Yes, but I didn't mean it seriously. You two are fine, aren't you?"

"Normally, I would say we definitely are fine. But he stopped in at the shop this afternoon and, I don't know, something in his mood bothered me. He wanted me to close the shop so we could have a cup of coffee and talk."

"Randy sit and talk in the middle of a workday? That is a bit weird. Did he say why?"

"He wanted me to take a vacation. Not a family vacation, just him and I."

"In the middle of your busiest time of the year?"

"That's what I said. It would be crazy for me to shut down in the middle of summer. I wouldn't even know who to hire to watch it for me. He's a businessman. He knows how that could kill my numbers."

"I'm sure he could understand that. Is that all there was to it?" Lucy was certain Ellie was reading something into a perfectly innocent request. Ellie tended to be the worrier in the family.

"No. He started talking about all the fun things we used to do and how boring we've become."

"Sounds to me he's pouting about something like a little boy. He needs some attention."

"Hmmm, maybe, but it seemed as though there was more to it than that. At first his demeanor scared me. I was afraid that something had happened to Abby. He reassured me that she was fine, but he acted as though he wanted to tell me something."

"Did you ask him?"

"I asked what was responsible for the mood he was in, and he kind of froze. He didn't say anything. Of course, a couple of customers walked in which didn't help. In fact, he seemed quite angry."

"What happened?"

"He quickly said we'd talk tonight and walked out. It was just so strange, Lucy. Something is up and I don't know what. His business is doing better than it's ever done and things at home have been fine. We never fight about anything. Our days seem to flow pretty smoothly so I can't imagine what's going on. Anyway, I needed another perspective."

"Talk to him tonight. Get it out in the open whatever it is. You can't deal with it until you do. He's too young for a mid-life crisis so it's probably just a phase." As she spoke, Lucy noticed the leg of a sage green pantsuit sticking out of her closet. She stood and pulled it out, inspected it for wrinkles and laid it on the bed.

"Really, El," she continued, "I wouldn't worry."

"I hope you're right. I knew you'd make me feel better. Good luck with your date tonight."

"It's not, I repeat, NOT a date. It's a meeting. I've got a plan to increase the profits of the camp and I want to pitch it to Flynn."

"Well, I wish you luck."

"I wish you luck as well, although I don't think you'll need it. Take him on a long weekend in September and shag his brains out. It'll make whatever's wrong all better."

Lucy heard Ellie chuckle on the other end. "Sex isn't always the answer for us old married folks, you know."

"Don't knock it 'till you've tried it. I've got to get ready now."

"Thanks for the session. See ya."

"Bye." She clicked off the phone and studied the suit on the bed. Classy, understated, perfect.

A familiar voice called to her from the front door. "Lucy, you here?"

Shooter. "Hey, just a sec." She closed the closet doors and went out into the hall that cut through the center of her house. "It's been a while. Where've you been?"

Shooter's tall frame nearly blocked the late afternoon sun streaming through the screen door. The aroma of motor oil met her nostrils, and considering he must have come straight from work at the garage, he was rather clean. He'd obviously changed into a clean T-shirt and jeans, which was unusual for him this early in the day. She smiled as she noticed the same beat-up camouflage cap he'd worn for ages scrunched over the sandy curls on his head. The too-tight shirt accentuated his meaty shoulder muscles and rippled stomach deliciously well. He did have a great bod. Must have been all the wrenching.

"Hi, I need to talk to you about something important."

Lucy placed her hands on his hips and leaned into him to brush her lips with his. "We can talk later," she said in a sultry voice. "I have a meeting tonight and you"—she pushed up the sides of his T-shirt to feel the skin beneath—"and I have to make up for lost time when I get back." She nipped at his neck and bit his ear lobe.

Shooter took a step back and pulled his shirt down. "Lucy, I don't think so."

Something wasn't right. Lucy stepped toward him. "Look, I'm sorry, but I have this damned meeting and I cannot miss it." She took his hand in hers and smiled coquettishly. "I'll make it up to you later."

"Lucy." He took another step back until he was in the corner of the hall by the front door like a caged animal.

"Okay, what's up?" He had rotten timing. As much as she didn't have time for whatever it was, he looked like he was about to have a major pout coming on and she had better give him some time. "Are you angry with me? Because if you are, I'm sorry, I didn't mean whatever it is and I've missed you."

Shooter placed his hands on her arms. "I need to tell you something."

Lucy placed her hands on either side of his head and guided his mouth to hers. Shooter closed his eyes and allowed her lips to play upon his. "Like I said, I've missed you."

"Lucy." He pushed her away roughly. "Listen to me."

Something in his voice caught her up short. "Okay, okay."

"First, I need my Dale Earnhardt hooded sweatshirt back."

"It's in the bedroom closet." He followed her down the hall and stood in the doorway as she retrieved the black shirt off the shelf where it had been neatly folded. As she did so, a neatly wrapped box fell onto the floor.

"Are you ever going to open that?" He was referring to the gift her father had sent her after graduating from high school.

"No, for the last time."

"Then why not throw it away?" He threw the sweatshirt over his shoulder.

"Butt out, Shooter." He knew better than to broach that subject.

"I give up." Shooter sighed.

She followed him into the hall where he turned to face her once again.

"Even though this has never been serious between us, I want you to hear it from me rather than from the all the gossips in this town."

"What's up? You didn't wreck your truck again, did you?"

"I met someone." Shooter shrugged and smiled. He looked like a little kid with his first crush. Lucy felt as though she'd been sucker-punched.

"You met someone?" It suddenly felt as though the air had been sucked from the room. "Is this why you've been such a stranger lately?"

"Yeah. You look upset." He angled his head before her. "You're not, are you? I mean, this was just for fun between you and me."

Lucy shot her chin into the air. "Of course, I'm not upset. Why would I be?"

"Well good, because you're too good a friend to me. You're getting that rosy thing up into your neck, though. Are you sure you're not mad?" He waved a finger toward her traitorous blush.

She put a hand to her neck. "I said no." She tried to tamp down the hurt that was filling her. This was stupid. They'd never declared undying love for each other. She simply thought she'd be the one to end it. *Damn ego.*

She steadied her voice before she spoke. "Who is it? Someone I know?"

"Nope. She's the new librarian over in Eagle River and teaches Sunday school at my mom's church."

"So, your mother introduced you?" *Alice, you witch.*

"Yep. Now don't go putting anything into that." Shooter held up his hands.

"It's kind of hard not to since your mother hates me."

"Well, you bucked her on the old school being torn down, and, well, Lucy, you get pretty hotheaded when you're mad. 'Course my mom can hold a grudge forever. But this has nothing to do with that." Shooter took a step toward her. "You'd like Marta, you would. I want you to meet her."

"Why? You want me to give her a few pointers?"

"That's mean."

"Yeah, it is. Sorry." They looked at each other a long moment. "So, you've come to tell me goodbye."

"We sure had fun," he said quietly.

"Yeah, we did." She couldn't deny that her feelings were hurt. Unable to look him straight in the eye any longer, she bit her lower lip to keep from spewing any other embarrassing remarks.

Shooter stood before her, lifted her chin with the tip of his finger. "It's time to move on. I want to get married, have some kids. Maybe put up a double-wide on the forty behind my parents' place."

"You think I don't?" She wished he wasn't so close. "Want to get married and have kids, that is. Although hell would have to freeze over before your mother and I could live on the same piece of ground."

"Yeah, that wouldn't have worked. 'Sides if you did want to get married and have kids, it wouldn't be with me."

Lucy stuck a defiant chin in the air. "How do you know it couldn't have been with you?"

Shooter chuckled. "Because you don't love me, and I don't love you. I don't know why. Things just didn't spark between us."

Lucy couldn't think of a single argument to his statement.

"Take care, Luce. The right guy will come along. I know he will." With that he brushed a kiss on the top of her nose and left her standing alone in the hallway biting her lip and feeling a bit unsettled. Not one for wallowing in a pool of pity, she gave in to melancholy for about a minute before anger set it. How dare he find someone else before she did?

Suddenly the sage pantsuit didn't fit the bill any longer. Reaching into the back of her closet, she pulled out a dress she hadn't dared to wear in ages.

Chapter Five

Ian found it interesting that Lucy had chosen an obscure destination like Harper's Landing for their meeting. Only ten miles from town, but off the main road and down a long, snaking drive through dense forest. Harper's Landing was situated along the south fork of the Flambeau River. The building itself was nothing special from the entrance off the parking lot, but the interior was a mix of rustic elegance and country charm. Log beams, fieldstone fireplaces, candles.

Ian sat at the bar, his back to the entry, and pretended interest in the aquarium teeming with freshwater fish along the back wall. *Where was she?* He checked his Rolex for the fourth time. Seven fifteen. She was fifteen minutes late, but it was beginning to feel more like fifty. He was impatient, edgy, but why? He knew why. His nerves had been raw ever since the phone call from his mother.

He'd spent the remainder of his day pushing the memory of the unsettling call from his mind. Mike being as sick as Gladdy'd described was dubious, and if he was, well, tough luck. Perhaps it was time for payback. Payback for a spectacularly shitty childhood. Rising above it had been hell, but he'd done it. Every phone call, every bit of contact with them brought it all back. Nothing ever changed when it came to his family. And if he remembered correctly, a jukebox had whined in the background of Gladdy's call, proving the lack of believability where they were concerned.

He lifted his water with lemon and drained the glass.

On top of it all, he was bored with this village, and his restlessness was getting the better of him. He needed a diversion, a release. Lucy Mitchell could very well serve that purpose. After all, while she most certainly wasn't his type, she was female and, who knows, she may clean up well. Yes, she just might do.

Ian set the glass precisely on the center of the coaster before him and found he was looking forward to an opportunity to spar with the intriguing Ms. Mitchell again, if that was her intent. Causing her anger to boil held the promise of great entertainment. He grinned at the thought of her invitation. She had spunk, he'd give her that.

Certainly, it was possible that her motives were otherwise. If Lucy was indeed interested in him, he could handle that. She could toy with him all she wanted. *The things a man has to put up with.*

"Can I get you another?" The bartender appeared to be in her late forties and trying desperately to hide it. She bounced her breasts with every movement and tossed her dishwater-blond hair like a teenager.

"No, thanks." He checked his watch again. "My dinner date should be here soon."

The bartender leaned on her elbows and set her bosom on the bar before him, as though they were sharing some intimate secret. "I'm assuming it's a 'she' and, if so, she better get here real soon, or some lucky girl's gonna come along and snap you right up." She winked at him and gave him a hungry smile that showed her dimples. The establishment lost some of its charm.

Ian leaned toward her. "I'll just have to do what I can to hold them off." He winked back at her.

"Excuse me."

Ian turned to find a composite of Lucy Mitchell. A delicious vision in a shimmering sapphire dress stood before him. His breath caught in his throat. Could this be the same angry storm cloud he'd encountered just this afternoon? She was breathtaking. From her swanlike neck, delicate shoulders, generous curves, to the long, graceful angles of her tanned arms and legs. And those legs, like those of a dancer, athletic and, God, they went all the way up to…to the daringly short silky sheath that flowed over her skin like rainwater. Her hair, gathered into an unruly ponytail earlier, hung in a fluid chestnut sheen that nearly touched her bare elbows. Ian forced the knot from his throat into his stomach and felt an ache gnawing in his belly.

If this was her secret weapon in her plea for the

camp, at the moment it was working. How the hell was he going to concentrate on the business at hand with her looking like that? Damn, this was unfair. Of course, if her agenda was to seduce him, this was going to be a walk in the park. For one night only.

Ian rose from his stool. The thought of running his hands down the silky curves before him was distracting. Unexpectedly, the promise this evening held blossomed exponentially.

"I hate to interrupt, but I believe I owe you an apology." Lucy moved toward him as though she were floating on a pillow of air. "Sorry I'm late," she said in a voice as smooth and silky as chocolate. "I hope you haven't been waiting long." She extended a hand toward him.

Ian hadn't expected to be blindsided this way. "Ah, no, not long." He stepped forward and took her slender hand in his while attempting to keep his gaze from tumbling down her body. If business was her intent, she was deliberately disarming him, and he could play that game as well, once he regained his wits.

He raised her hand to his lips and feathered a kiss above her knuckles. He held her gaze with his own and could easily see she was a bit uncomfortable at the unexpected feel of his lips upon her skin. To her credit, she easily recovered and flashed a confident smile. He slowly lowered her hand, keeping her fingers cradled between his thumb and palm.

"Aren't you the charmer." Lucy appeared to be studying him. She withdrew her fingers from his embrace. Her lips curved in a seductive smile.

Ian couldn't stop the grin from spreading across his face. "I could say the same. You're a woman full of surprises, Ms. Mitchell, full of surprises."

"Call me Lucy and…" She wet her lips with the tip of her tongue. "I hope that's a compliment, Mr. Flynn." She was flirting with him, and he loved every sweet second of it.

"It most definitely is, and the name is Ian." This was promising to be a highly amusing evening, although it didn't change the fact that she wasn't going to get her way, had she planned to continue the argument regarding the camp. But for the present, Ian fully anticipated an enchanting diversion. "I must say, you were well worth the wait."

"I hope you feel that way at the end of the evening, Mr. ah, Ian." Little did she know, he was counting on just such an outcome.

The hostess approached them. "I have a table for you if you'd follow me."

Ian watched Lucy turn on her heel and follow the hostess. The silky fabric of her dress caressed the enticing sway of her hips in a way that made him hungry, and not for food. *What would she look like without the dress?* Damn, he hadn't had a woman in forever, it seemed. Hadn't had the time. Want and need shot through him like lightning with a sense of urgency and heat that was quite deliciously distracting. Far be it from him to ignore any opportunity, business or otherwise.

Especially one as tempting as Lucy Mitchell.

The hostess seated them at a small table next to the windows just off the river's edge. Weeping willow trees swept the opposite riverbank with slow, lazy caresses. A swan, regal and majestic, floated on the languid current. Ian held a chair for Lucy, and as she sat, he had an overwhelming urge to run his hand across the exposed skin on her back. He wanted to touch her, feel her skin, and sample the promise of its softness. The hostess handed them menus, took their drink orders—an Old Fashioned for Lucy and another water for Ian—and left them to themselves in the dining room bathed in candlelight.

"Afraid ordering alchohol may impair you in some way?" She was teasing him.

"No. Never developed much of a taste for it."

The intimate candlelight seemed to illuminate the appearance of the woman across the table from him with a golden aura that heightened her cheekbones and coaxed forth the flecks of fire in her sable eyes. For once, the fire wasn't borne of anger. He wasn't at all certain what he read in them tonight, but her anger seemed to have abated. The glow of candlelight lent an angelic sheen to her hair. But this was no angel, of that he had no doubt. The slight shadow of a nipple pushed upon the front of

Moonlight Bay

her dress and he averted his eyes fully appreciating the sensual stirrings within him.

"Nice place," he offered as he scanned the menu. When she didn't answer immediately, his eyes slanted in her direction. "On my drive, I couldn't help but think this area could be a superb location for a golf course and country club. The lay of the land, the gently rolling landscape, it would be perfect." The remark was meant to spark a fire under her cool exterior, and he was certain it did just that, but only by the slight blush forming just below the perfect line of her jaw.

Lucy kept her eyes on the menu, scanning from top to bottom while she replied. "Why don't you buy the entire county while you're at it? Seriously, I know of an old dump you could turn into a ski resort and an abandoned veneer mill in Peeksville you could rebuild into one of those swanky day spas. Why, we could turn every square inch of Price County into a getaway for the rich and the famous. Think of the piles of money you'd make." She waved a graceful hand.

Ian put down his menu and laughed. "A community activist and a comedian. Why, Lucy, you become more intriguing every time you cross my path." He liked a sense of humor and rarely ran across a good one.

She shot him a disapproving look, but something in her eyes didn't quite carry it off. It occurred to Ian that he was already enjoying himself more than he had in quite some time. To hell with the dinner choices, the only thing in the restaurant he wanted was right in front of him.

"I like you, Lucy." She seemed a bit startled; he liked that. "You're quite a woman."

She unraveled her napkin and nearly knocked her water goblet over. "You don't even know me," she said once she recovered.

"That could be remedied, right here, tonight."

His comment brought her up short and rendered her speechless. She'd obviously come ready to knock him senseless with the dress and the makeup and the hair, but hadn't prepared herself for his flirtation as well.

Lucy picked up her menu and gestured toward his. "We need to order." Concentrating on the dinner choices seemed a welcome distraction for her. Perhaps she needed a moment to regroup. Ian had no doubt that behind the oversize menu, she was squirming in her seat.

"Tell me something about yourself, Lucy. Have you lived in this area all of your life?"

"I have." He noted the pride she felt at saying that. "Except for my time at UW Eau Claire. I teach physical education at Butternut Creek High, and my girls' volleyball team nearly went to state last year. My sister, Ellie, owns the coffee shop we sparred in yesterday. Ellie's husband is an accountant, and I have a niece, Abigail, whom I adore. That's it. My life in a nutshell."

"Is there a Mr. Mitchell?"

"No." The finality in her voice said "next subject" loud and clear.

"Ever? You've never been married?"

"How about you? I don't see a ring on your finger." Her eyes held a challenge.

"Too busy raping and pillaging small villages. What's your story?" She clearly didn't appreciate his attempt at humor.

"None of your business."

He chuckled. "Touchy subject?"

"I want you to know that I am very devoted to my summers at Moonlight Bay. I see firsthand what the experience does for the campers. There's no better reward than a child leaving camp with a heightened sense of confidence and worth. Self-esteem is so important to a child. Don't you agree?"

His eyes shifted from the perusal he'd been giving her, toward the windows, then down to his fork, which he picked up and then set back down. "Yes, I suppose," he answered her.

"Now it's your turn. Tell me about Ian Flynn." Damned if he didn't like the way his name sounded on her lips.

Ian took a sip from his water glass. "There's not much to tell. I started my company with a friend, right out of college, and bought him out a few years later. I'm expanding our holdings to nearly every part of the state. There's land near White Cap that we're looking at now. I have to say that I spend nearly all my waking hours to making this company the success that it is." He felt his chest expand with pride.

"Sounds like fun." She looked at him over the rim of her drink. He ignored her jibe.

"Last fall I acquired a large tract of land along the Flambeau River, just north of here. I have plans to lot it off, build a few cabins, and sell it all. It'll bring in a tidy dollar when all is said and done."

"I don't care about your money. I meant personally. You do have a personal life, don't you? Work can't be the only thing in your life." She leveled a condescending gaze upon him.

Obviously, he'd failed to impress her.

"My personal life is just that, personal."

"Fair is fair. Is there a Mrs. Flynn?" She was trying to look innocent, but innocent she was not.

"There's only one Mrs. Flynn and she's my mother. I dare say, one is all this world needs. No, I am not married, never have been." Her attempt to throw him off track by turning the conversation to personal matters amused him.

"Okay. So, your relationship with your mother is complicated, and your view of marriage is, well, not good." Lucy folded her hands in her lap. "All right, Ian, I'd like to discuss the sale of the camp."

"Don't you think you should approach Mrs. Duncan?" Honestly, he didn't know what more he could say to make her understand the futility of her plea.

"I've spoken with Lida. She's explained her reasons and I accept them."

"Then it seems to me it's a moot point. The sale of the camp is what she wants. It's also what my company wants, and we are proceeding as such. I'm not sure what more there can be to discuss." He fingered the rim of his glass as gazed at her. "I was under the impression this was more of a date, not a business meeting."

She smiled sweetly and asked, "Do I look that hard up?"

"Lucy, you're something." Ian took another drink. "And when I figure out what that is, you'll be the first to know."

He leaned his elbows on the table and brought his face nearer to hers. "The last thing I would guess is that you would be hard up. Any woman who looks the way you do must have men running after her in droves. I'm just not in the habit of doling out my time to lost causes. Business or otherwise."

"I'll bet not." Their eyes held for a brief, sizzling moment. "Look, Ian, I'll try not to be a smartass if you'll try as well. I know it'll be hard, but please do the best you can."

Ian smiled first. "Deal," he answered, just as the waitress set their salads in front of them, and for a few moments they ate in silence.

"All right, Lucy, what did you hope to accomplish this evening?" He sat back in his chair and studied her as she wiped the corners of her mouth and set her fork down.

"I'm looking for some way to save the camp. That should be obvious. Moonlight Bay is important to a lot of people. The kids need a place to spend their summers away from the city. Butternut Creek needs the revenue that is generated from the influx of travel to and from the camp every week."

"There're other camps out there. Don't you mean you need to have a place to go?" Okay, so he was still being a smartass. Some habits die hard. But he knew he'd screwed up by the insulted look on her face.

"Just what are you getting at?" She was clearly angry and Ian didn't fault her for that. He should have kept his big mouth shut. "I'm trying to have a civilized conversation with you, but you continue to throw insults at me. Give it a rest."

He felt thoroughly admonished.

"Sorry. Look, I've seen the payroll records. You work for minimum wage. The others don't. Therefore, you must be independently wealthy or not exactly motivated to achieve and I don't think either of those is the problem."

Lucy pointed her leafy fork at him. "There are more important things in life than a big paycheck, and I'm thinking you have a lot to learn about life, in general. Besides, I'm sure you've noticed the camp is in financial difficulty, and I didn't want to be part of the problem. What I'm suggesting to you, Ian"—she paused a moment—"is that we explore ways to make the camp profitable, to allow it to stay in business."

"Just hear me out, please." She took a deep breath before proceeding enthusiastically. "Okay, I believe the answer to the camp's financial woes is to make it profitable year 'round."

"Waste of time." She ignored him.

"The camp would be a perfect getaway in the winter. We could draw upon the logging heritage of this area by opening the lodge to serve logging camp style meals. Think of it, Ian. The lodge would be perfect with just a few decorating details to bring out that logging camp feel. The long tables flanked by benches that are already there would be perfect. We'd have a fire crackling in the fireplace and folk music in the background, and the meals could be served family style."

He shook his head and began to respond, but she cut him off.

"Just hold on, I'm not finished. The land around the camp has rolling hills that could be used for sledding and tubing, the trails could be groomed for cross-country skiing, and the lake cleared for ice skating. Just think of it, the evergreens heavy with snow under the night sky. We could build a fire along the shore and roast marshmallows and hot dogs, serve hot chocolate, maybe have a local come out and play guitar. It would be the perfect winter recreation area for families. The place would be a hit. I'm sure of it." Her face was glowing with excitement.

"The cabins are not winterized, are they?"

"Well, no, but we wouldn't use the cabins in winter. Families could come for the day. Church groups could come out, community groups, Scouts, 4H groups. I see real potential here."

There was no easy way to let her down. "Lucy, I don't know how to explain this so you'll understand, once and for all. I'm not going to save the camp." He could see by the look on her face, she wasn't done and for a moment, he was certain she had a rather crude suggestion for his idea.

"Ian..."

"No, it's not what I want." He took a sip of his water. "Lucy, you have this fantasy about some backwoods retreat for families that simply isn't going to happen. Why would I want to collect a couple of bucks from a kid sledding down a hill when I could get hundreds of thousands from selling condos? Your ideas are purely the sugar-coated result of living in a dream world."

"I don't think you're seeing the big picture here. There's more to life than money."

"So says those that don't have any. Face it, the camp is nothing more than a babysitter for spoiled, rich kids. Let me tell you my vision for Moonlight Bay." He straightened the silverware in front of him until it was aligned perfectly. "I see expensive condominiums, tennis courts, a gym, a golf course. The kind of place that would bring a whole new clientele to this part of the state, infuse money into the economy, help this town be more than it is, bring jobs into the area. These are the kind of people that could make a difference here. They'd come to get away from the stress of their city lives and spend serious dollars in this town. Think what that could do for Butternut Creek, for your school, for your sister's business."

"I suppose they'd leave their children at home with nannies." Her tone was terse.

He ignored her. "From what I can see, your way of life is threatened and you're simply frightened by that prospect. Now it's your turn to hear me out. I think I have an idea that may appeal to you. If you'd like a way to earn more money than your teaching salary, I'm thinking we could hire you to look after the condominium complex. Of course, I'd have to explore your qualifications, discuss training, but I'm planning a small apartment to be built within the complex to house a caretaker. I'm thinking you could be that person. Hell, you'd be perfect. It would be helpful to have someone who knows the area. You could even earn extra as a guide for people who don't know their way around. Think of it, Lucy, you could live right on the premises rent free. You wouldn't be giving up a thing." He spread his hands wide. "It's the perfect solution." He was quite pleased with his idea.

"I'd rather be sucked up by a tornado." If it was possible to see a person's blood boil, he was seeing it first hand. Red began to creep up her neck and her nostrils flared. She pushed her salad plate away from her.

"What?" Honestly, was there no way to please this woman?

Just then, the waitress delivered their meals, much to Ian's relief, although he was a bit nervous she'd tip his plate into his lap and leave him sitting there.

He cut into his filet, took a satisfying bite and noticed she was staring at him.

"Your scallops are calling your name." He waved his fork in her direction.

"Do you know what an asinine idea that was? I thought you were just rude, but now I know you're stupid as well. You've completely missed the whole point of my concern with this." She closed her eyes and shook her head.

"You could just say 'no thank you.' Now eat." He cut into his steak again. "I'm done, Lucy. I'm tired of this subject."

They ate in silence for a few minutes. Silence that Ian was immensely grateful for.

Lucy held her fork in midair, a buttery scallop skewered at the end. "Did your parents ever send you to camp, Ian?" She popped the scallop into her mouth and licked her lips.

Aw, jeez, not again.

He finished chewing his steak, then dabbed at the corners of his mouth. "No." He'd said it a bit too loud. The woman didn't know when to give up when she wanted something. Damn it all, she was...well...she was a lot like him.

"Didn't you ever wonder what it would have been like? I'm sure you must have known other children who enjoyed summer camp."

"No." He had to steer the conversation in another direction. "Tell me, what do you do outside of the camp, since you're so adamant about having a life."

She ignored him. "What did you enjoy as a child?"

"What every other kid enjoys."

"Like what? Tell me."

"Riding a bike, playing ball, the usual." How the hell had the tables suddenly turned? Ian did not enjoy this interview at all. He'd answered her question, but it was the other children in his neighborhood he'd spoken of. He wasn't about to tell her his only toys had been wooden blocks he'd taken from a construction site down the street. He'd spent hours in the dirt outside constructing roads and buildings, sometimes whole cities. He'd loved to make something from nothing, see the possibilities. He hadn't even owned a bike until he'd earned one himself mowing lawns and performing odd jobs in the rich section of town. He vowed someday he'd be living there as well. Now he did.

"Were you happy as a child?"

This line of questioning definitely had to stop. "What does that have to do with anything? My childhood is none of your business."

"Because, as clichéd as it may sound, children are our future, and it's important that they have a place to go that makes them feel loved and appreciated, especially when their home life may not be the best. It may mean the very difference in the path that child chooses to take. Ultimately, it affects all of us. A camp like ours can be the catalyst for something wonderful. I know it works, I've seen it." Her face softened as she continued. He hoped that was a sign she was letting go. "Look, I can see it's hard for you to relate. I suppose you were you brought up in some fancy boarding school or spent your summers at the golf course, or traveling Europe. Not every child has those opportunities. Some have no opportunities at all."

That's enough.

"Take a breath, Lucy." He watched as she stopped her line of questioning and gaped at him. "I've been badgered enough, thank you very much." He watched as she snapped her jaw shut and then took a sip of her water. "I think there's more going on here than a discussion of how to save a lost cause."

"Such as?" He liked the way her eyebrows knit together in consternation.

Time to have a little fun. He didn't want to give her time to think about it, so he launched into his assault. "There's a chemistry between us, don't you think?" He kept his voice smooth. The same voice he used to charm an unwilling business opponent. "We're attracted to each other, plain and simple. That's really what this evening is about, isn't it? Why else would you have chosen such a romantic setting? I'm sure there are plenty of other eating establishments in the area. This one seems the perfect setting for a first evening together." He ran a finger down her forearm, felt his crotch warm, and tried to keep his eyes off her cleavage. "You're a beautiful woman, Lucy Mitchell. Beautiful and tempting, and I'll bet there's one wild fire beneath that cool exterior."

"Our food is getting cold." Lucy turned her attention to her plate and, thankfully, shut the hell up.

She tackled her food as though she hadn't eaten all day, which was a good possibility considering the cling of her dress.

"Would you care for dessert?"

"No." She dabbed the napkin at the corners of her mouth.

The waitress cleared their dishes as an uncomfortable silence settled between them.

Her back straightened against her chair and her eyes focused on some distraction behind him.

"Lucy...something wrong?" Ian looked over his shoulder, noticed another couple leaving their table, then angled his head into her line of vision.

"Uhh, no. No, nothing at all. I just..." She dabbed the napkin at the corners of her mouth again. "Would you excuse me? I need to use the restroom." She rose and left her napkin on the table. "I'll be right back."

****

Lucy's heart was booming in her chest so hard that she could barely breathe. She wove her way through the dining room and into the entry of the restaurant.

"May I help you?" The hostess smiled her way.

"No, thank you." Lucy wished for privacy.

She watched through the leaded-glass window as her brother-in-law and a big-haired Barbie doll crossed the parking lot, his hand resting on the small of her back. The touch spoke of intimacy, and a black feeling of dread spiraled through her. The two stopped in front of Randy's car, the woman smiled at him, and then rose on tiptoes. Randy gave her a quick peck on the lips and placed his hands on her shoulders as he stepped back.

A waitress rounded the corner with impeccable timing. "Table four left their car keys."

"They just walked out," the hostess said. "I'll see if I can catch them."

"I'll take them out for you," Lucy interjected. The hostess looked unsure. "They're friends of mine."

The hostess and waitress exchanged a look and Lucy realized she needed to do a bit of cajoling.

She pointed a finger at the hostess. "Aren't you Marion Steinhagen's granddaughter? She lives across the street from me."

"You're the one that helps her with her flower beds in the spring. That's so nice of you."

"Well thank you. Now about those keys. I can save you a trip." Lucy plastered the sweetest smile she could muster across her face.

The waitress shrugged, and the hostess said, "Okay. Thanks." She dropped the keys into Lucy's outstretched hand.

Lucy stormed between the parked cars focused solely on the two people across the lot, her high-heeled shoes jet-powered by rage.

"Randy, you forgot your keys." She stood, one hand on her hip, the other jiggling the forgotten keys.

Randy's eyes registered his shock while his girlfriend slinked around the front of the car. As if that would keep Lucy from bounding over the top and strangling her. It was too tempting a scenario.

"Who the hell is this?" The pile of hair spoke. Randy sent her his best "shut up" look.

"Luce, ahh, I'd like you to meet a business associate of mine." He nervously gestured to the blonde behind the car. "Cindy..."

"What business is this now, Randy? I didn't realize you were dabbling in prostitution. Wow, an accountant *and* a pimp. Now that's what I call diversified." Anger filled her, consumed her, and threatened her control. An inferno of rage that this man could betray Ellie and Abby.

"That's not fair, Lucy. This isn't what it seems."

From the front of the car, came, "Randy, honey, should I get in the car?"

"Randy-honey" looked like a caged animal. "No, Cindy, you can't."

Lucy jiggled the keys in her hand. "Hence, the keys,

Cindy."

"Now, Luce, like I said, we need to calm down. This isn't what it seems." He held up his palms with a pleading look on his face.

"Of course, it's what it seems. Can't you come up with a better line than that? Do you think I'm blind? Do I look that stupid?"

"Ellie's at fault here, too, you know." He pointed a shaky finger at her, but his confidence was clearly blown.

Lucy took a step toward him and he jerked away in response. She shook the keys at him. "You bastard, Randy. How dare you blame Ellie. She's been a good, kind, and loving wife to you and a terrific mother to Abby, your daughter. You remember Abby, don't you? How can you do this to her? Is this the thanks Ellie gets for sticking by you when you didn't have two pennies to rub together? You should be ashamed of yourself.

"And you..." She turned her attention to the cowering heap of hair on the other side of the car. "You've got yourself a real prize here, honey. Of course, you look like just the kind of girl Randy deserves."

"Stop it, Lucy." Randy's defense of the tramp enraged Lucy all the more.

She took two more steps toward him. "You son-of-a-bitch. You'd better come clean with my sister tonight, or I'll make you pay. I mean it, you had better tell her before she hears it on the street, unless she already has. I won't allow her to be strung along this way." With that she drew her arm back and tossed the keys into the brush at the edge of the gravel parking lot.

Randy's eyes registered panic as he watched the keys sail overhead. "Luce...shit."

Lucy spun on her heel and marched back toward the restaurant. Heaven help the next man that crossed her path.

Ian Flynn stepped through the restaurant door, her purse dangling from one hand and a smirk curling one side of his mouth.

Chapter Six

Ian suddenly had the feeling he was standing in the path of a very angry tempest hurtling in his direction, daring someone, anyone, to cross her stormy path. It was an opportunity Ian could not resist. He stepped directly into her path. She moved to the left and he did the same. She swerved again, causing him to adjust his stance once more.

Comforting a woman on the rebound was not what he'd planned this evening. He'd succeeded in suppressing her inquisition into his childhood and thought he'd rekindled the seduction he'd begun. But now, well, drying tears was not his forte, although she hadn't produced any. Damn, he didn't have patience for this kind of thing.

"Threw you over, did he?" The venomous look in her eyes said it all.

"Get out of my way, Ian." Her beautiful, sable eyes lit with licks of fire, and the prettiest shade of pink dusted her neck and cheeks. "By the way, nice purse."

He glanced down at the black leather bag he'd reluctantly taken care of for her. She tore the purse from his hand and continued toward the door.

"Poor slob should have known better than to cross you." He said to her backside as he followed.

"I really don't need your commentary at the moment." She swung the purse backward in his direction, striking him in the upper arm, but never missing a step. In one fluid movement Ian beat her to the door and covered the knob with his expansive hand.

"I'm taking you out of here before you accost anyone else," he said.

"No, you're not." She tried to wrestle the doorknob out of his hand with no luck. "I have to pay the bill. This was my invitation, remember?" Her slender hand didn't stand a chance against his.

As she continued to struggle with the knob he held

captive, he leaned forward until his mouth was next to her ear. The lavender scent of her hair threatened to rob him of his senses. "The bill has been taken care of."

"Oh, no, I'm paying." She circled his wrist with both hands and pulled, but to no avail. Her determination was admirable.

"I'm as feminist as they come, but it's too late for that now."

"Oh, give me a break." She yanked once again, but he held fast.

It was time to move on. "Come, Lucy, your work here is done." He released the knob and quickly took her by the elbow, directing her away from the door. She jerked her elbow free from his grasp, but he captured it once again and steered her across the parking lot.

"You're the next person on my list if you don't stop handling me."

"Don't tempt me, Lucy. You wouldn't stand a chance. I'm taking you home so you can lick your wounds in private. Another display like that and you'll have yourself a nasty reputation." She jerked once, but he simply increased his grip on her elbow.

"You're taking me home...I don't think so." The stubborn set to her jaw was nearly comical. She pulled away once again, but with a hand on the small of her back, and the other clenching her elbow, Ian propelled her toward his car. She suddenly dug her heels into the gravel and stopped their forward motion.

"Who do you think you are? I'm not going anywhere with you." Her eyebrows were all squiggled together in the cutest way, and she pinched her lips into a tight little bow. It was damn near kissable.

"Thanks a lot, Lucy. You better hope I find my keys," came from the man in the bushes.

Lucy jerked her head in his direction. "Screw you, Randy. Those keys are the least of your problems."

"That's enough." Ian felt as though he were scolding errant schoolchildren. To Lucy he said, "Every set of eyes in the restaurant is probably glued to the windows right now." He pulled her closer. "I'm the person who's keeping his head here. You're not driving when you're this upset, so get in." He opened the car door and waited.

"I'm not getting in your car. For all I know you're some kind of psychopath. You are a *man* after all." She fairly spat the word, as if it were the foulest word in the English language.

"Glad you noticed, but either I'm driving you in my car or yours. I couldn't, in good conscience, send you out on the road in this state of mind." Having her so close did something strange to the pit of his stomach. "Now, where's your car?"

"Good conscience? I didn't think you'd know what that means. Anyone with a good conscience wouldn't take the camp away from the kids who need it."

"Don't be mean, Lucy. It doesn't suit you. Now, tell me, where's your car?" The pressure of his hand on her elbow increased, and he gave it a warning jerk. "Tell me now, or I'll throw you out into the bushes with the other two."

"Fine, it's the Taurus over there." She directed his gaze with the tilt of her chin.

"Where?" His eyes searched, but all he saw was a sorry-looking rust-bucket in bad need of a wash. He eyed her. "You don't mean..." Ian felt a grin spread across his face.

Parked in the corner of the lot was, indeed, a white Ford Taurus that Ian guessed to be about fifteen years old. Rust dotted the wheel wells, each quarter panel sported a dent, the red pinstriping stopped abruptly mid-door, and the antenna was bent. What a piece of crap.

She stuck her chin in the air and said defiantly, "Yes, that's Toty."

"Toty?"

"You heard me. Toty." She avoided his gaze.

"I really hate to ask, but why is your car, such that it is, named 'Toty'?"

"Really, it's kind of self-explanatory." She gave him an impatient glare before rolling her eyes.

"You've got me on this one. Explain." He released her elbow, crossed his arms over his chest, and waited.

Lucy held a palm up. "She totes me here and totes me there, and that's all I expect of her. She delivers every time. Unlike some people I know."

"Toty." He pressed his lips together and

contemplated the word. "Interesting. Well, I'm driving, so get in."

"Absolutely not."

He steered her toward Toty's passenger side, keeping one hand on her back, using the other to hold the door open.

An odor assailed his senses like nothing he'd experienced in a long time.

"What's that smell?"

"Skunk. If you weren't such a city slicker, you'd know that."

"Skunk? Where?" He searched the ground, then the perimeter of the parking lot.

"I hit a skunk on the road a few days ago. It's not so bad, once you're inside. Of course, you're not going to find out." She jostled against the hand on her back, but he held her firmly in place.

"Unfortunately, I will. Get your ass in the car. Now." His patience had hit its limit. She looked at him a moment, speechless, pulled the keys from her purse and slapped them into his hand. "I'll come back to pick up my car in the morning." With that he put a hand on her shoulder and gently forced her in.

Ian slid into the driver's seat, trying to dismiss the awful aroma. If she wasn't so pissed off at the man in the bushes, he was certain she'd be relishing in his discomfort.

With one quick turn of his hand, old, smelly Toty came to life and they were off, turning out of the parking lot, past the two heads bobbing in and out of the brush searching for the keys Lucy had sent into orbit.

"He'll think twice before crossing you again...the man, not the skunk. Of course, that poor creature paid for the day he crossed your path, the skunk, not the man."

"A man *would* think this situation is funny."

Ian felt his pulse quicken at sight of the city limit sign, knowing he was near to getting out of this rust-bucket she called a car.

"Turn here," she ordered and pointed to the left. "I live in the white house, second from the end. The street is a dead end."

Hmm, Ian was sure there was a joke there

somewhere, but didn't dare go near it. He parked Toty in front of an old rambling house that looked a bit displaced among the more modern homes around it. This house, he mused, should be near a barn and have a tractor parked outside, not curb and gutter. At the very least it should have a B&B sign out in front of the porch, which was badly in need of a paint job and new railing.

She hadn't fallen apart yet, but it was coming. Ian was certain of it. He quickly lit from the car and sprang to her side to open the door, although she beat him to it.

"I'm walking you to your door." He fell in behind her.

"No, you're not," she said with a good dose of finality and promptly swung her delicious little derriere up the walk. It reminded him of the way she'd stormed from Lida's office the very first time he'd seen her. She wasn't nearly as fetching in her shorts as she was in the blue silk that now embraced her backside. Suddenly he found himself wishing he could bury his hands in the cascade of her chestnut hair, taste her creamy shoulders with his lips.

He watched her for a moment, hands in pockets, before following. "It's the gentlemanly thing to do and I'm doing it."

She stopped, peered at him over her shoulder with an eyebrow arched, an absolutely fetching picture. "Gentlemanly? Now you're the comedian." She was so cute when she was angry.

She continued up the walk, across the porch, and stopped. She held out her hand and waggled her fingers. "Keys."

He tossed her the keys and waited while she unlocked the old-fashioned front door adorned with an oval etched-glass window. As she angled her body through the doorway, he zipped in behind her, much to her obvious displeasure. The tears would soon be flowing in great rivers and for some reason he couldn't quite fathom, he wanted to be there. Was it to gloat? That would be mean. It certainly wasn't to wipe her cheeks and offer encouragement. Could it be that he was intrigued and wanted to see what a devastated Lucy Mitchell looked like? Probably. Maybe there was just a glimmer of a chance he'd get lucky. No telling where comforting could lead. Needy girls were usually not his type, but, well, he'd do what he could.

****

The gentlemanly thing to do? Who did Ian Flynn think he was kidding? How dare he push her around like...like some disobedient child. She was sick and tired of men always thinking they knew best.

It rankled to be manhandled the way he'd treated her in the parking lot. Leave it to a man to think a woman couldn't even open her own door, much less drive a car, just because she was upset. That would be the day. Lucy Mitchell as a damsel in distress. The last thing she needed was rescuing. Ian Flynn was not in control of this situation, or any other that concerned her, and it was about time he realized that.

Lucy clicked the hall light on. *To hell with Ian, to hell with all men.* She clicked it off again, slammed her purse onto the small table in the middle of the entry, and advanced on him. She placed her hands on his chest and pushed him against the wall. He opened his mouth to say something, but too bad for him. Before he could utter a single word her lips were upon his, enveloping, crushing. She drank in the sweet sensuality of his taste and scent. She wanted his body. She wanted to forget the pain of the betrayal being played upon her sister, the pain she'd known from nearly every man that had come into her life.

His arms came around her, his head lowered as his mouth took hers in response. She slid her hands from the smoothness of his face to the back of his neck, where her fingers wove into the curl of his hair. She continued to bruise his lips with her own. His tongue entered her mouth, and she commanded with her own. And the heat grew.

"It's hot in here...I can't stand it," she whispered against his face, breathless.

"We need to do something about that." His words were all the coaxing she needed.

Their eyes locked as she released his hair, ran her hands down the sides of his neck, cupping the crest of muscle over his chest, feeling his nipples under the material of the shirt, fingering his rib cage, then sliding south to pull the shirt from his pants. Hungrily, she pushed it up as he raised his arms. Carelessly, she tossed the shirt toward an overstuffed chair in the corner. She allowed her eyes to savor the broadness of him, the sculpted muscles, and his golden skin. He was perfect, and this was only the top half.

Ian ran his hands up her arms to rest on her shoulders. Slowly, sensuously, he lowered the straps of her dress, allowing it to slide to the floor and puddle about her feet. A hot prickle of desire shimmied down her spine intoxicating her brain and stirring the pit of her stomach and destinations beyond.

"Tell me, Lucy," his voice was deep, throaty, "do you make a habit of seducing men in your entry way in full view of the street."

"Shut up, Ian." Lucy slipped her fingers under his belt and pulled him away from the wall. His hands cupped the curve of her derriere while his lips attempted to capture her mouth. She dodged him, tugging him behind her to the bedroom down the hall. Once inside the room she swung him around, careful to keep the advantage.

"You keep hauling me around by the belt, you'll put my back out."

"Shut up, Ian." With hands on his shoulders, she pushed him back onto the bed, landing on top of him. She savaged his lips once again while Ian pushed the panties from her and unhooked her bra. Finally, she was naked, and his fingers were drawing exquisite bursts of pure pleasure that she hadn't experienced in a very long time. And somehow, in her need to savor this moment, she lost all desire to be the aggressor. In one delicious, fluid movement, she was beneath him and in glorious surrender, completely willing to be owned by the body of Ian Flynn.

****

Surreptitiously sliding from the bed, Ian collected his clothing strewn about the room and dressed while admiring the chestnut fan of hair spread about the pillow as she slept, face down. Her creamy shoulders beckoned to him. Thoughts of pulling back her hair, running his lips over that skin, dipping his hands beneath the sheets, threatened to override his senses. But he needed to keep his head, keep his desire at bay. Lucy was on the rebound and somewhere in the heat of making love to her, he'd come to care that her feelings not be complicated once again. Curious, Ian thought. He didn't remember feeling that way before, ever.

Lucy Mitchell intrigued him. A beautiful, yet earthy type of woman. She did not use her beauty as her ticket in life. There was so much more to her than that. A temper for certain, but she deeply cared about the children of the camp. She had family that was important to her. And she'd just been jilted, or had she? For all Ian knew, Lucy'd run right back to the man who had openly betrayed her the evening before. For that reason alone, Ian needed to bypass waking her this morning. The idea of welcoming the morning together, in her bed, was an intimacy he couldn't handle.

He quietly slipped from the room despite a few annoying creaks of the hardwood flooring. Once in the hallway, lit only by broken squares of moonlight on the floor, he paused to take in the surroundings he'd paid little attention the night before. The wall opposite her bedroom door held framed pictures.

A simple wooden frame depicted two little girls, one in a maelstrom of blond curls, the other in dark braids, arms around each other squeezing tight, toothy grins upon their faces. Another showed an elderly couple in golfing attire holding clubs, waving and looking the picture of happily retired under a brilliant sun with palm trees in the distance. A smaller frame had Lucy hoisting a trophy high, surrounded by teenage girls in a gym, a volleyball net in the background, all of them triumphantly holding up one finger, signifying number one. Yet another looked to be a school portrait of a young girl in pigtails, and another of this same girl with Lucy making goofy faces at the camera. Finally, a picture of Lucy in the center of a group-hug of campers with the camp lodge in the background. Ian felt he was seeing her life spread out before him in photos. It looked like a nice life.

There was one more. A small family in front of a Christmas tree. He recognized the woman as her sister Ellie; a small child sat contentedly on her lap and behind them a blond man. The unfortunate man in the parking lot the night before.

He now understood the heat of that confrontation. He was her brother-in-law, not a lover. He felt a bit ashamed at his cavalier attitude toward the scene she'd caused. Her brother-in-law was going to be one sorry schmuck once Lucy got hold of him.

He moved to the front of the house. To his left was the dining room. Four old-fashioned wooden chairs surrounded a round claw-footed table and a buffet stacked with books and files.

To his right, French doors flanked the entry into the living room. He couldn't make out much in the darkness, but the walls seemed to be papered with a flowery pattern, the room held an overstuffed chair and sofa, a wooden rocking chair in the corner piled with pillows. Overall, the home looked comfortable, welcoming, in contrast to the tempest that lived here.

Despite the creaking floor and cry of the door hinges, Ian slipped from the house. The motel was approximately two miles away on the opposite side of town, he guessed. With luck, the walk would do his befuddled mind some good. The events of the previous evening, while enjoyable, exciting even, confused him to the core.

Streetlights illuminated faded pools of light on the pavement as Ian walked through the village. Few homes were lit against the soft velvet of early dawn. A woman peered out her kitchen window; a solitary pickup truck pulled up to the corner, then turned. A bent old man stopped sweeping grass from his front stoop to raise a hand in greeting. A young man on a bike sent missiles of newsprint hurtling through the air. As he came toward Ian he called, "Mornin'," and launched another paper onto a porch. Ian bobbed his head in response.

It was a good morning, and Ian couldn't have wiped the evidence from his face if he'd wanted to. Small town life had never appealed to him, but he was feeling so good this morning that the Rockwellian feel of it warmed him. With a satisfied bounce to his step, he continued his trek down the cracked and swollen sidewalk.

The brisk morning air urged his senses to life with its dewy, sweet scent as the dusky pink of dawn began to push the black of night from the eastern sky. He'd slept fitfully alongside Lucy for a short time before giving up and watching the gentle rise and fall of her seemingly blissful slumber. Conflicting emotions coursed through him, waging a battle that denied him peace of mind and sleep. While he'd thoroughly enjoyed the course the evening had eventually followed, she'd turned the tables on him, and it was confusing. His experience as the "seducee" was unfamiliar territory.

Lucy Mitchell's seduction had taken Ian by surprise. And it was a rare occasion that Ian Flynn was caught off-guard. His past with women consisted of sporadic affairs that meant little. His primary concern in a partner had been social status and business connections. He'd only said the dreaded "L" word once, and the result had been disastrous. He'd never make that mistake again.

Ian thought back to the scene in the parking lot. He had to chuckle at the memory of the keys sailing into the brush and the perplexed faces of Lucy's brother-in-law and his date. Good luck, Buddy. He had more than lost keys to worry about. He'd unleashed Hurricane Lucy.

For the first time in what seemed forever, Ian Flynn's emotions were a jumble. Lucy had turned him inside out, and he didn't like it one bit. He stopped walking for a moment, taking in the sight of this sleepy little town coming to life around him, a solitary figure in the early morning shadows, as the streetlight above him blinked once, gave a dying *zzzt* and burned out just as the realization of his situation hit home.

He was stuck in this town only another day or two. The complication of a woman, especially a woman he was beginning to care for, was not in his best interest. He made a decision. Avoid Lucy Mitchell at all cost.

****

Lucy pushed the covering of hair away from her face and stretched the sleep from her naked body. Her body tingled with glorious nips of revisited pleasure and the aftermath of complete ecstasy. The leathery scent of Ian lingered deliciously on her awakening limbs, and somewhere deep within her she wanted to feel his body against hers one more time. Her lips curved into a fully satiated, delicious smile. Somewhere in the middle of their lovemaking, she'd replaced the angst-driven desire to control with an acquiescence of leisurely pleasure as her body responded to his, touch for touch, climax to climax. She nearly trembled with remembrance.

Stretching her arms above the sheets, she rolled to her right, but the bearer of her wonderful mood was gone. Nothing left but an indentation in the pillow. The smile she wore slid from her face and the glow of satisfaction was replaced with hollow disappointment.

"Ian?" The sound of her voice seemed to echo off the hardwood floors. The coo of a morning dove outside her window was all that greeted her. "Ian." Silence, an empty, cold silence.

He'd gone. Her heart sank into the hollow pit of her stomach. What had she expected?

Flinging the sheet from her, she swung her legs over the edge of the bed, sat up, and ran a hand through her unruly hair as it spilled over her shoulders. It stung that Ian had so readily accepted her the night before, only to casually disregard her with the dawn of morning. She pushed away the swell of emotion. With a resolute huff, she straightened her shoulders and set her jaw in a determined line. She wasn't going to waste any more of her precious time on Ian Flynn and his casual dismissal. With a little luck, he'd leave town shortly and she wouldn't have to face him again. There were more serious issues at hand than her bent pride.

Damn Randy for what he'd done. How dare he betray Ellie in this despicable manner, throwing away the life they'd made, the family they'd created. Lucy simply wouldn't allow her sister to be duped into thinking he was the devoted husband she counted on. If Randy had confessed to Ellie the night before, her sister would need a shoulder. Ellie would need her.

So many questions whirled through her mind that her head began to pound. Had Randy confessed his betrayal? Had Ellie weathered the blow, or had she dissolved into an abyss of depression and pain? Had a terrible argument taken place as a result, or had Ellie known in her heart what was happening to her marriage all along? And little Abby. What would be the impact of this mess upon her life?

She glanced at the clock. She had just enough time to

check on Ellie before heading to the camp and her first lesson at nine. If Ellie needed her, Jule could fill in.

She left her unmade bed and stepped into the shower. As the cool water streamed down her body, she couldn't help thinking of Ian, touching all the places he'd touched, as she washed away his scent. It still stung that he'd left her without a single word, without a kiss goodbye, without a "hey, thanks for the roll in the hay." Nothing. Even though she'd clearly been the aggressor, she felt used somehow. She'd more than likely given Ian exactly what he'd hoped for when he followed to her door. How ridiculous it now seemed that he'd driven her home under the guise of concern for her driving under the duress of the scene in the parking lot with Randy.

And then to top it off, *she'd seduced him*. In taking control of the situation, she'd played right into his hands. How stupid could she be?

****

Lucy parked Toty in front of Ellie's Pantry, completely shocked to see the lights on and the open sign in the window. Ellie was certainly dedicated to her business, but this was inconceivable.

Ellie had her back to the door when Lucy entered. "El, how're you doing?" she cautiously asked.

Ellie's blond head turned in her direction as a welcoming smile spread across her face. "Oh, hi, Luce, didn't expect to see you so early." She turned back to cleaning the espresso machine.

"I had a few minutes and thought I'd stop by." She studied Ellie's back. She certainly didn't seem upset. *The bastard never told her.* Lucy wished she'd gone straight to the camp this morning. "Did you get to have that talk with Randy? You know, about his request for a vacation and the strange mood he was in?"

"He came home so late and looked so tired and drawn that I didn't bother to grill him about it. We'll see what he's like tonight. Hopefully it's like you said, a phase."

Lucy pushed her hands into her pockets and shrugged.

"Yeah, I hope so."

"By the way," Ellie turned from her chore, motioned Lucy to come closer, and with the counter between them whispered, "How was your date, I mean, meeting last night?"

Lucy was a bit perplexed by the whispering. "Didn't accomplish a darned thing except..." At least this would give them something to talk about rather than Randy's infidelity. "Well, we slept together."

Ellie's eyes widened. "What?" She quickly clapped a hand over her mouth. "Lucy, you have to explain this." She waved her hands as if to slow traffic. "I don't want the intimate details, but how did this happen?"

Good question. How *did* that happen? She felt her face warm and realized she certainly couldn't tell her sister everything. She couldn't explain it herself. She shrugged in response.

"Oh, come on, you have to do better than that." Ellie was still whispering, her hands clasped in front of her as though she were praying. "Sleeping with someone on the first date, or should I say business meeting, isn't exactly your style."

"I know, I know." Lucy covered her eyes. "This is Shooter's fault. If he wouldn't have thrown me over for Marion the librarian, I wouldn't have had all that pent up...well, you get the picture." It was just a little lie. Shooter wasn't even on the periphery of her thoughts this morning.

"Shooter left you?" Ellie reached a hand toward her.

"Yeah, no biggie." She squeezed Ellie's hand and let it drop. "Really, the writing was on the wall. I just didn't open my eyes." She shook her head and spread her arms wide. "But this...I don't know what came over me."

"I do. You've taken a good look at him, haven't you? Wouldn't take much for most women to succumb to a specimen like Ian Flynn."

"I suppose." He did have some pleasing attributes. "Why are we whispering?" Ellie's eyes grew wide as the creak of a door echoed. The shop's bathroom door opened, and Lucy turned to see Ian coming toward them. Her body responded to him with an unwanted primal twist of lust in the pit of her stomach. Lucy bit her lower lip in anticipation of a messy situation.

Ian was obviously taken aback by her appearance, although he shouldn't have been surprised to see her in a shop owned by her sister. He could have had the decency to stay away, of all mornings. A tremulous spasm raced up her spine. What if he spilled the beans in front of Ellie regarding Randy's illicit behavior?

"Lucy." His acknowledgement forced the breath from her lungs. She felt lightheaded. He continued toward them, each step coaxing her temperature to rise another uncomfortable degree.

Lucy glanced furtively at him, trying in vain to avoid the questioning eyes of her sister, but failing miserably. The shop suddenly seemed awfully stuffy, the air heavy with unspoken, unresolved emotion.

She forced down the knot in her throat. "Ian." Her eyes darted nervously between her one-night-stand and her sister.

Ian came alongside her, pulled out his wallet, and thumbed through the bills while Ellie, obviously nervous, rang up the charges, voided them, and rang them up again.

"That'll be five dollars and twenty-five cents."

Ian set a ten-dollar bill on the counter. "Keep the change." Lucy noted the strength his hand displayed, the fine wisp of dark hair.

Ellie's eyes widened. "But that's..."

Lucy watched out of the corner of her eye as Ian's face broke into a smile. "Just keep the change," he said in a voice as sweet as one of Ellie's famed cinnamon rolls. "You have a wonderful place here, a nice addition to this town. You should be proud."

Ellie looked positively stunned. "I...I am. Thank you."

When his gaze swung toward Lucy, his chiseled features lost all hint of a smile. "Lucy," he said in a sober tone as he passed by her, barely giving her a nod, and left the shop.

Lucy felt as though a cold front had moved through, leaving her breathless and chilled to the bone. The ring of the cash register brought her attention to the questioning eyes of her sister.

"Lucinda Mitchell, you've got some explaining to do." Ellie was looking at her with a motherly stare, and all thoughts of her tryst with Ian faded. Randy and his betrayal crashed through her brain.

Lucy glanced once more at the door and saw the red Porsche cross the parking lot. "I really don't want to talk about it."

Ellie's brows formed a line over her caring eyes. "I take it the evening didn't go as planned."

That was an understatement. Lucy lowered her head. "No, no, it didn't." Her head began to ache. "Can I have a cup of coffee, please?" Caffeine would help.

"Sure." Ellie poured her a hot, steamy brew in a to-go cup. "Are you going to tell me, or am I going to have to drag it out of you? How in the world did you end up in bed?"

Lucy took a cautious sip. A sigh escaped her. "There's nothing to tell. It was my fault. We shouldn't have taken it so far. The night was a complete failure. I just...I can't talk about it right now." She took another sip, feeling Ellie's eyes on her.

"You're in a strange mood this morning. It's a little scary. Are you sure I can't do anything to help?" Ellie tilted her head to one side. "You know, he seemed nice for a split second there."

Lucy's head was pounding and her heart racing. "Yeah, real nice." How lame that sounded. She hoped her sister would leave it at that and allow her to change the subject. "How are you this morning?"

"I'm fine." Ellie shrugged. "Abby passed from Minnows to Sharks yesterday thanks to her Aunt Lucy. Her instructor says she'll probably go right on to Whales within a couple of weeks. She's quite the little fish."

"Great, I'll pick her up tonight, and we can work on her dog paddle at the beach." With a little luck she could get Abby out of the house and out of the path of the brewing storm.

"Sorry, she has a birthday party tonight for Sarah Tanner."

"Oh." Drat. Dare she probe any further? She needed answers. "So, Randy really didn't have anything further to say last night?"

"Nope." Ellie shrugged. "Actually, now that I think of it, he wasn't any better this morning, so who knows what's up. I'm clueless as to what could be causing this mood of his. Got any ideas?"

Oh crap. Lucy glanced at her watch nervously. "I have to go or I'll be late. See you soon." She took a gulp of her coffee and gave her sister a lingering look before rushing for the door.

"Luce, are you sure nothing is seriously wrong?"

Lucy turned and flashed her a smile. "It's fine, El. You have a good day, okay?" She pushed the door open.

"Yeah, Luce, you too."

Lucy stepped out into the crisp morning air. It was going to be an interminably long day, and the emotions building within her needed release. The loss of the camp, her sister's sham of a marriage, and Ian's abandonment this morning tormented her. She craved resolution, or at the very least, a good venting. Low and behold, the Bluebird Motel was just ahead.

Chapter Seven

Ian slammed the door to his motel room, watched the cheap painting on the wall reverberate with the percussion, kicked off his shoes, and promptly stubbed his big toe on the bedpost. After releasing an expletive or two, he tossed his keys onto the dresser, watched as they sailed over the top and dropped over the edge. *Damn.* His day was getting off to a hell of a start.

He'd had amazing sex with a beautiful woman and spent the night in her bed. All should be right with his world, but, curiously enough, it wasn't. Ian prided himself as being on the controlling side of any situation, personal or business. Somehow he'd completely lost control of this one, and the line between personal and business seemed smudged like chalk on a well-traveled sidewalk. Lucy'd invited him to dinner, to which he'd foolishly agreed, and then she'd blindsided him with that slinky blue sheath she called a dress, made him stand by while she accosted her brother-in-law in the parking lot, and then proceeded to soundly seduce him. How had she managed to completely thwart his objective when, truth be told, his objective had been fulfilled? It made no sense at all.

Be honest with yourself, Flynn. He'd had no intention of meeting her for business. It had been purely personal, purely physical.

Closing his eyes, he could still revel in the sweetly seductive scent of her hair, taste those lips, feel that body. His hands tingled in remembrance of the sensation of delving over and into the contours of her. *Get a hold of yourself, man.*

Lucy Mitchell was nothing more than an interesting diversion on this trip to the boondocks to seal a deal. Yet she'd gotten to him. Interesting as she was, he certainly didn't have time to waste on an affair, especially one that was doomed from the start. After all, time was money. Clichéd as it was, that had always been his mantra. So why did this one-night stand with a potential thorn in his side cause him a second thought? Curious, no, maddening was more like it.

His head was throbbing, as was his toe, and his foul mood darkened with every minute that passed. He stripped each piece of clothing from his body, carefully placed each item neatly on the bed before entering the shower. Warm pulses of water soaked his body as he lathered. Too warm. He needed to cool down—his body and his thoughts. Delicious memories of Lucy's supple skin against his own washed through him, and he was forced to adjust the temperature of the water even cooler. Try as he might, he couldn't wash her from his thoughts. He was haunted by the scent of her, the prickles of sensation she aroused, the loss of control as want gave way to need, and the exquisite release followed by the peace he'd found sleeping beside her.

Peace of mind. Something Ian hadn't known in this life, an unattainable state of being that didn't apply to him. As long as he kept working, he didn't have time to think about the messiness of relationships and that's the way he liked it. As of late, this race he was running was beginning to confuse him at times. The forces that drove him with such clarity in the past had begun to fail him. With a shake of his head he cleared the psychobabble from his mind. He didn't have time to decipher his evening with Lucy. Business needed tending.

But he couldn't shake the feeling that something was different with her. That, this morning, he was different.

Ian stepped out of the shower to an insistent rap, rap, rap. He chased the last of the water from his hair before wrapping a white towel around him. Probably the manager of this two-bit joint, hoping he'd stay on a while longer to feather his pockets. He should be so lucky.

Through the peephole, the living, breathing storm cloud known as Lucy Mitchell waited, and the vibe she was exuding was not pleasant. He looked at the towel wrapped around his waist, thought to quickly throw on a pair of pants, but what the hell.

He peered through the peephole again. Yes, she was definitely angry. Her eyes were narrow slits and her mouth a thin line of general pissed-offed-ness.

What the hell did he do now? Could it be she was looking for a repeat performance of the previous night? Funny, she didn't strike him as the insatiable, sex-nymph type. One just never knew. He wanted to be annoyed at her for coming to his room. Really he did, but certain parts of him seemed awfully glad to see her.

****

Lucy felt her jaw drop open at the sight of Ian in nothing more than a towel. She snapped her mouth shut. He wasn't going to get the satisfaction of knowing she was a bit daunted by his lack of attire.

It was nothing special, just your standard motel towel, but she couldn't help but notice the rippled stomach glistening with water and the fine line of dark hair that disappeared beneath the towel. She had a whole new appreciation of motel towels.

Slowly, her eyes traveled up his torso, past the dark nipples surrounded by the soft brush of chest hair, to the rise of pectorals to the angles of his face underneath wet spikes of dark hair. She hadn't counted on this and was ever so sorry she'd followed him to, of all places, a motel room. *Stupid.* Just plain stupid.

Berating herself wasn't going to help her now, and she certainly wasn't going to allow Ian Flynn the fun of unnerving her with his nakedness. But honestly, words failed her.

She watched, speechless, as the corners of his mouth curved into a salacious smile.

"Back for more?" The teasing, sarcastic tone of his voice failed to match the caustic glint in his eyes.

"You wish." She began to step forward, but he wasn't budging. "Are you going to let me in, or not? I have a bone to pick with you."

"A bone?" His smile widened under an arched brow.

"Give it up, Ian. Let me in. I'm not having a conversation with you dressed in a towel in an open doorway. I don't need all of Butternut Creek talking about us. There's enough gossip in this town as it is."

He pushed the door wide and turned away. She followed him into the room. Very neat and tidy, just as she suspected. There was nothing messy in Flynnville.

With his back to her, he smoothed his hair in the

mirror. "Get to the point, Lucy, I have a property to look at in Vilas County in an hour and a half, and as you can see, I'm running a little late."

She fought to regain the sheer anger that had brought her here. But for the life of her, she couldn't find it. Something about having a half-naked man standing in front of her was damn distracting.

When she failed to respond, he turned around to face her. "While you're trying to find your tongue, I'm going to dress. You don't mind, do you?"

Before she could answer, he pulled the towel from his waist in a single fluid flick of his hand and tossed it casually into the corner, revealing two very nicely rounded cheeks. It was as though the air had been sucked from her lungs. He stepped past her to the suitcase perched on the desk without so much of a glance.

"Are you laughing at me?" she asked when she regained her wits.

"No, should I be?" His smug attitude was absolutely maddening. Time to cut to the chase.

"Would a simple goodbye have killed you this morning?" She hadn't planned to sound like such a nag, but there it was.

"Well, I..." It was clear he thought this was a joke. "It's not as though we're a married couple."

"I suppose in the big city it's nothing to spend the night with someone, then slink out on them in the morning without so much as a word. But in a small town things are different. I have never had a one-night stand. I have more principles than that. Besides, people aren't so callused here. They have more common courtesy than I'm sure you're used to. You are a rude man, Ian." *What has gotten into me?* She wasn't one to run after a man, but seeing him at the shop caused her some sort of breakdown of common sense. She had to see him again and his lack of a goodbye was the only excuse she could come up with. She felt like a fool but would be damned to let him know it now.

"I take that to mean you followed me here to seduce me again, so you can say we did it more than once, and therefore what happened last night doesn't qualify as a one-night stand?" He picked up his watch from the nightstand, still naked, checked the time, and said matter-of-factly, "I suppose I could give you about ten minutes."

A rapid flood of heat filled her. "You arrogant ass. I wouldn't dream of treading on your busy schedule."

"You want me to pencil you in?"

She was amusing him to no end, and it was infuriating. Problem was she wasn't quite sure what she did want, or why she'd followed him, or why she was feeling like a schoolgirl with a crush.

"You're pissing me off, Ian. I'm sure you know that's not why I'm here."

"Calm down, Lucy."

"Don't tell me to calm down." It was hard to stay focused with a butt in front of her, albeit a hairy, and, well, nicely formed one at that. *Stop it*. "For crying out loud, put some clothes on."

"What do you want from me? An apology? Well, you've got one. Lucy, I am very sorry I didn't say goodbye this morning. There, are we all better now?" He glanced at her over his shoulder.

"Why you condescending, smug jerk."

"Let's not resort to name calling, shall we? I could say you owe me an apology as well." He stood and turned in her direction. *Oh, Jeez, put it away. Please.*

"Me? Why should I have to apologize to you? Could you cover that up?" She waved a finger in the direction of his member and tried to avert her eyes.

"You could apologize for using me for sex simply to make yourself feel better." He pulled a pair of boxers from his suitcase and slipped them over one ankle, then the other, and finally covered the source of her distraction.

"What in the world are you talking about?" She'd missed something somewhere in this stupid repartee they were calling a conversation.

"I know it must have been devastating to find him with a woman other than your sister. But I don't appreciate being your emotional punching bag."

"Oh come on, you're a man. Men live for that kind of thing." She had to chuckle at that. "Men sleep around all the time to make themselves feel better or younger or sexier. If that is what I did, and I'm not saying it was, poor you."

"I'll ignore your broad generalization of my gender in light of what happened with your brother-in-law, for now. I take it your sister doesn't know."

"No, Ellie has no idea." Her chest tightened with emotion she couldn't begin to lay before him. "She's going to be devastated."

"I'm sorry. I really don't know what to say." He spread his hands and shrugged.

"There's nothing for you to say. It's a situation involving my family that needs to be resolved, but we can handle it. Mitchells stick together. Don't worry about us."

Silence fell between them. He pulled on a pair of khaki pants and a blue polo shirt that matched the color of his eyes. She stood before him, not knowing what to say or do, suddenly feeling out of place. After all, they'd shared an intimacy the night before, borne of need and frustration on her part. She could admit that, but not to him. Watching him dress shouldn't feel like such an invasion, but it did. Regardless of what they'd shared, she didn't belong here, with him, alone in his room.

"I need to get on the road, or I'll miss my meeting." He stood before her, looking very much the success he obviously was, expensive-looking shoes, a gold watch on his wrist, everything neat, perfect.

"Sorry." Why did she say that? She'd come here for *his* apology. This was suddenly so awkward. She was allowing him to dismiss her as an errant child. "I won't keep you then."

He turned from her without a word, without a smile, and started for the door.

"Wait." She felt so inexplicably sad at the moment. This day had barely begun, and already it was a complete and total mess.

"Lucy, I really don't..."

"Your collar's goofed up." As she reached to straighten the corner tucked in at his throat, her fingers brushed his skin and sent a flood of warmth through her. Her eyes reached for his and held them. It was only a moment, but a spark of something deep, inexplicable, passed between them. She felt it just as profoundly as she felt her heart pounding in her chest. With shaking fingers she unfolded the collar and stepped away.

By the look on his face, she could tell Ian wished she hadn't done that, hadn't touched him with that simple, intimate gesture.

"I probably won't be back until late." It was a comment one spouse would say to another. This was ludicrous. But as crazy as it was, she'd seen a chink in his armor, a fissure of emotion when she'd touched his collar.

"Goodbye, Ian." She pushed past him and into the bright morning sunlight.

"Lucy, wait." He followed her out. She stopped as she was lowering herself into her car. "I hope your sister comes through this."

Why did he have to go and say something nice?

****

Later that afternoon Ian drove the winding ribbon of road through the forest that took him to the camp. Why, he wasn't quite certain. He really didn't have a reason. The meeting that had promised to take all day had wrapped fairly quickly and he had time on his hands.

Of course, he reasoned, seeing Lucy wasn't his motivation for driving to the camp. He needed to speak with Lida, check on her progress with the required paperwork. With a bit of luck, she may have made a dent in the mountain of papers on her desk. And, if time permitted, he'd walk the perimeter of the camp, take more notes, and refine his landscaping ideas. Of course, he could turn these details over to a professional, but Ian preferred to put his own stamp on his properties.

He parked his car along the road close to Beaver Cabin, preferring to get some needed exercise by walking the path through the trees that eventually curved to parallel the lake.

"Hey, Mister."

Ian glanced one way, then the other, before he saw him. It was the boy again, crouched down at the water's edge. The boy rose and came toward Ian dressed in swim trunks. His knees were scuffed with dirt, as were his feet and hands. His bony shoulders and skinny arms were freckled by the sun, and his hair was a spiky mess.

"Still looking for that snake?"

"Naw, I'm just hidin' out again." He cocked his

brown-haired head to one side and eyed Ian. "You wanna give me a ride in that car?"

"Not right now." Actually a part of him almost did.

"Why not? Looks like it's got a lotta snot." This kid had more guts than most adults.

"Snot?"

"Yeah, power, you know." He looked at Ian as though he were dense.

"It does. Have a lot of snot, that is."

"A Porsche, huh?" Jonah pointed his freckled nose in the direction of the car on the hill.

"It's a Porsche 911." Ian never tired of saying that. The car had been a gift to himself after an obscenely successful deal.

"Okay, so when you gonna give me that ride?" The boy stared him down with a steely gaze.

"I'm not getting you in trouble with Lucy. She's not someone you mess around with." Well, actually, she was. He found himself grinning at the thought.

"What's one little ride gonna hurt? You scared of a girl like Lucy?" Jonah pursed his lips and crinkled up his freckled nose in disgust.

"I'm not, but I'm not at her mercy the way you are." Although being at Lucy Mitchell's mercy was not all that undesirable.

"There you are, Jonah Bates. You are in big trouble." A tanned young woman with straight, blond hair came jogging through the trees.

"Aw, Jeez." Jonah hung his head and kicked the dirt.

The blonde came toward them and thrust a hand in Ian's direction. "Hi, I'm Jule Sutherland." Her skin was flawless, her smile wide with blue eyes that sparkled like the water behind her. And her curves were in all the right places.

Ian accepted her hand. "Ian Flynn."

In a voice he could describe as nothing but perky, she said, "I've seen you around a few times. Are you here to check out the camp for your son or daughter? It's a great place, really it is. I've been coming up here for about six years now. I could show you around more if you'd like. We've got a lot to offer, we really do."

"Sutherland. You aren't from the Madison area, are

you?"

Jule's eyes became wider, if that was possible. "Why do you ask?"

"I've done business with Senator Sutherland."

"Oh, how cool. He's my uncle, Stan."

"Really?" Ian felt the wheels turning in his brain. She looked to be twenty-one, maybe twenty-three tops, but still...

"In fact, Uncle Stan and Aunt Delle are coming up here in August to vacation in Eagle River." She smiled so sweetly up at him. "That is just *way* cool." Okay, her vocabulary needed work.

"Hey, I'm leavin'." Jonah turned and started to advance toward the lake once again.

"Just a minute, Bud, you're coming with me." Jule grabbed his scrawny arm.

"Yeah, I figured." Jonah resolutely stopped in his tracks and pointed a dirty finger in Ian's direction. "I still want a ride in that car."

"Not today." Not ever. He didn't need dirt and pine needles and God only knows what else, all over his interior.

"Come on." Jule pulled him behind her. "Lucy's starting swim class." She glanced back at Ian and batted thick eyelashes. "Why don't you come down and watch?"

"Maybe I will." He stood with hands in his pockets and watched them go. Suddenly he couldn't think of a single other thing to do this fine afternoon than watch Lucy in action.

Children were gathering on the dock jutting out into Balsam Lake as Ian leaned along the porch hanging off the log-hewn lodge. Lucy was nowhere in sight. He was told Lida was resting and Jule was attempting some semblance of order with her uncontrollable little mob of swimmers. Movement to his right caught his eye.

Lucy advanced along the path from the changing rooms looking very athletic in her lavender swimsuit, white shorts, lusciously tanned limbs, and white deck shoes, with stylish sunglasses covering her eyes. A silver whistle on a string bounced on her chest as she walked. Lucky whistle. When she saw Ian standing along the porch, she stopped to peer at him over her glasses.

"Good afternoon."

"Good afternoon to you, Lucy." He felt his attitude drastically shift for the better.

She furrowed her brows together, still peering at him over the glasses. "Come to lord over what will soon be all yours?"

Ian chose to play her game and chuckled. "You could say that."

"Well, aren't we lucky." In the distance the buzz of a jet ski disrupted the glassy sheen of the lake sending a spray of water behind it. Lucy turned her attention to the noise and Ian followed. "Darn jet skiers. We're trying to get the DNR to regulate when they can and cannot ride. Some of them are such a nuisance."

"Why is that?"

"Because they're annoying when you're trying to teach a class, much less sleep in or go to bed early. Some pay little heed to the swim area. It's dangerous. Anyway, if you are here to see Lida, she's napping."

"I know. Something occurred to me. I never properly thanked you for the invitation to dinner last night." He watched for her reaction. Just as he predicted, a blush crept up the silky skin of her neck.

"You paid for it." She pumped a shoulder in nonchalance. "It was a mistake, pure and simple. The dinner didn't accomplish a thing. A complete waste of time." She fixed her eyes on the children waiting for their lesson.

Her words surprisingly stung, and Ian wanted to sting back. "Oh, now Lucy, it wasn't a complete waste of time. You were able to catch your brother-in-law in a, shall we say, terribly compromising situation." He suddenly wished he could take the words back.

Lucy's face reddened further. "How dare you. Unless you're dead from the neck up, I'm sure you could see how upsetting that was, and for you to throw it in my face is despicable. Not everyone can have the perfect little family I'm sure you have at home."

Her words bit into him. She couldn't possibly know how wrong she was. He swallowed the bitter pill. "You're right, that wasn't nice. I apologize. But, you have to admit, it was a stroke of luck to have caught him stepping out on your sister. The truth needed to be known. Unfortunately, your sister will be the one to pay." He canted his body in her direction. "I do care, you know."

"The hell you do." The muscles in her face tightened. "Okay, forget I said that."

"Let me know if there's anything I can do." He honestly couldn't remember the last time he'd said that, if ever.

"Thanks...well...I have to go." She turned and walked toward the beach.

****

Please leave, Lucy thought as she made her way through the children gathered before the dock. The last thing she needed was an audience, especially if that audience was Ian Flynn. She took off her shorts and shoes and tooted the whistle around her neck. "Today's lesson," she explained to the group of eight- and nine-year-olds, "is to see how far you can swim."

The students groaned. Out of the corner of her eye, Lucy spied Ian walking through the sand. He sat on a park bench shaded by pine branches overhead. Knowing he was there caused a curious heat that spread through her like wildfire. She couldn't wait to get in the water.

She clapped her hands together twice to get the attention of the students. "This will help build endurance. Don't you want to see how strong you're getting? By the time you leave here, you will be able to swim across this whole lake if you want to."

Behind her, the young man on the jet ski sluiced through the water at breakneck speed. Lucy turned her attention to the interloper and shook her head in disgust. There was nothing she could do since he was staying outside the boundaries of the camp swim space. "Okay, kids, let's get used to the water first."

The children began wading cautiously into the frigid, tamarack-stained water of the spring-fed lake. The more adventurous dipped their heads below the surface; others shivered against the cold and rubbed their arms against gooseflesh. On the dock Lucy braced herself with a hand and swung her body into the waist-high water. She wasn't about to allow the shock of the water to register, nor would she, in view of the unwanted onlooker.

"All right, campers, now that we're acclimated, let's line up on shore. I need the Beavers over here, closest to the dock, then the Otters, next the Badgers, Eagles, and Porcupines. Come on, nice straight lines." She positioned a few of the children and then went back before them. Something wasn't right. "Hey, does anyone know what happened to Jonah?" Toward the shore she called, "Jule, I thought you had Jonah."

"I did." She shook her blond mane from side to side. "Where did he get off to now? Golly, this is getting old."

Darn right it was. Lucy knew she should have gone for him herself. Something was going to have to be done about the errant Master Bates. She hadn't wanted to bother Lida, but it was time to bring Jonah in line.

"Carlos, do you know where he is?"

"Nope, I don't know." His face betrayed him.

"Are you sure?" Lucy crossed her arms over her chest while the boy shook his head. "Brad, could you look for Jonah?"

"Sure thing," a tall, lanky young man dressed in camp attire called back.

"Check for him up around Eagle. I saw him there about an hour ago. And if not there, try Beaver or Porcupine."

Brad waved as he made his way up the path.

"Okay." Lucy clapped her hands to regain the attention of the swimmers. "We're going to make this a race." A few of the heartier swimmers began to cheer while the others groaned.

"First, we're going to swim out a little farther than we have been. See the third buoy out there?" The children nodded. "You have to swim out there, touch the buoy and come back in, tag the next in line, and that one will go."

"That'll be hard, Lucy," one boy spoke up. "'Sides, the Otters always win." To which the Otters cheered enthusiastically, while the others jeered.

Lucy attempted to calm them by holding out her hands and tooting the whistle. "Well, we're going to make this interesting. The second swimmer in your line must join the line to their right, and the fourth swimmer must join the line to their left. This way we'll mix up the teams a bit."

There was some confusion, which Lucy quelled. Before long, the sound of the whistle signaled the beginning, and the swimmers were off through much splashing and cheers from the others. Lucy cheered along with them, clapping her encouragement, giving instruction. And completely forgetting the presence of Ian Flynn on shore, that is, until she turned her head in the direction of the lodge and found him staring at her. All of the sudden, the water wasn't so cold.

****

Ian found himself enjoying the scene before him. Lucy Mitchell certainly had a way with children. A thought occurred to him. A thought that brought him up short. Lucy would make a great mother. Why would such a thought ever come to him in the first place? He'd never planned to have children of his own. Much less with someone like Lucy Mitchell. *What the hell, he didn't want a wife or kids*. Life was complicated enough as it was.

A mangy bundle of hair rubbed against his leg. He looked down to see Gabe's wet, drippy tongue, and droopy eyes.

"I don't want a dog either." Gabe panted and inched closer, causing Ian to move his leg, which didn't matter. The dog moved closer still.

"Don't you have someone else to annoy?" The dog wasn't very intelligent or he'd seek someone who appreciated him.

Ian chose to ignore the dog and turned his attention to the race in the water. He rose and moved closer to the edge of the shore. Gabe followed. Lucy turned toward shore to urge forward a swimmer whose team was a full length behind the others. As he watched her encourage the little girl, an object came into his peripheral vision. A silver canoe glided from behind massive pines toward the middle of the lake. With Jonah at its helm.

He cupped his hands around his mouth and called to Lucy. When her eyes met his, he pointed in the direction of the canoe.

Lucy placed one hand on her hip and shielded her eyes with the other. She emerged from the water and sprinted to the end of the dock. "Jonah," she called, her voice echoing off the water, "Jonah Bates, you get that canoe back here right this minute." Jonah continued to paddle toward the center of the lake. Lucy stamped her foot on the dock. "Jonah, you stop right now. I mean it."

The swimming race came to a halt as the swimmers stopped to watch the disobedient camper. "You turn that canoe around and get back here, now!" She was losing her patience. Not a good sign. "I'm not kidding, Jonah, if I have to swim out there myself, you're coming back to shore."

Jonah stopped paddling as the canoe continued forward gliding effortlessly through the water. His shoulders slumped in acquiescence, and he raised the paddle, then dipped it back into the water and began to turn the canoe toward shore.

It was a good thing corporal punishment was no longer acceptable as the boy was pushing the limits. Of course, Lucy could never lay a hand on any child, Ian was certain, even this one. The errant boy's disobedience grew from a need to be seen and heard, and loved. Ian knew this only too well.

Lucy turned to check on the swimmers behind her, and then back to Jonah. He had to chuckle at the prospect of Lucy getting her hands on the boy once he returned to shore. Lucy may have met her match in Jonah.

It was almost as though in slow motion, Ian saw the jet skier heading in Jonah's direction at a dangerous rate of speed. Ian tried to call out, but the sound of his voice seemed drowned in the buzz of the machine. As the canoe swung sideways, the jet skier attempted to swerve out of the way.

"No," Ian yelled as they collided. A spray of water and a deathly crunch were followed by the swamping of the motor, and then silence. The canoe was upside down and the jet ski bobbed along empty, the skier visible only by the flotation device he was wearing. Jonah was nowhere to be seen. Ian experienced panic unlike anything he'd ever known. He wanted to scream, but couldn't find his voice. He wanted to run, but his feet seemed cemented by the terror of the situation.

He saw Lucy immediately dive from the dock and begin frantically swimming toward them. Suddenly he was able to break free from his fright and act.

He ran toward the dock, shedding his sandals, keys and wallet and shirt. As he passed the stunned counselors on the shore he yelled, "Call an ambulance." He propelled himself down the dock and dove through the air and into the chilly water. As he surfaced, he saw Lucy swimming just ahead. He gulped for air and followed her. Together they reached the overturned canoe just as it broke into pieces and slipped beneath the waves.

"Jonah, Jonah, where are you?" Lucy's scream echoed off the water. "Oh, God, this can't be happening."

"Stay calm, we'll find him."

Ian jerked his head from side to side. No sign of him anywhere. Their eyes met and without communicating verbally, they knew what they had to do next. Ian bobbed his head in acknowledgment before they disappeared beneath the surface. Together they searched the murky depths of Balsam Lake. Lucy went up for air first, then Ian. After gulping fresh air, he dove, frantically reaching into the darkness for any sign of the boy.

Eyes strained against the muddy water, his hands flailing to and fro, he was grasping for anything that resembled a child. A small, lifeless hand brushed Ian's fingers. Adrenaline rushed through him as he grabbed, but missed. Then he snared an arm and pulled Jonah to the surface just as Lucy came through the waves a few feet away.

He wrapped an arm around the boy's limp torso as best he could while keeping himself afloat. Forcing the knot from his throat he barked, "Jonah, boy, can you hear me?" The limp form showed no sign of life.

Lucy swam to them, placed a hand on Ian's shoulder, the other on Jonah's wet, matted hair. A trickle of blood streamed down his forehead forming tiny red tributaries across the side of his face. "Jonah, honey, Jonah, wake up." A sob escaped her. "We have to get him to shore."

"Can you manage him on your own? I'm going to check the skier and tow him in."

Fear was evident in her eyes. She gave a short, clipped nod of her head and reached for Jonah.

Ian gently transferred the boy into Lucy's arms as she immediately began paddling with her free arm toward the shore. Ian watched her for a brief moment. Beyond the two figures bobbing in the water, the shore was lined with campers, counselors, and Lida Duncan wringing her hands before her.

The skier floated nearby, face up. Ian guessed he was around twenty-five. As Ian neared he moaned. Luckily he'd had the sense to wear a life preserver. His body seemed intact as it floated, arms thrown out to either side. Ian pushed his way through the water to the man's head and held it in his hands.

"Are you all right? Can you speak?" The skier's eyes fluttered open, closed, then opened again.

"Yeah...I think I'm okay," he whispered weakly.

Ian reached beneath and supported his back. "Do you feel any pain?"

The man coughed once. "My arm. I think it's broken."

Ian scanned both arms. The right seemed fine, but the left was swelling just above the elbow and taking on a purplish hue. "We need to get you to shore. Just relax and I'm going to pull you in by the back of your life jacket." He secured a strap on the back. "Ready?" Without waiting for a response, he began to tow him toward shore where he could see Lucy and Jonah just reaching the sandy beach and people running to help.

Ian's lungs burned and his paddling arm ached. He was thankful for the life preserver that made this transfer all the easier. He stretched his feet searching for the bottom, but felt nothing. His body was letting him know that it had been far too long since he'd swum.

Keep your eye on the prize. It had been his mantra when he'd begun his business. Now he repeated that line over and over as he pulled himself and the skier through the unforgiving waters. He focused on the shoreline, ignoring the frantic rescue attempt that he knew was surrounding Jonah. He needed to get to shore. That's all he asked.

Suddenly, his foot touched something. There it was again. He touched his feet upon the sandy bottom and released a grateful and exhausted sigh.

He quickly pulled the man to where the water was knee-high. Brian raced into the water to help. They each grabbed a shoulder and gently glided him onto the sandy beach.

"I'm a first responder," Brian said and to Ian's relief, took over examining the young man. Ian plopped into the sand butt first, caught his breath, then crawled between the campers to where Lucy was bent over Jonah.

Lida and Jule herded the children away from the scene. Many were crying; some appeared to be in shock.

The skier groaned, then turned his head to watch what was happening alongside him.

"Will he be all right?" the skier asked.

Lucy did not take her eyes from Jonah. "What were you thinking, to behave that way on this lake? You knew there was a camp full of children here. You've been violating our beach area nearly every day. What did you expect would happen?"

The young man's face crumpled. "I know. I'm sorry." With his good hand he reached up and pinched between his eyes as a tear trickled down his cheek.

A cough brought their attention back to the boy on the sand.

"Jonah, honey," Lucy spoke to him. "Please be all right."

Lida raised her hands to the heavens. "Oh, thank the Lord."

Jonah coughed once more, a deep racking cough, and then began to vomit. Ian helped Lucy turn him onto his side. When the vomiting stopped, she guided his still-limp form onto his back, once again. A few of the counselors sank onto the sand in relief while the children cried and clung to each other. Jule applied a towel to the cut on Jonah's forehead that quickly stained with red.

Ian placed a shaking hand on the boy's bony chest. He fought the nearly overwhelming urge to gather him into his arms and hold him tight. His eyes scanned the small body that seemed devoid of life save for the shallow breaths causing his rib cage to expand and contract ever so slightly. His eyes met the fathomless depths of Lucy's, and a current of shared emotion flowed between them as strong as any tidal wave. The boy began to whimper and tears rolled down each cheek.

Lucy kissed his cheek and took one of his hands in her own. Ian took hold of the other. Jonah's hand was so small and so cold that he sandwiched it with both of his.

"You'll be okay, buddy. Hang in there." Ian hoped Jonah didn't detect the total lack of confidence he had in that small bit of encouragement.

He'd never felt so helpless in all his life. He felt as though he might hyperventilate. A tremor began in the pit of his stomach and spread throughout his body. He breathed deeply, hoping to gain control. The fact remained: this little boy could easily have died, may still, but Ian had found him on the bottom of the lake and brought him to the safety of Lucy's arms. He'd never saved a life before. Had never held a child before. The reality of the situation and the emotion roiling within him were almost too much to bear. He couldn't stop shaking.

Lucy raised tearful eyes to his as the siren of an ambulance, followed by that of a police car, echoed through the trees. Relief flooded through him and he bit back tears of his own. The ambulance drove through the grass to park next to the beach, followed by a sheriff's squad. As EMS workers flew into action and officers questioned, Ian made his way to the back of the crowd and released the breath he hadn't realized he'd been holding. His knees buckled and he sank to the sand. Gabe was instantly beside him. Ian wrapped an arm around the furry, panting dog and hung on.

Chapter Eight

The family waiting room at Mercy Memorial held the air of a grandmother's living room. Overstuffed furniture, afghans and plushy pillows. Despite the comforting atmosphere, Lucy was anything but comforted. Guilt was chewing her up and spitting her out. And she was exhausted.

Why hadn't I called the police on the stupid skier? I should have paid more attention to Jonah. He was my responsibility. The canoe should have been padlocked.

She and Ian took turns at the window and otherwise paced back and forth silently. She was afraid if she tried to speak she would dislodge the knot in her throat and sob. She was not inclined to patience, which made the wait for word on Jonah's fate excruciating.

A man in hospital whites walked past. Lucy jumped from her chair, but he paid her no heed. Ian turned from the window, then went back to whatever it was he was so intent upon on the outside. She returned to her chair, hugging her arms and rocking back and forth.

Her hair hung in stringy waves, and wet spots appeared through the sweats she'd thrown over her swimsuit before jumping into Ian's car for the race into town. She could see Ian's shorts were still damp and his shirt studded with sand. He began to pace, then stopped and sat on the sofa across from her, elbows on his knees, hands knit together, studying a thumbnail.

Unable to stand the pressure any longer, she rose and went back to the window. Two floors below, a young man pushed a wheelchair across the parking lot, his passenger, a woman cradling a newborn baby. The stark fragility of life struck her with blunt force. The fear forming a stifling ball in her chest made it hard to breathe.

He'll be fine. Jonah will be fine. Oh Lord, help him to be fine.

Silently, she repeated the prayer. It was so painfully hard to sit by and do nothing. She rubbed her arms as though she was cold, but realized it was the nervous energy of not knowing what lay ahead.

Ian joined her at the window.

"Look down below." Lucy pointed to the couple in the parking lot leaning over their precious bundle. "They're celebrating the birth of their child while Jonah is fighting for his life with no one here for him but a camp counselor and a..." She looked his way, pumped a shoulder in a half-hearted shrug before turning her gaze back to the window.

"A guy with a car with a lot of snot, as Jonah would say," Ian finished the sentence for her. Lucy raised an eyebrow at that. "He wanted a ride in my car right before he took off in the canoe." Ian hung his head and jammed his hands into his pockets. "If I'd have given him that ride, he'd have missed that jet ski." He puffed out a breath and shifted his gaze to the window. He looked exhausted.

Lucy cocked her head to one side as she regarded him. "Watch it, Flynn, your soft side is showing."

"I'm not such a hard-ass, you know." He shrugged. "Not all the time anyway."

Lucy folded her arms in front of her again. "I should have done a better job of keeping track of him."

"That boy is a challenge at best. You could have done a million things different. We all could have. But in the end we saved his life. That's what counts."

Lucy, fighting to retain control, shook her head in protest, her voice throaty. "Don't make excuses, Ian. He was my responsibility and I failed him." If he didn't make it, she could not fathom life beyond this unforgivable moment of irresponsibility.

Ian turned toward her, a stern look upon his face. "Stop it right now. Beating up on yourself isn't going to help. Pity and self-loathing accomplish nothing."

"I took him for granted because, well, he was always there, every summer, all summer, and we've gotten used to his behavior. That's not fair to him. None of this is." Her chin quivered, but she brought it in check. "Why does it take a tragic accident to show us the value of people?"

Ian was silent a moment. "You know," he said gently, "you saved that boy's life today. That's pretty amazing."

Lucy didn't meet his gaze. "We don't know that yet. Besides, you're the one who found him at the bottom of the lake. We wouldn't be here at all if it wasn't for you."

"Maybe so, but you knew what to do once he was on shore. I didn't have a clue." Ian turned back toward the window.

"Who'd have thought you and I would be a team." She tried to smile as she said it, but couldn't quite carry it off. *Hold me, Ian.* Why couldn't she say it aloud?

As if he read her mind, he slipped an arm over her shoulders and Lucy felt some of the tension give way as she allowed her head to lean into his shoulder.

They kept their vigil at the window until Lida broke the silence some ten minutes later.

"Have you heard anything yet?" She bustled into the room. Lucy and Ian indicated they had not. "I tried to call his parents, but the secretary at their church wasn't in. I left a message for her to call me here. She's the only emergency phone number they gave. She's going to have to contact them in whatever country they're in this year, as missionaries. I also checked on the young man who hit little Jonah."

Lucy crossed her arms and shook her head in disgust. "How is the jerk?"

"Now, Lucy." Lida leveled disapproving eyes on her. "He's very broken up over this and feels just awful. He's lucky that all he received was a broken arm."

Lucy pointed an angry finger at Lida. "How lucky was Jonah? He's the only one I'm concerned with."

"Calm down, Lucy," the older woman admonished. "He, his name is Eric Gavin, would like you both to stop by so he could thank you. Eric's just as anxious as all of us regarding Jonah's condition."

"I'll bet. He's worried whether we'll file charges against him."

"Lucy..." Lida warned.

Just then a tall, white-haired gentleman dressed in hospital scrubs walked through the double doors of the emergency room toward the family waiting room.

Lucy and Ian rushed forward. Lida stood alongside

them.

"He's one lucky, little boy." The doctor smiled, introduced himself as Dr. William Thomas, and shook hands with each of them.

"Thank God." Lucy breathed in relief. Ian nodded his head in agreement. Lida wiped at her eyes with the tissue in her hand and sunk into a chair.

"When can we see him?" Ian asked.

"In a few moments. He's being moved to another room. We're going to keep him overnight for observation. He ingested quite a large amount of water and, since he was unconscious for a while, we're keeping an extra eye on him. We'll be monitoring his lungs to make sure they're clear before he can be released."

Lida spoke first. "Certainly. We're still waiting for a call back from his parents, but I left the number for the hospital. I have all his insurance information in my purse, but, oh dear, I seemed to have left it in my car."

The doctor smiled. "Someone from Admitting will be here in a moment, and they'll help you with all of that. If you don't mind, I'm going to see if our patient is settled yet. The nurse will let you know when you can see him. It shouldn't be much longer."

Ian extended his hand. "Thanks, Doctor."

"You people saved this boy. I ought to thank you. Once I check him again, you'll be able to spend some time with him." He left them, and Lida went back to her car for the insurance information, leaving Ian and Lucy alone.

The relief that swept through Lucy was beyond containing. She let loose with an exuberant "yes" and wrapped her arms around Ian's shoulders.

****

Ian hadn't expected her reaction, hadn't hated it either. Her joy was contagious. It was as though the emotion she was feeling transferred from her body against his, straight to his heart. He encircled her with his arms and held fast. He hadn't felt the equivalent of an emotion so pure in a very long time, certainly nothing on this scale. In a matter of hours he'd gone from terrified to joyous. For someone who didn't express a whole lot of emotion, this day had been a marathon.

He could have held on to Lucy, held on to this

moment forever. It, she, both felt so good. When at last his arms relaxed and her body shifted away, disappointment washed through him.

With eyes he couldn't quite read, she said, "Thank you, Ian. Thanks for being there today. We made a good team."

For once, he was completely speechless. This was territory he had never traversed before. He'd never before found himself in a life-and-death struggle, never been thanked for an act of goodness on his part. Hell, he'd never performed an act of pure goodness before, not that he could remember anyway.

Cautiously, Ian and Lucy entered room 212. In the dim light of the stark hospital room, Jonah's body laid upon the bed, deathly still, a white sheet across his chest and tucked under each arm. His face seemed ashen, dark circles rimmed his closed eyes, and his breathing was shallow at best. A shock of brown hair fell across his forehead, barely covering the white bandage that shielded the cut caused in the collision.

Ian stood on the side of the bed nearest the window while Lucy stepped between the bed and the bathroom door. Gingerly, she took his small hand in hers and Ian leaned on the bed rails and watched. Poor kid. He looked like some little refugee you'd see on the evening news.

"Jonah, sweetie, it's Lucy." Jonah failed to respond, and Ian held his breath. Lucy raised teary eyes to him just as Jonah moaned and jerked one arm.

"Maybe we should let him sleep," Ian whispered.

"I just want him to know someone familiar is here. His parents might not get the message right away, and I don't want him to be alone. I'm sure once they find out they'll come, but until then I don't want him to feel alone or afraid."

Just then Jonah's eyes fluttered open, then closed again. "They ain't comin'."

"Jonah?" Lucy wiped a tear from her eye with a knuckle. "Jonah, how do you feel?"

"Like I been hit by a jet ski," he answered in a raspy voice. He coughed, sending a spasm through his skinny frame.

Ian moved to touch the boy's head, thought better of

it, and returned his hand to the bed rail. "Hey, big guy, you gave us a scare."

"Aww, I'm okay." The boy's bravery in face of the seriousness of the situation impressed Ian, and something akin to pride sprouted within him.

Lucy stroked the boy's mussed hair. Ian noted the calming affect she had on the boy. "You're going to be just fine. The doctor said so. You'll probably be able to leave here tomorrow. Mrs. Duncan's attempting to contact your parents, although she hasn't gotten through just yet. She's going to keep trying. They'll be so worried."

"I heard what you said, and they won't, ya know." Jonah weakly pulled his hand from Lucy's and pushed his body onto his side to face Ian.

Lucy looked perplexed. "Who won't what?"

"You said they'd come here as soon as they find out, but they won't. They'd miss too much time with the natives they're tryin' ta save. That's what's important to them, ya know."

Ian studied Jonah's face. The boy's eyes glazed with tears and his chin trembled, but not for long. As soon as his tough façade began to crumble, he set his chin and with a stubborn shake of his head, the tears stopped, and his eyes held a look of strength that Ian could identify with all too well. A neglected child learns self-reliance at an early age. It was a shame, but such was life for those not gifted with the kind of family he was certain Lucy Mitchell was privileged to have.

Lucy set a hand on his shoulder and gently positioned him onto his back again. She placed a hand under his chin and turned his face to hers. "They love you, Jonah. We all do. They'll be very worried when they hear what's happened."

"Maybe, but they won't come." Jonah kept his eyes on the ceiling.

"Yes, I'm..."

"Can we get something for you, Jonah?" Ian broke in. "Maybe a book, or a candy bar, or some ice cream maybe?"

"No, I don't want nothin'. I'm kinda tired is all." He puffed out a weary sigh and closed his eyes.

Ian placed a hand on Jonah's bony shoulder. "Then we'll let you sleep."

"Yeah, I'm tired." He blinked once, closed his eyes and before long, the steady rise and fall of his chest told them he'd fallen asleep. Lucy crooked a finger, luring Ian into the hall. The look on her face sent up a warning.

Lucy whirled on him, arms crossed over her chest. "I was trying to assure him in there. Why did you cut me off?"

Ian placed his hands on his hips and canted his body toward hers. "Because he was trying to tell you that his parents aren't going to care that he's in the hospital and you were trying to tell him he was wrong. He knows his own parents better than you do."

"No self-respecting parent would leave a child by himself in a hospital room miles from home."

Ian crossed his arms over his chest as he stood before her. "Want to make a bet?"

"Do you know something I don't?"

He watched her beautiful, sable eyes narrow on him. "Just leave it alone, Lucy. I didn't think he needed to be given any false hope, that's all."

"Everyone needs hope, Ian. Everyone," she said in a lowered voice.

He knew she was right, but he also knew what it felt like to be on your own emotionally as a child. Jonah was tough, he'd be all right, and he didn't need to be placated.

"Are you heading back to the camp, or are you going home?" Ian asked.

She shook her head. "I'm not leaving here. I can't leave him alone. Not like this."

The next words out of Ian's mouth startled him as much as they obviously startled Lucy. "I'm staying with him."

"You? No offense, but you're not exactly the nurturing kind." An amused grin spread across her face.

"I'm not leaving. Besides, I don't have anything pressing to attend, whereas you do."

Lucy's brows came together in question. "I do?"

"Don't you think it's time you check in on your sister? I'm guessing she's been on your mind, and if her husband fessed up, she'll need a shoulder."

Lucy was thoughtful a moment.

"You're right. I can't imagine how she's taking the

news that her husband...it's too much to think about." She studied the ceiling before meeting his eyes. "If you don't mind, I will check on Ellie. Thanks."

"Lucy." Something was different between them. Friendship, maybe. Affection, possibly. He wasn't quite sure. "You were right when you said we were a good team."

Her face lit in a wide smile. "Let's go back in so I can tell Jonah good night."

Jonah was sound asleep. Lucy gingerly brushed a hand over his head and to Ian said a simple "thanks" and left. Ian went to the door of the room and watched her leave. He returned and pulled a chair to the side of the bed and with his legs propped on the rails of Jonah's bed, settled in for the night.

****

The Barlows lived in a fashionable neighborhood, or as fashionable as a neighborhood could get in Butternut Creek. The homes were newer, the lawns more manicured, the vehicles parked in the drives more expensive. Lucy pulled into the yard and walked to the front door with the etched glass that she'd admired so. The thought of what she would find on the other side of this door nearly caused her to turn and run.

"Ellie?" The house was dark except for a slash of light at the top of the stairs. "El, are you up there?"

"Yes, I'm here. Come on up."

She didn't sound as though she were in a state of devastation. Lucy felt as though weights were tied to her feet as she pulled herself up the curved staircase. Taking a deep breath for strength, she entered the spacious bedroom and found Ellie sitting cross-legged on the bed, folding underwear and looking positively serene. Country music filled the room from CMT on the screen of the small television in the corner.

"Ellie?" Lucy studied her sister.

"Hey. What's up?" Ellie's eyes belied any distress. She pointed the remote at the television and reduced the volume. Blond curls wreathed her round face. She wore a white shirt, open at the collar, and blue jeans. Lucy realized the irony as she thought Ellie had never looked better. Then Ellie's face clouded over as her eyes traveled the length of her younger sister. "What happened to you? You look like you've been to hell and back."

The burden of the last few hours weighed heavily upon her. Lucy sank onto the corner of the bed. "I'm good."

"You liar." Ellie angled her head to one side. "You're not fine, that's plain to see." Her eyes studied her sister up and down. "You're a mess. Come on, fess up."

Obviously, Randy had yet to confess his awful sin. Lucy puffed out an exhausted breath and pinched the bridge of her nose to fight the headache building.

"Actually, I've had quite a day. You have a minute?" Lucy flopped back on the bed.

Ellie forgot the laundry and focused on her sister. "Of course, what's going on?"

Lucy propped herself on her side and told her sister about the accident and Ian's assistance. The seriousness of the situation with Jonah hit her full force as she told the story. By the time she got to the vigil she and Ian had kept at the hospital, her insides were quaking with nervous tension.

"Thank God, you found him. Just think what might have happened."

"I know, but let's not dwell on that. I can't. Jonah's fine, and we'll go from here. Ian's spending the night with him at the hospital." She watched as Ellie's eyebrows arched in surprise.

"He's spending the night with an injured child? I'm very impressed with your Mr. Flynn. He's hiding a bigger heart than I thought."

Lucy found herself speechless. The thought of the dragon otherwise known as Ian Flynn suddenly morphing into an angel of mercy just seemed, well, not quite right with her world. Time for a new subject.

"Anyway..." Lucy steeled her emotions before asking the next question. "Where are Randy and Abby?" She watched for any sign of upset. There was none.

Ellie reached for a pair of Randy's boxers, folded them in half and then in half again before setting them aside. "He's at the office finishing some paperwork, and remember, Abby is at Sarah's birthday party." Ellie glanced at the clock on the nightstand. "Actually, she should be here any time now."

"Oh." All words escaped Lucy at the moment. What exactly was a sister to do in the face of such a dilemma? Her gut told her that the news needed to come from Randy, yet her sisterly protection/support system was kicking in big time.

Unfortunately, the raw emotion of the situation with Jonah along with Randy's betrayal was nearly overwhelming, and exhaustion was getting the better of her. Much to her chagrin, tears stung at the corners of her eyes and a slight tremble began in her chin.

"Lucy?" Ellie angled her face in front of Lucy, concern clearly etched into the otherwise soft features of her face. "Please tell me what's wrong."

"I'm just tired." Lucy felt her face redden. "No, it's, well..." The last thing she wanted was to break Ellie's heart. "No, it's nothing." She'd blown it. Ellie always said she wore her emotions on her sleeve. How she wished she could change that.

Ellie began filling the laundry basket with the neatly folded whites. "I know what's on your mind, what's got you twisted in such a knot." One corner of her mouth drew up in a grin.

"You do?" Lucy tried to stem the pounding of her heart.

"Yes, Lucy-Goosy. Do you think I'm blind?"

"Well...no." Lucy felt the blood drain from her face. "What?"

"Ian Flynn. Remember him? The guy you spent the night with and now the knight in shining armor who saved Jonah." Ellie waved a hand in front of Lucy's face. "You with me there?"

Sweet relief flooded through her. "Yeah, I guess I'm kind of confused by the events of last night and then today." *Oh please, Ellie don't ask anything more.*

"I can understand that. You've never been one to jump into bed with just anyone. This guy must be different. This must be the mother of all crushes for you to have allowed him to seduce you on the first date."

"I don't think I'd go that far, and for your information, I seduced him." She waited for Ellie's response. She wasn't disappointed. Ellie's mouth formed a perfect *O* and her eyes followed suit. "And on that note, El, I have to go." Lucy reached across the bed and gave her sister a quick squeeze on the knee. "See ya." She strode toward the bedroom door.

"I just don't know what to say to that so...bye." Ellie grinned and gave her a thumbs-up.

Lucy left, her heart breaking at the knowledge of the pain that was to come. It was time for Randy to fix this mess, and fix it he would, if Lucy had anything to do with it. A heady rush of adrenaline replaced exhaustion. She had to find her brother-in-law.

****

Fifteen minutes later Lucy pulled Toty into the parking lot alongside the log-hewn building that served as the office for Barlow Associates. She could see Randy's car parked in the back. The front office appeared to be dark, but a beam of light across the floor told of activity of some kind in the back. Lucy opened the door and stepped inside, unsure what she would say to the skunk her sister was married to, but she had to say something. It was unforgivable that he hadn't confessed to Ellie.

Lucy slipped through the front door and followed the light. Soft voices and a tinkling of female laughter came from behind the slightly opened door. Holding her breath for fear of discovery, Lucy peered around the edge of the door. Randy was sitting behind his desk, eased back into his chair and smiling warmly at the blond mass of hair Lucy had seen him with at the restaurant. Sudden, swift anger pushed Lucy over the edge as she bolted through the door and into the light of the office.

Randy sat straight in his chair, his hands gripping the armrests. "What the hell...?"

"Randy, you son-of-a-bitch." Lucy stormed across the room and landed a fist in the middle of his desk. "How dare you leave Ellie in the dark about the state of your marriage?"

The blonde seated at Lucy's elbow began to rise from her chair. In one fluid movement Lucy grabbed a handful of hair at the top of Blondie's head. In a high-pitched voice the woman whined, "Owww, let go of me, you bitch."

Lucy twisted the hair in her hand. "I'm just taking out the trash, that's all." With that she guided the blonde out of the office by her hair and nearly threw her into the reception area.

Randy bolted from his chair and rounded his desk. "Who the hell do you think you are to come here, where you're not wanted? Get the hell out of my office."

"I'm not leaving until you and I talk, but first you better get rid of the trash out in the other room or I will." Lucy gave him the meanest look she could create.

The fierce expression on Randy's face caused her to quake with anxiety, but she fought to conceal it. There was a good chance he might throttle her, but she didn't care. Randy turned to the door. "Cindy, it'll be okay. I'll call you later."

Cindy pushed against the door as Lucy attempted to close it on her. "Did you see what she did to me, Randy? I'm going to call my attorney. You'll pay for this you..."

"*Cindy.*" Randy wrestled the door from Lucy. "Just go home. I'll talk to you later." His voice boomed off the log office walls.

From over his shoulder Lucy called, "No, he won't, because I'm going to knock some sense into his head. Obviously, he's lost what few rocks he had when he took up with the likes of you."

Randy turned his attention to his sister-in-law. "Lucy, that's enough."

Lucy took a step toward him. "Don't you tell me 'that's enough.' Don't tell me anything." She gave him a push to his shoulder and, for a second, she thought he was going to push her back. To his credit, he didn't.

From the other side of the doorway Cindy snickered. "Randy, honey, you want me to call the police?"

Randy turned toward Cindy. "No, we don't want to make this a bigger mess than it already is. Just leave. I'll see you later."

"No, he won't." Lucy shoved Randy in the back, knocking him into the door and he banged his head.

"Dammit, Lucy." He whirled on her just as Cindy pushed the door open and hit him in the opposite side. "Owww." He brought both hands up to his head.

The mass of hair came around the door. "Randy...honey, I'm so sorry."

Randy's face was now a dangerous shade of red. "Get

out, Cindy, now."

Cindy huffed once, then disappeared into the darkness.

Lucy waggled her head and upper body as she stuck out her lower lip and imitated Cindy's whiny voice. "Raaaandeee."

Randy rubbed the emerging bumps on his head. "Lucy, knock it off." The sound of the outer door slamming echoed through the office. He went to his desk and wearily dropped into his chair.

"Well." Lucy stood before him, her hands on her hips and tapped an impatient foot. "What sorry excuse have you got to explain this mess?"

"Sit down." He looked up at her with eyes that seemed to express sadness rather than guilt. "Please, Lucy, please sit down so I can talk to you."

"No. Do you know what you've done?" Could this really be the man she'd loved as a brother all these years?

"Come on, Luce, please." He pulled his hands down over his face. "You and I have always had a good relationship, haven't we? Please, just listen."

Reluctantly, Lucy sat in the chair so recently vacated by the blonde. "There's no excuse for this, Randy, so please don't try to pass one off on me. Do you realize the hurt this will cause Ellie? This is going to devastate her. Besides, what were you thinking to take that bimbo to dinner at a restaurant only a few miles from town? That was plain stupidity on your part." Lucy settled back into the chair. She was going to be sick. The sight of him nauseated the hell out of her.

"I know." Randy raked his hands through his hair, the color that, until now, hadn't reminded her of dog shit, but there it was, plain as day. He was doing his best to look haggard. Lucy wasn't buying it. "I'm just getting tired of hiding. It was dumb, I know."

"I don't think you *do* know. Ellie loves you. God knows why, but she does." Lucy bit her lower lip in an effort to control the tremble beginning in her chin.

"Where did you find that, that...person?" Lucy flung an arm in the direction of the door.

"She's the secretary for LJ Motors over in Eagle River. I do their books now and, well, she was helping me.

I have a feeling I'm about to lose a big client. Her father is the owner." He pulled a hand over his face.

"Did you have to sink so low as to mess around with such a piece of trash as that? I used to think you had a brain."

"Oh come on, you and I have always been friends. Don't act like I'm some parasite you've had to accept all these years. We've been family. Correction, we are family."

Lucy bit back the ball of resentment clawing up the back of her throat. How dare he speak to her of family? How dare he expect her to sweep his betrayal under the rug as if it were simply a hiccup in their relationship? "I want to know what you're planning to do about this. I expected that you were going to be honest with Ellie last night. I can hardly bear to face her, knowing what I know."

"You don't know a damn thing." Randy glared at her across the desk. His fist pounded the desk in front of him. "I've been a good husband and father, and I've seen to Ellen's needs, but I need something too. Ellie is a great person, but I want some excitement. We married too young, and people change as they age. I don't blame her for anything, but I..." He set his elbows on the desk, clasped his hands in front of him and hung his head. "Oh, I don't know. I screwed up."

Lucy leaned forward on the desk. "That's an understatement. I don't want to hear your excuses. You know what's right and what's not. You've messed up the best thing that's ever happened to you." She studied him for a moment as she remembered the man she'd thought he was. His betrayal was inconceivable. "Randy, how could you?" This time she was unable to stop the tears that formed rivers down her cheeks.

A tear slipped down his face as well. "I know it. I love Ellie, I really do. I don't want to lose her." He buried his face in his hands for a moment before looking to Lucy. "I couldn't believe it when I saw you there, at the restaurant. I...it was all wrong. Cindy's not what I want, and I realized that the moment I saw you and knew that I'd been caught. Maybe that's what I wanted, to get caught."

"At Ellie's expense." Randy handed her a tissue and she dabbed the tears away. She wanted to believe him, but he didn't appear to be suffering enough to assuage her anger and disappointment.

"You had pretty bad timing tonight. When you walked in here, I was getting ready to tell Cindy goodbye." He wiped his face dry with the palms of his hands. "I want my family, Lucy. You can believe that."

Lucy stood before him. This was too much. "I don't believe a word you say, Randy. How can I?"

"I love Ellie. I just ran a little off track, that's all." He refused to look at her.

"A little off track? Infidelity is more than a little off track, I'd say."

"Just let me explain."

"You broke a sacred trust between you and your wife, not to mention your daughter. That can't be mended just by saying, 'oops, I got a little off track.'" She was incredulous at his sorry attempt to justify his actions.

"I know, but Ellie doesn't need to know about this. It'll only hurt her." Now he truly looked frightened. "Please, Luce, I don't want to hurt her. I truly don't."

Lucy shook her head and pointed a finger at him. "You're telling her tonight. I'll not have her in the dark any longer. I mean it, Randy. You tell her, or I will. I can't bear the guilt I feel for not going to her right away. She deserves to hear this from you, not from me."

"So I'm supposed to pay for your guilt? You want me to hurt her so you'll feel better?" His face reddened with anger.

Lucy pointed a finger in his face. "Don't pull that manipulation on me. Don't even try. It won't work."

Randy withered in his chair. "Luce, I can't. I can't hurt her like that."

"Ha! That's rich. What do you think you've done every time you left her to be with that piece of trash?" Lucy was incredulous. Were all men this stupid?

"She doesn't need to know," he answered in clipped words.

"Have you forgotten how rumors fly in a small town? I'm sure people are talking already with you wining and dining her within a few miles of town and meeting her here in your office. Where was your head?" She held up her hands and shook her head. "Don't tell me, I know, but look at the hurt you've caused. Of course, people are talking, and it's only a matter of time before someone slips. And, how do you know Cindy won't want a little revenge once you dump her? She could spread it all over town, or tell Ellie. You have no choice but to tell your wife what you've been up to. I don't want her hurting, but she deserves the truth and she deserves to hear it from you."

The room was silent for a moment.

Randy stood from behind his desk. "You're right. I'll tell her tonight. I...I don't want a divorce. I don't want my daughter having to divide her time between us. Maybe we can go to a counselor, or, oh, I don't know. I'll make this right, I promise."

"I don't know how. My suggestion is that she throw your sorry butt out, cut her losses, and begin again."

The color drained from his face. "Don't say that, we have a daughter to raise. Lucy, please don't give up on me." His eyes pleaded with her. "Ellie puts a lot of store in your opinion. I want to save my family. I swear I do."

"You should have thought of that before boinking that bimbo you had in here. Face it, you screwed up and now you're going to pay. A counselor isn't going to help you hang on to the best thing that ever happened to you. Ellie won't put up with this for one second. She's going to send you packing as well she should."

She went to the door and stopped, turning to face him. "Look Randy, Abby deserves a happy family and as much as I want to see you thrown to the curb, I want that little girl to have what her mother and I didn't. You damn well better make this right."

Chapter Nine

From the door of the hospital room Lucy watched as Ian and Jonah shared a bowl of Cream of Wheat.

"Sure you don't want some?" Ian smiled at her over the spoon at his mouth. "I haven't had this in years, but it's rather good."

"It's not bad," Jonah added in a gravelly voice.

"No thanks, but I have something for Jonah." Lucy revealed the gift bag she had hidden behind her.

The boy's eyes rounded. "You do?"

"I thought you deserved a little something." She handed him the bag. She and Ian shared a smile before turning their attention to the boy.

Jonah tore into the bag, leaving blue tissue paper strewn about the bed. Gingerly, he pulled out a box. "It's a model car."

"I hope you like it. I heard you like cars with a lot of snot." Lucy's eyes found Ian's. "It's a replica of Tony Stewart's race car." She pulled a chair to the edge of the bed and sat across from Ian.

"I know." Jonah studied the box intently. The bright light in his gray eyes warmed Lucy's heart.

"I thought we could spend extra time in the evenings putting it together. I don't know much about cars, but maybe you could teach me a thing or two. Would you like that?"

Jonah nodded. "Thanks, Lucy. This is pretty cool."

"Nice idea." Ian's gaze held hers. It was as though she was seeing his heart melting before her eyes. He was different this morning. Perhaps she was different as well.

Lucy left them to drive to Ellie's with her heart pounding in her chest. She'd worried all night and prayed she'd handled the situation with Randy correctly. If she hadn't, she may be paying for her miscalculation for the rest of her life.

"Hey, sweetness, where's your mom?" Lucy placed a

hand on Abby's tousled locks. Sitting cross-legged on the carpeted floor of the family room, in her pink Barbie pajamas, Abby sucked on a red Popsicle. SpongeBob SquarePants danced across the television screen, and she giggled.

"She's upstairs in her room. I think she's sick today," she said without taking her eyes from the screen.

Fingers of dread spread through Lucy. "Why do you say that?" She held her breath, not really wanting to hear the answer to her question.

Abby pumped her shoulders in a shrug. "I dunno. Her eyes are puffy and her nose is red. She's kinda sniffly."

"What's up with a Popsicle so early in the morning?" Lucy squatted down to Abby's level and smoothed the golden hair on her little head.

"Mommy said I can have anything I want this morning." She licked once, and then shrugged. "This is what I want." With a crook of her finger, Lucy caught a red drip just as it left Abby's chin and for lack of a tissue, licked it off her finger.

"I'll see if your mommy needs something, and then I'll make you breakfast." Lucy stood and surveyed the family room and the kitchen beyond. Everything seemed spotless and in order.

"Mommy always makes me breakfast right after SpongeBob."

"Okay, I'll come down in just a little bit and make us all something yummy. How about scrambled eggs and toast?"

Abby scrunched her nose at the suggestion. "I'd kinda like pannycakes. Can you make 'em to look like teddy bears? My mommy can." Piercing blue eyes offered Lucy a challenge.

"I'll try." She hesitated before continuing. "Is your daddy here?"

Abby returned her attention to the screen. "Nope. He went to work before I got up. I want him to take me to the park today to see the new tornado slide."

Lucy blew out a sigh of relief. "Okay, I'll be back." Abby giggled at SpongeBob and his cohorts. Oh, to be that young and carefree again. Lucy hurriedly climbed the stairs to the master bedroom.

Ellie sat at the window seat in the elegant bedroom, rocking back and forth. Her swollen eyes were unfocused, her usually smiling lips down-turned, her face stained from tears. She was still in pajamas, her hair a straggly mess. Lucy felt her breath catch at the sight. Never in her life had she seen Ellie look so despondent, not even when their father had left them so many years before. His abrupt abandonment had left Lucy angry, their mother heartbroken, and dear Ellie had rallied immediately to take care of everyone and everything.

A thought occurred to Lucy. She'd never once seen Ellie grieve over that long-ago betrayal. Ellie had been too busy mothering her mother and her sister. Of course, Lucy hadn't grieved either, simply because she wasn't about to allow dear old Dad the intrusion into her emotions. Lucy squared her shoulders. She'd be damned if Ellie would shoulder this betrayal alone.

"You knew, didn't you? That's why you came to the house last night." The pools of Ellie's eyes were unfathomable depths of pain. Lucy knew the expression on her sister's face would haunt her forever.

Lucy cautiously approached, silently praying she hadn't handled the situation all wrong. "Oh, Ellie, I'm so sorry. Please don't be angry with me. I wanted to tell you, but I thought it should come from...him."

"I don't even want to hear his name." Fresh tears flowed freely. She dabbed at them with the crumpled tissue balled in her hand. "I should've known all along. God, I'm so stupid." She choked back a sob.

"No, Ellie." Lucy searched frantically for the right words to help her sister. "You loved him, and because of that you trusted him." She patted Ellie's knee, feeling completely inadequate.

"All those late dinner meetings, all those conferences out of town. I should have known. He hasn't been interested in me in so long I...I can't remember when. Who could blame him, I suppose. I know I've let myself go lately." She blew her nose into the tissue and handed it to Lucy who quickly delivered the soggy blob to the wastebasket in the corner while Ellie pulled out another. "I've seen those women on talk shows who've been cheated on, how they all thought it would never happen to them, and I always thought, 'come on, the writing was right there on the wall the whole time.'" A sob broke forth. "Oh God, I can't believe this is my life too." She raised red, puffy eyes to Lucy with a pleading look of desperation.

Lucy's eyes welled in response. She spread her hands, as though attempting to pull the perfect words from the air around her, but they weren't coming. What she really wanted to do was run from the house, hunt Randy down, and kick his ass. But she was needed here, and here she'd stay. She'd never felt so inept in all her life.

"I'm sorry you're going through this, El. I wish I could come up with some magic solution to make it better, but I can't." She pushed back tears of her own. "I'll tell you one thing. I don't want to hear another word about you letting yourself go. El, you're the only person I know who's as beautiful inside as you are on the outside. He's a damn fool to hurt you this way."

When Ellie wrapped shaking arms around her midsection, Lucy feared she was going to be sick. "Tell me how you found out." Bleakly Ellie stared out into the morning light, her voice marked with exhaustion.

"I saw them together. It was at Harper's Landing the night I took Ian to dinner." The mention of Ian's name brought a queer pang to the pit of her stomach, which she promptly dismissed in light of the more important issues at hand.

Ellie's eye met hers briefly, before dabbing at her nose. "Harper's Landing? You mean he didn't even have the decency to leave the county with her?" Ellie turned from the window. She looked about the room as though she were searching for clarity, understanding, anything to wash away the reality, but reason seemed to elude her. "That's not a large place. He must have known you saw them, didn't he?"

"Oh, he knew all right." Tears had begun to spill down Lucy's cheeks and she wiped them dry with the palms of her hands. "I sort of made a bit of a spectacle of myself, of all three of us actually."

Now she had Ellie's full attention. "Lucy, what did you do?" The memory of foiling Randy's rendezvous with the bimbo gave her no comfort this sad morning as she hoped to assuage her sister's pain.

Lucy related the story of the unfortunate confrontation in the restaurant parking lot and then of the argument in Randy's office the night before.

Ellie stared off into space for a moment, and then, miraculously through her tears, she burst into laughter. "You actually pulled her by the hair? Oh, Lucy, that's priceless." She reached for another tissue as she was crying and laughing at the same time. "You're priceless. Thanks for sticking up for me."

Lucy chuckled. "I half expected the police to be at my door this morning with a charge of assault and battery." She was thoughtful for a moment. "You should have seen the look on her face when I dug my fingers into her hair. I couldn't wait to wash my hand, it was so sticky. Ish." She jostled her fingers in the air for effect.

They were thoughtful a moment, and then Ellie dissolved in tears again. "God, Lucy, what will I do now?" She balled another tissue in her hand and pounded her fist on her knee. "I have a daughter to raise and, darn it all, I didn't want her to have the same kind of family life we did. And now look, here we are all over again."

Lucy wrapped Ellie in her arms. "I'll help you figure it out, I promise. You name it, I'll be here for you and Abby."

"Oh, how do I tell Abby?" Ellie's shoulders shook with sobs while tears ran afresh down Lucy's face. "I can't do it, I just can't."

"She doesn't have to know anything just yet. Give it a few days before you tackle that."

Ellie blew her nose. "She's a smart little girl. She'll know something is wrong."

"Randy was never home much anyway. She may not realize there's a problem. I'm just saying wait until you can do it calmly, without falling apart. Maybe you could do it together, to reassure her that she still has two parents—even though one's got his head up his ass right now."

****

At eleven that morning, a subdued Jonah Bates was released from Memorial Hospital into the care of Lida Duncan with Ian by her side. As the odd threesome walked across the parking lot Jonah said, "Wish Lucy was here."

A look passed between Lida and Ian before he answered. "She had some business to take care of this morning. She'll see you later." Silently Ian wished Lucy the best of luck this difficult morning. He had wanted to counsel her regarding the situation with her sister, but that sort of thing was not exactly his forte. Another first in what was promising to be a long line of firsts the longer he stuck around this sleepy, yet endearing, hole-in-the-woods.

Lida's round form bobbled from side to side as she walked. "I hope she's all right. She called early this morning and asked Jule to take her classes."

"She's fine. You know Lucy, solid as a rock." He hoped the situation with Ellie and her husband hadn't escalated into something ugly. He knew too well the ugliness that could come from the dysfunction of family life.

Ian left Jonah in the care of Lida at the camp and drove to Conover to meet with a client. It had been a long, boring day. His mind kept wandering, and it had been embarrassing. At one point, his client asked if he'd like to take a break, maybe get some air.

Driving back into town later than he'd anticipated, Ian was exhausted and anxious to crawl into his bed. Strangely enough, when he reached the motel, he deliberately drove by and took a right onto Main Street. The only sign of life there were the twinkling lights embellishing Theatre North and the few cars parked out front. He took a left onto Lucy's street. Funny, he thought as he felt his spirits lift, that his day should end here, in front of her house. Anticipation spread through him, filling him with thoughts of being welcomed by her smiling face, maybe a glass of iced tea, and, well, whatever else the evening may hold.

His eyes searched for the welcome of her front porch, a light in a window. He pulled his car over to the curb and parked in front of the house before hers. The windows of Lucy's simple home were dark. Toty was absent from the drive, no sign of her. Disappointed filled him, although he didn't understand the complexity of that emotion. What did he expect of dropping in on her at ten at night? It's not as though they were having an affair. They didn't exactly have a friendship. Of course, the tone of their relationship seemed to have taken a turn with Jonah's accident. What were they? He was confused by the very fact that he was confused in the first place.

Lucy Mitchell wasn't his type, not even close. Ian's women were of the same mold—classy, elegant, well-mannered and, most importantly, well-connected. Yet there was something nagging at him, a yearning he wasn't at all certain how to satiate. The comfort of a familiar face would have soothed his unsettled psyche.

What was it about Lucy that seemed to have him knotted up inside? Was he simply craving more of the torrid lovemaking they'd shared? While that was certainly satisfying, something had changed when they'd saved Jonah. Maybe, somehow, he'd been the one that had been saved.

A ridiculous thought, he silently chided. He had a life most would admire. A successful, challenging career, more money than he knew what to do with, no responsibilities other than to himself and his firm. No wife, no children to burden him or slow him down, no family to bother him at all.

That last thought lingered like a bad taste in his mouth, weighing heavily on his shoulders. The words "no family at all" worked at him to pierce his armor, an armor that lately seemed made more of liquid than steel. Besides, it was a lie. He had family, if you could call it that.

Probably a lack of sleep muddling his brain, clouding his thoughts, making him vulnerable to these nonproductive meanderings. He watched her simple, unassuming house, willing a light to signal her presence, for Toty to magically appear in the drive. He pictured her on the porch, her curves draped in a dress sprinkled with tiny flowers, waving him in.

He sighed and massaged the bridge of his nose. He felt unsettled, restless. The thought of going back to his motel room alone didn't appeal to him in the least.

Slowly, he shifted into reverse and backed down to the corner, turned his car around, and drove toward the only place he knew he could find solace tonight.

****

Lucy pulled her car through the gates of the camp, to the side of the road, and parked between two evergreen trees. She sought relief from the oppressive heat of the day, and solace for her turbulent heart.

Even in the dark, she knew the path through the trees and down the hill to the lake. The clouds overhead shifted to the east to reveal a full moon that illuminated the forest around her. Slowly, she picked her way along the path, ferns brushing her ankles as she went, a sleepy breeze fluttering through the birch trees above her. Soon she was at the lake, a ribbon of moonlight weaving through the rippled wake of the breeze, the stars coaxing diamonds from the black depths below.

Her eyes searched the shoreline until she found the canoe kept among the rocks tethered to the trunk of a poplar tree. Lucy carefully untied the knot, threw the rope into the canoe, and settled herself inside. She picked up one of the two paddles lying inside and pushed herself away from the shore. The canoe scraped the sandy bottom before effortlessly sliding into the tepid waters.

As she glided to the center of the lake, the stillness enveloped her tattered emotions. Off to the north, a light shone golden in a distant cabin. To her left, a campfire blazed alongside another cabin, sending the pungent aroma of burning wood and leaves wafting over the water. Lucy pulled her paddle from the water, closed her eyes, and allowed the canoe to glide under its own power as she took in the scent of the campfire. A lonely loon called for a mate, sending forth a haunting entreaty. The sound echoed through the black of night while moonlight spilled upon her, filled her with comfort. She felt utterly alone, and ultimately at peace.

Whenever life's complexities seemed too much, this place had always been balm to her soul. It was inconceivable that, should Ian's plans come to fruition, this place would be lost to her, lost to them all.

She eased her body into the belly of the canoe and propped the oar between two benches and stared up at the night sky. Her soul was fraught with too many unsettling emotions. If only she could seek answers to all of life's mysteries from the stars above.

Silently, she sent a prayer heavenward, a prayer for the pain of her sister, for Jonah, for Lida and the challenges facing her, and for the life of the camp she loved. It was a shame the tranquility of this lake would be shattered by Ian and his condominiums. Ellie's problems were not unsolvable, just an ugly bump in the road they'd have to weather. And no doubt, Ellie would recover, but it would take time.

Ellie was a gentle soul, sometimes too loving for her own good. She would need time to grieve, time to wallow before she went ahead with the rest of her life.

It was good riddance to Randy Barlow, if being rid of him was Ellie's choice. If it wasn't, Lucy would have to forgive him and that would not come easily. As far as Lucy was concerned, any man who could deal this type of pain to someone who'd stood by him and loved him deserved all the bad that came his way. Her father was living, breathing proof of that.

The thought shattered the tranquility of her respite and she guided the craft toward shore. Rings of moonlight flowed from where the paddle dipped into black, and a silvery ribbon spread in the wake of the canoe's path.

The craft bumped against the bank, and its wake lapped along the shoreline to herald her arrival. Carefully she balanced her weight as she negotiated her footing out of the canoe, checking her footfalls on the rocks, one hand keeping the canoe close. She retrieved the rope in the bow and tied it to the tree trunk just as a squirrel scurried from the fern cover of the forest floor.

Lucy jumped at the sound, splayed a hand upon her chest and breathed a sigh of relief as the little scamp chattered from a branch overhead.

Just then she heard a soft voice behind her, barely a whisper on the evening breeze.

"Lucy."

She gasped and turned.

Ian Flynn. Moonlight wreathed his dark head and shoulders against the black of the nighttime forest. For a brief moment, time stood still and the world melted into black until all that remained was Lucy, with her heart beating wildly in her chest, and Ian, before her, sheathed in the silvery light.

Then she recovered her wits. "Ian, what are you doing here? Are you following me? You nearly frightened me out of my shorts." She hoped he didn't latch on to her comment about the shorts, but it was too late.

"Frightening you out of your shorts isn't a bad idea. But am I following you? No...and yes." Through the black of night she could see the glint in Ian's eyes, hear his smooth, silky voice. "I didn't feel like sleeping. Thought I'd see what the lake was like at night." His gaze scanned the perimeter. "It's quite beautiful here, peaceful. More captivating than during the day." He returned his gaze to her. "Something about the night seems to add a different element to the beauty of everything here. Why is that, Lucy?"

For a brief moment, she was speechless. "It would be a shame to see it all go, wouldn't it?" Her eyes sought his in silent challenge.

He shoved his hands into the pockets of his pants. "Lucy, I plan to protect the beauty of this lake. I wish you'd understand that."

"I wish I understood as well, but I don't and frankly, I can't deal with anything more right now. This has been a trying day to say the least. I came here seeking solitude, and it's just not working at the moment." A strange shiver went up her spine, and she rubbed her upper arms.

Something akin to concern clouded the shadows of his face. "I...it's just been a hell of a day and...well, in light of what Ellie's going through, you're not the gender I should be dealing with at the moment."

"How's she doing, if you don't mind my asking? I assume your brother-in-law has confessed his sins."

A few short days ago she would have found his concern dubious, but this was a different Ian. "He's confessed and she's struggling. Thanks for asking."

"I like your sister, what little I know of her. She strikes me as a kind person, more decent than most."

"She is." Why did he have to look so handsome?

He turned from her and seemed to study the placid lake. "I left Jonah in Lida's care this morning. Have you seen him?" She studied the shadows of his profile a moment.

129

"He's doing well. I saw him this afternoon." She chuckled. "He's not being a very cooperative patient. Poor little guy. Although I will say he seems to appreciate being here now more than ever before." The memory of Lida trying to make him eat squash at dinner made her smile. "Unfortunately it takes tragedy to appreciate those around you."

"Did his parents ever show? Did they at least find time in their busy schedule to call him?"

"No, they didn't. They spoke with Lida and once they learned he'd be okay, they simply asked if he could finish his term at the camp. They've just begun a mission project and didn't want to leave before they finished. That's got to hurt, but you know Jonah, he's a trooper. I think we're his summer family. It's too bad, but you know, we see a lot of children like that here. It's why this place is so important."

Ian ran a hand over his hair and massaged the back of his neck. "Lucy, I don't need to be badgered by you right now. Can we drop this subject? I promise you a knock-down-drag-out argument one of these days, but not tonight."

Something told her not to antagonize him any more than she already had. Neither one of them had the energy for another sparring match. She crossed her arms over her chest and said, "I'll hold you to that. What do you propose we talk about? The weather, gas prices—we really don't have much in common, you know."

He stopped his self-massage and turned a stony gaze to her. She'd obviously said something wrong. The way he continued to stare at her was a bit unnerving.

He bit his lower lip and seemed thoughtful for a moment. "We've slept together. Maybe we could talk about us."

His words sucked the breath from her lungs. For a moment, she simply stared at him. Before she could find her voice, the muffled chime of a cell phone broke the silence. Ian's features took on a hardened expression of annoyance as he dug into his pocket, snapped the phone open, checked the caller ID, and firmly snapped it shut again.

"Must be something important for someone to call at

this hour," Lucy ventured cautiously. It had suddenly occurred to her that she'd never asked if he was attached to someone in Madison. "My guess is business or a girlfriend."

"It wasn't business, and no, it wasn't a girlfriend." He replaced the phone in his pocket and slanted his eyes in her direction. "There isn't a girlfriend, hasn't been for quite some time. I seem to be married to my business too much of the time." The corners of his mouth curved into an amused grin. "So, to digress, I'll ask again, what about us?"

Us? Oh, I'm really not up to this. "I'm sorry, you've lost me with that one. What 'us'? Sure, we had dinner one night." She gave a nonchalant shrug. "We slept together once; we've even had a few, shall we say, discussions. But as far as us being an 'us,' I don't quite know what you're getting at." She knew she sounded ridiculous, but this subject made her uncomfortable, plain and simple.

Ian took a step toward her, his broad shoulders blocking her view of the lake. "Come now, Lucy, you don't strike me as dense by any means. We're attracted to each other, you and I. Don't ask me why, maybe the old adage 'opposites attract,' but I think you feel it as much as I. Or quite possibly, we're very much alike."

"I do? We are?" His self-confidence irked her. "You're attracted to me but can't imagine why. Well, that's a real smooth pick-up line, Ian, and answers the question why you're not seeing anyone with technique like that. I think you'll have to explain yourself." Her flight response was fighting to kick in.

"On second thought, never mind. I need to go. I've got an early lesson tomorrow. See ya." She took a step but met resistance with the grip of his hand on her arm. The sizzle that simple contact sent through her was unnerving, to say the least. Slowly, cautiously, she raised her eyes to his.

"Ian, really..." God, they were so close that she could feel his breath upon her face.

Ian crushed her against him, his arms encircled her. "Lucy, don't fight it." Before she could respond, his lips came down on hers and captured her body and soul. She attempted to free herself, but he held her firmly within his embrace.

She bent her head back to seek release from the entrapment of his kiss and whispered, "Ian, I don't think..." Before she could complete the sentence, his lips caught hers once again, but she wrenched away. "Really, I spent the evening trying to comfort my sister"—she dodged his lips again—"from the pain her husband has caused and to be honest, Ian...stop it now...spending time with a man isn't all that appealing at the moment."

"Well, get over it." His lips crushed hers while one hand came up to cradle the back of her head. And she couldn't deny her feelings any longer. She wanted him.

All rhyme or reason flew from her brain, like the flight of a hummingbird flitting between advance and retreat, tasting both, unable to relinquish either. Unable, or unwilling, to find any plausible argument against the onslaught of his advance, she surrendered to him. She slid one hand along his back, the other cupping the back of his head.

His lips coaxed hers apart, tasting, savoring. Heat washed over her, gripped her, making her feel as though her body were liquid, washed together with his in a tidal wave of desire. Passion stirred in the pit of her stomach and spread fevered fingers through her body. His arms pulled her tight against him, and she answered with the press of her breasts against the rock that was his chest. His lips sought that sensual area just below her ear and under her jawbone and the desire to become one with his body consumed her. Wanton desire tingled along every inch of her. His hands splayed on her back, massaged between her shoulders, then slid to cup her buttocks as his lips again found hers. Between the crush of their bodies, she felt the full measure of his desire for her.

A sigh escaped her lips as her hands sought to claim him as well, feeling the taut mass of muscle over his shoulders, the sinewy ripples down his back. So hard, so sexy. She pulled his hips against hers as they kissed. All thoughts of the unsettling events of the last two days melted, replaced with one solitary goal: the final destination of this emotional and physical melding.

Ian released her lips and held her head in his hands. He smoothed her hair, resting a hand on either side of her head. "Lucy, I want to make love to you. Right here, right now."

She answered him with a kiss and together they sank to the earth below. The strength of his hands guided her back to lie on a soft bed of fern and woodland grasses. As she lay between Ian and the soft earth, her need for him increased tenfold. It felt so natural, so right, to be here with him. He shifted his weight on her as his lips came down upon hers and they clung together hungrily. Lucy arched against his body, driven by the desire to pull his heart into her very soul...at least until a pine needle poked her in the side and she jumped in response.

"Ow," she said, a bit too loudly into his ear, and he jerked away from her.

Ian covered his ear with one hand and with the other lifted his body from hers enough to let her catch her breath. "What...happened?"

"Something just stuck me in the side." Feeling quite giddy as she spoke.

"Well, it wasn't me." Through the moonlight that kissed one side of his face, she saw the curve of his lips and knew he was smiling.

"I know that." She placed a hand on his shoulder and gave a teasing little shove. "It's Mother Nature jolting me into reality."

"You think so?" His eyebrows formed a lovely arch frosted by moonlight. He lightly brushed her lips with his.

"I know so. She's probably saying, 'What are you thinking?'" Honestly, she didn't want this to end, and yet, now that they'd been interrupted, the consequences of making love with him again frightened her. Truth be told, she cared for him more than she wanted to admit. Yet, this was too beautiful a moment to let reason and good common sense ruin it.

"I think she's just jealous. What do you think?" His face hovered above hers, nose to nose, and his grin gave way to a more serious expression. She had the uncanny feeling he'd read her mind. "Do you want to be here with me?" He kissed her lightly again, as though to sway her answer.

In the shadow of the moonlight, his eyes shone upon her, drinking her in, communicating with her soul, telling her that no matter what, they would be all right.

In a rushed whisper, the words left her. "Yeah, Ian, I want to be here, with you." Her heart began thumping wildly in her chest in anticipation. "Make love to me."

His gaze caught hers and held her there, suspended in time, the two of them in the moonlit forest, under the evergreens, kissed by the cooling woodland-scented breeze and underscored by the lonesome song of the loon dancing on the water.

It was then that his lovemaking took on a different tone. A slower, gentler rhythm than the night she'd seduced him in her bedroom. He kissed her deeply, caressing her softly, exploring her curves ever so gently that it nearly drove her insane. Her body ached for more as his hands slipped under her shirt. A sigh escaped her at the sensation of his hands upon her skin. He caressed her breasts as she slid her hands along the length of his back until she found the hem of his shirt and worked her hands beneath it and felt as though she were feeling him for the first time. His skin was surprisingly soft in contrast to the hardness of his muscles.

His caresses drove her mad with desire. She couldn't stand it one moment longer. As if he had known, he raised up enough for her to push his shirt to his shoulders, where he quickly tore it from his torso and tossed it into the woods. Then he watched as she pulled her shirt over her head and gave it a carefree toss into the night sky.

His hands came over her breasts as she arched in response, and then around to her back and in an instant she felt her bra release. She wiggled her arms free of the restraint and gave it a toss overhead where it hooked on a pine branch and hung as a white flag of surrender above her.

He kissed her fully, deeply, breathing life to her soul. The rapture of nature's beauty only heightened the thrill of communicating in that most basic of ways. Body to body, breath to breath, heat matching heat, until the exquisite release left Lucy thoroughly exhausted and gloriously satiated.

The haunting cry of a solitary loon echoed into the night.

Chapter Ten

"Ian," her voice skittered upon the surface in a whisper as they circled each other in the cooling waters, and he ached to kiss her mouth. The sound of his name upon her lips was a soothing song to his senses. Their naked bodies caused a gentle undulating of the blackness enveloping them.

She said it again, "Ian." He could no more ignore her beckon than stop his heart from beating. He swam toward her through silver-tipped waves. Nearing her, he dipped his head beneath the black water, and rose before her, nose to nose, body to body.

"Lucy." Rivulets streamed into his eyes and he blinked them away before they would surely evaporate from the heat generated between them.

Silvery moonlight dusted her creamy shoulders and the dark sheen of hair framing her face. "You're a different person when you're so relaxed," she said. A gentle smile played upon her lips and reminded him of a mythical sea goddess.

He smiled back. "I'll take that as a compliment." He ran a finger the length of her jaw bringing it to rest upon her lips.

Funny, he couldn't remember the last time he'd felt so carefree, so at home. He was swimming naked in a lake after making love with an absolutely captivating woman in a bed of ferns. This was not Ian Flynn, driven workaholic. Something was happening to him. This was some back-to-nature nut's idea of the perfect date, not his. Yet, this was the most peaceful evening he'd spent in so long that the memory of it, if there actually was one, had long ago faded.

"I'll bet you've never skinny-dipped before." She pushed back from him and tipped the back of her head into the water, allowing her body to float near the surface.

"How can you tell?" He watched her, thoroughly

enjoying the view. Her breasts rose, then faded from view.

She kept her eyes on the stars overhead. "There's the Little Dipper." She pointed skyward and he followed her gaze. "You overachievers seem to have a problem letting go. I see it in the parents that drop their kids off. Too devoted to their yuppie keeping-up-with-the-Joneses lifestyles. Too bad, so sad." She raised her head, her eyes mischievous. "By the way, look out for the muskies in this lake. There have been some big ones caught here."

"Muskies?" His voice rose a decibel or two.

"You know, the big fish."

"I know it's a big fish, but why would I need to look out for a fish? Should I be expecting the theme song from *Jaws* to echo over the lake?"

"No." She chuckled. "But they might mistake certain parts of you for bait."

She was kidding, right?

He pushed himself toward her. "Then you had better help me hide it." He slid his hands around her backside and pulled her to him, feeling the heat for her grow within him.

"Oh, Ian, you're so romantic." She was mocking him. "How many girls have you used that line on?"

He chuckled as he answered her. "I can honestly say you're the only one." He covered her lips with his as she encircled him with her arms. The kiss grew more heated until he ached with want of her. She drew her legs around his torso, her breasts pressed against his chest and, as he entered her, she ran kisses along his neck. It was not long before they shuddered in simultaneous, exquisite release.

****

Lucy was damp in her clothing. They'd used Ian's shirt to dry off, and now they sat on the hill that rose from the lake among a stand of birch trees, the white of the bark in stark contrast to the black of night. He was dressed only in his shorts, the wet shirt laid upon the ferns. She sat between his legs on the soft earth enjoying the warmth of him, the way his hands smoothed her hair and rubbed the gooseflesh from her arms, the strength of his body supporting hers.

He bent his head so that his mouth was next to her ear. She could feel the warmth of his breath on the side of her face. "Tell me, Lucy, why do you love this place?"

She rested her hands on his knees. "It's what we give the kids here, a sense of belonging, acceptance."

"I want to know about *your* feelings for this place, not the kids." He ran his hands along her arms and interlaced his fingers with hers. "I want to know what makes you tick."

She liked the way it made her feel to have him wrapped around her in this way. She felt safe, totally protected from the world around them. A world that could dish out so much unhappiness. She thought briefly of Ellie. She wanted someone to hold her sister this way, to chase away the pain. A lump formed in her throat, but she forced it back.

"After our parents divorced, our neighbor, Mrs. Malach, took Ellie and me to church with her on Sundays. I guess the congregation took pity on us and gave us a free scholarship to the camp when I was eight and Ellie was ten." The warm memory of that special gift filled her once again. It was something she would remember for the rest of her life. "We were scared to death, but we had each other and that took the fear out of going someplace different." Pictures tumbled through her brain like rain. "We had such fun that summer."

"What happened between your parents, if you don't mind my asking?"

"My dad up and left us for Miss Dorothy Dyrkaz, Ellie's sixth-grade teacher." The anger that usually accompanied that memory was absent, replaced by a deep-seated emptiness. A hole in her chest she knew would never be filled. "Try living with that in a small town."

"I'm sorry." Ian's legs tightened about her as though to chase away the hurt. It was nice, but not necessary. She'd put that memory in its place a long time ago.

"Evidently, Miss Dyrkaz had quite a nightlife going. Anyway, it was humiliating. My mother worked to support us during the day and was too busy for us at night while she tried to replace him. This camp, this place, gave me what I needed at that time. Ellie and I begged and pleaded every summer after that first time to return and somehow Mom found the money. I suspect the

Duncan's gave her quite a break on the price so we could continue to attend."

"From what I've seen, they've certainly been generous." Whatever that meant, she chose to ignore his statement.

"As soon as we were old enough, they offered us jobs, and we lived out here all summer long. Ellie stopped working here when she married...him, and I haven't missed a summer yet. Sounds pretty boring, doesn't it?" Someday, she'd see other places, but not yet.

"Not at all." She sensed a chink in his armor. "You're wonderful with the children. I've watched you. This is what your life was meant to be, Lucy. You're more to them than a mere swim instructor and counselor. They look to you for understanding and patience. A kid needs that."

"Why have I just told you all of this?" She angled her face to view his. "I don't get this deep with anyone but Ellie."

"Maybe it's time you did."

She suspected he was speaking of himself. There was more to Mr. Ian Flynn than she'd allowed. She was certain of it.

****

It was with great enthusiasm, despite a lack of sleep, that Lucy approached her students the next day. She'd spoken with Ellie as she dashed about the house getting ready for work. Her sister assured her she was in better spirits and was on her way to open her shop, determined not to let Randy disrupt her life more than he already had. Abby was still unaware of the conflict between her parents. At the camp, Jonah was thriving, albeit stubbornly. The students were rowdy as usual, but the chaos didn't faze Lucy. Life was great, beautiful in fact. The sun was shining and Lucy loved everyone and everything around her.

More than once her gaze swept the premises for Ian, but he hadn't materialized. Within minutes of beginning her first class of the day, the sound of a car pulling into the parking area alongside the lodge gained her attention as she was helping a student with a pitiful version of the dog paddle. She turned her head just as a blur of red caught the corner of her eye. He was here. Ian was here, and it wouldn't be long before she'd see him standing on shore, waving, smiling that wonderful smile of his. She'd have to find a way to take a break from her class to say good morning and hope that the other counselors wouldn't guess what they'd shared the night before.

Lucy attempted to push the bemused thoughts from her mind to focus on the task at hand, but within minutes, that same car engine sounded behind her. Before she could focus, the car and its driver were gone in a flash of red. Surely, he'd simply run to town for something, a meeting, gas, a carton of milk, loaf of bread...Surely he'd be back to say good morning. He wouldn't leave knowing she was just a beach away.

But he had.

The morning seemed to pass agonizingly slow once Ian had gone. When noon finally arrived and he still hadn't returned, red flags began to wave. Where was he and why hadn't he come to the beach to say hello or even offer a wave? Any kind of greeting would have been better than pretending she wasn't a mere hundred feet away. Worse, she suddenly thought, what have I done to myself? She cared about Ian, it was just that simple.

It wasn't as if they'd professed their undying love the night before. No, it was one night of unbridled passion that let loose in a torrent of great sex and skinny dipping. And now, here she was, pining over the fact that he hadn't come to see her this morning. This was the kind of thing Jule would do.

Yet, something had changed between them. He'd become important to her, he mattered. They'd shared parts of themselves she was certain neither had revealed in a very long time, if ever. She was falling for Ian Flynn, falling hard, and as unnerving as that realization was, it was there all the same. Now she had to deal with it and, unfortunately, the fear that he didn't feel the same was eating away at her.

Still, a "Hi, Luce, howya doing, great sex last night, huh?" would have been good. Well, maybe not quite like that, but a hello would have probably sufficed and tempered the anger and confusion filling her.

At two, when Ian still hadn't returned to camp, Lucy

couldn't stand it any longer. She went to Lida's office. Lida was at her desk in a red sweatsuit, a purple bandana over her hair, eyeglasses sitting on the tip of her nose.

"Was Mr. Flynn here earlier today?" Lucy asked after they exchanged greetings.

"Why yes, and a crabby cuss he was. Now, where do you think I left my purse? I swear, if it was stapled to my arm, I'd still lose the dang thing."

Lida, focus, you're not telling me anything. "Is he going to be hanging around here all summer? I mean, I don't want him bothering you. You have enough to do without some citified investor lording over you." She hoped she sounded convincing.

"Oh, I don't mind him. This sale has been a great relief to me, and we can't forget that he saved our Jonah." Lida leveled a brief gaze on her before opening a desk drawer to search for the missing bag. She closed the drawer and opened another.

This wasn't going to be as easy as Lucy'd thought. *Oh well, might as well try the direct approach.* "Where'd he run off to so fast this morning?"

"Ian? He went back home, I guess. Oh, here's my purse. My, my, should have known it was stuck in here." From a drawer in her desk she pulled a black vinyl bag that was near to bursting from the seams.

"What do you mean, he went back home?" Dread began to work its way up her spine.

"You know, he asked for you." Lida stopped digging through her purse to raise a quizzical gaze on Lucy.

Lucy felt her spirits rise. "He did? What did he say? Did he leave a message? What did you tell him?"

"My goodness, all these questions. I told him you had taken the children on a hike through the bogs."

"A hike through the bogs? I was at the beach with the beginning swimmers. The hike isn't until three." Lida was never good at paying attention to the schedule. "Did he leave me a message?"

"No, he didn't. He stormed out of here like there was a fire somewhere." Lida began shifting papers on her desk.

"Where do you mean by 'home'? When will he be back?"

"He's on his way back to Madison, so you don't have to worry about his lording over me. He said he'd call me sometime. It didn't sound like he'd be back anytime soon."

Lida's words hit her with the force of a hundred-year-old balsam crashing to the ground. Something like the way her heart hit the floor, with a resounding, deadening thud.

****

Ian ducked beneath the yellow police tape, crossed the weed-infested yard, and entered the dilapidated, gray house that sat on a corner lot in one of Milwaukee's seedier districts. He entered through the dirty, rusted screen door into the living room and immediately wrinkled his nose at the stench of cigarettes, spilt beer, and death. The house was as gloomy as he remembered. The same ugly plaid sofa was nearly threadbare and pushed against the paneled wall. The same filthy brown recliner sat in the corner nearest the door. Everything was brown or had a film of brown.

Every cell in his body screamed "run as fast as you can."

The kitchen was a mass of dirty dishes that had been sitting there for how long, he couldn't imagine. Every surface was moldy, dusty, smudged, or torn. It made his skin crawl to think people lived like this, to think he'd once lived like this. The seed of anger began to germinate within him and gnaw at his insides.

He was dog tired from the drive, and his weakened mental state allowed the flow of memories to assail his senses. The echo of drunken arguments and terrifying threats seemed to reverberate off the walls. Many was the night he'd lay awake listening, ready to hide in the closet should the melee spill into the hovel that was his room. The stench of beer and cigarettes and filth was so strong that Ian felt the bile rise in his throat. It was a smell he'd never wanted to experience ever again. As his eyes swept from living room to kitchen and back again, his heart clenched with the loneliness and the disillusionment he'd experienced as a child in these very rooms. It took every ounce of strength in him not to turn and bolt.

Behind him, the screen door screeched, then banged.

Ian jumped at the sound. A young woman, in her

early twenties, a small curly-headed child propped on her hip, stood between him and the door.

"Okay if I come in here?" the woman asked.

She had thick, sandy colored hair pulled into a spiky ponytail, no makeup; and, in fact, the pallor of her skin and dark smudges under her eyes suggested she'd been pulled through hell and back. She was dressed in faded blue jeans ripped at the knees and a well-worn black tank top with a motorcycle on the front. A tattoo of what appeared to be a dolphin arched upon her upper arm. Both wrists were adorned with bangles and she had several rings on her fingers. Her general appearance screamed cheap, and easy and repulsive.

He eyed her cautiously before turning his attention to the child. He couldn't tell if it was a girl or a boy because of the cap of soft brown curls nearly covering its eyes and the bottle in its mouth, held in place by a chubby hand. The child's clothes did nothing to disclose gender, green overalls with dirty knees over a once-white tee shirt now stained with food.

"May I help you?" he asked, continuing to assess her.

The woman's eyes flew open wide. "Ian?" She bumped her hip to shift the child's weight, then took a step forward.

Recognition hit him full force like a steel trap around his heart. "It's been a long time, Colleen." Ian searched deep inside for some lurking tenderness toward his only sibling, but it eluded him. She was simply another problem to deal with before resuming his life.

Colleen's eyes filled and she took another step toward him. He held his breath. If she expected an embrace, it wasn't going to happen. He barely knew this girl before him. Correction, this woman.

"I take it, the child is yours," he said, pulling in his chin so that he looked down his nose at the two.

Twelve years younger than he was, Colleen appeared a misguided teenager with a baby to boot. A child raising a child, although she had to be past twenty by now. Any bond between them had dissolved years ago when Ian left vowing never to return. Yet, he had returned a few times, and the visits ended so dismally that he'd stopped all contact other than the calls he received from Gladdy when they were in some sort of trouble.

Colleen stopped just short of Ian, much to his relief. He didn't particularly care to be smeared with kid drool.

"Yeah, she's mine." Colleen bounced the child once and said, "This is Katie Rose." At the mention of her name, the little girl pulled the bottle from her mouth, held it toward Colleen, and smiled, showing tiny white teeth in the middle of rosy cheeks.

"A good Irish name, don't you think?" Colleen kissed the rounded cheek.

"Yes..." He wasn't quite sure what to say. It was a nice name, but a name wasn't going to carry her through life. A child needed a proper home with loving parents. He highly doubted the little girl had any of that. Of course, he hadn't had those advantages and he'd turned out all right. "How old is she?" He tried to hide the fact that Gladdy had failed to mention she had a grandchild, that he had a niece.

"She's a year and a half."

"Well, I suppose I should ask, how are you?" He was perfectly aware how cold he sounded, but dammit, every bit of contact with his family caused the same clenching of his stomach, the same steel wall around his heart. Colleen must have been fifteen the last time he saw her. She'd certainly grown up. Unfortunately, she appeared to be following in her parents' mold.

They stood in silence, neither knowing how to bridge the gap that had always separated them. A picture flashed before his eyes. It was a well-worn memory of his parents cooing and aahing over his little sister after they'd come home from the hospital, then leaving her in the care of her big brother while they went to celebrate down at Slickey's Bar. He'd been twelve years old, left with a newborn and he'd known it was just the beginning. When Colleen had turned six, Ian had had enough.

Katie cooed and sucked on her bottle again.

"Have you talked to the police?" Ian asked. "What exactly happened in this...this hole they called a home?"

Colleen bit her lower lip and nodded, tears forming again. "Yesterday morning, in the bedroom. The door's shut. You don't want to go down there." Tears spilled down her face and Katie's face clouded over at the sight of her mother crying. "He was in a coma by then and...she shot him and...then herself." Colleen wiped the tears from her face and smiled at her daughter. "Mr. Tesinski, next door, heard the shots and called the police. He said he wasn't surprised. Dad was so sick, he was dying, and Mom was devastated. She didn't know how she'd cope on her own. Aside from his Social Security checks, they didn't have any money."

"They could still afford beer and cigarettes, couldn't they?" He felt nothing but utter disdain for the people who had been his parents.

"That's mean, Ian. They had problems, but they weren't bad people."

"I guess we remember things differently. I remember being raised in a bar night after night and never having anything. What was different for you?" Suddenly his blood was boiling. Anger was seething through him so strongly that he could barely see straight.

Colleen set Katie on the filthy, worn carpet where she toddled over to the television and began twisting knobs. Colleen stood before him, hands on hips, her eyes matching the anger he was feeling.

"You know, Ian." She pointed a purple chipped nail at him. "Maybe if you'd have stuck around and tried to help them, things would have been different for all of us. Cripes, you're only two hours away, but it could have been on the other side of the damn world for how often you came around."

"Wanting parents who worked hard, paid their bills, and preferred evenings with family rather than barflies isn't so much to ask. By the way, how would you know what I wanted? We barely know each other."

"You think I didn't want those things? At least I was here to help while you were off making your millions." She practically spat the words at him. "That's all you care about anyway." She began nervously chewing a fingernail, her hand shaking as she did so.

"You don't know everything. I tried to get help for them. Years ago I tried to get them into treatment. I bailed them out of all their debts and begged them to get into AA. But you want to know what I got in return? Do you?" Colleen looked at him with big eyes as anger roiled in him with a force he could barely contain. "I was told to mind my own business and dear old Dad informed me that Mother screwed around on him so much in the beginning of their marriage that they weren't sure who my father was." He stepped toward her. "Don't you ever defend them to me. They are beyond my compassion."

He and Colleen stood for a long moment in reflection before the blast of the television cut through the stale air followed by Katie's howl. The child had inadvertently pushed the "power" button. Colleen raced over to switch it off and picked the little girl up to bounce on her hip. She kissed Katie's cheek as the child calmed and curled tiny fingers through the string of colored beards around Colleen's neck.

Ian studied them and suddenly a thought occurred to him. "You haven't been living here, have you?" The thought of Katie living in the same house where a murder/suicide took place bothered him more than he cared to admit.

Colleen kept her eyes on her daughter. "Katie and I live with my boyfriend, Woody, over on Avery. He fixes Harley's." If she thought that would impress him, she was mistaken.

Colleen came across the room toward him. "Here," Colleen thrust the child toward him. "Hold her. I need a cigarette."

"No..." Ian balked, but Colleen thrust the child into his arms. Katie sucked on her fist while looking at him with curious eyes. She'd be an adorable little girl, he had to admit, if someone cleaned her up.

He tried to push her back toward her mother. "No, I don't know much about babies, and I don't think this is a good idea."

Colleen turned her back to him and headed for the door. "She's not going to spit up on you and her diaper's clean." She stopped just short of the door and drew a pack of cigarettes from her jeans pocket. "What's the matter, don't you like her? How can you not like a baby?"

"It's not that."

"Well, she's not going to break. 'Sides, she needs to know her Uncle Ian." She stuck the cigarette between her lips and disappeared through the door.

Uncle Ian. That sounded nice. Reluctantly, Ian studied the child in his arms. Katie cooed and placed a chubby hand upon his face. At first he winced, not sure where the little tyke's hands had been. Within moments he warmed to her touch. She was lighter than he'd expected, soft, and wonderful smelling, despite outward appearances.

Katie slapped her hand upon his face once and then giggled. Ian noticed the tiny white teeth that shown with her smile. Her eyes were wide with innocence and sparkled as blue as an autumn sky. Her cheeks were rosy and fat.

He couldn't help but smile. Katie smiled back, and his heart seemed to expand until it ached.

****

There wasn't much of a funeral. A few friends from Slickey's Bar showed, but that was all. Mike and Gladys Flynn hadn't contributed much to the community, or what little family they had, and it was reflected. Colleen stood beside him at the gravesite, weeping openly and dressed more for a Goth reunion than a funeral. The gargantuan she referred to as Woody stood behind her, failing to hide his boredom with the whole affair. Ian felt it was his duty to comfort her, but he honestly didn't know how. She was his only sibling after all.

He studied the faces around the two coffins, searching for some indication that he'd somehow missed the kind of people his parents had been. Some small piece of kindness, decency, spirit of generosity. But there was none. Not one of Mike's former co-workers had come to offer condolences, none of the women of the neighborhood. Just a few of the regulars from the bar. It was sad that the sum of their lives came down to the few mourners who'd bother to come to stand at their gravesite. *Who would come to mine?*

The thought sent a shiver down his spine.

After the short graveside service, Ian drove Colleen and Katie back to the home they'd known as children. Woody had gone back to the shop and given them some time alone. Ian had paid a maid service to come in the day before and do what they could to clean the entire house. Especially the blood-spattered bedroom that he had completely gutted. The carpeting was replaced and the bedroom furniture hauled away. In silence, they inspected the house that, although smelled clean, still clung to a deathly presence.

Colleen was the first to speak. "Place looks nice. I suppose you'll be disappearing again." She had the saddest eyes he'd ever seen.

Ian raked a hand through his hair. It had been an exhausting couple of days. "I'm not far away. Here." He pulled out his wallet. "Here is my business card. I'll write my home address and cell number on the back." He took a pencil out of the drawer under the telephone and scribbled the information on the card.

Colleen took the card from him. "I hate to see you leave. I feel like I won't see you anymore. Katie won't know her only uncle."

The screen door banged and the stout form Ian recognized as the neighbor stood before them. The man hadn't attended the funeral.

In a nasally voice the man said, "I was hoping to catch you both today."

Ian extended a hand. "Hello, Mr. Tesinski." The neighbor reluctantly shook.

"I, ah...well, I'll just come out and say this." He shifted his generous body from one foot to the other. "I was hoping you'd sell me this property. It butts right up next to my garage, and I'd like to expand my yard. I've had my eye on this for quite some time and I even spoke to your father about it, but, well, we never got along and, he told me to shove my offer you know where." The man rolled his eyes in disgust. "Let's face it, it's an eyesore. Of course, you seemed to have cleaned it up quite nice. But your parents, they let the yard completely go to weeds and this house, for heaven's sake, it was a shack before you came along, no offense."

"None taken," Ian said.

"I thought I'd take it off your hands. It would be one less thing for you two young people to have to worry about." A bead of sweat trickled down the side of his chubby face, and he rubbed his hands together as though he were anxiously awaiting dinner.

Colleen spoke up. "It sounds like a good idea, don't

you think?" She looked to Ian.

Ian crossed his arms over his chest, scratched his chin thoughtfully. "Could your offer have anything to do with the highway improvements coming through this area?"

Mr. Tesinski had a surprised look on his face, although Ian suspected the man knew exactly what he was talking about. "I don't know..."

"Oh, come on, Mr. Tesinski, I'm a developer. I know that the state plans to revamp the highway through this area, and the city plans an industrial park and many other improvements along this stretch. All the land owners will be compensated quite well for their homes."

"That...that has nothing to do with my offer," the old man sputtered. "I know you two kids have your hands full right now. I'm just offering to help you out."

"You mean to help yourself out. No thanks. We'll hold onto it for now."

"I'm just trying to help out a neighbor and this is the thanks I get." His fat face was getting redder by the second.

"Goodbye, Mr. Tesinski." Ian ushered him to the door. The man continued to utter protests. The door banged behind him and Ian shut the inside door to drown him out.

"Way to go." Colleen grinned, and it struck him how pretty his sister was underneath all the embellishment.

Ian shook his head in disgust. "Old fart. His greed was coming through loud and clear. For once I agree with Mike, he can shove it."

Colleen checked on Katie, who was busy with the television buttons, then said, "So there's a development deal for this area? This is the first I've heard about it. Of course, I'm not much for reading the newspaper."

"Maybe you should and, yes, this property will be worth something to the state, should you decide to sell."

"Me? This belongs to both of us, doesn't it? Or does it have to go back to the bank?"

"No. The house is free and clear, has been for a while. I've had the house put in your name."

"My name?" Colleen was clearly confused. "Why?"

"I don't need it, and clearly, it would help you and

Katie. You can move in here if you care to. Otherwise, you can rent it out. It may take a while before the deal with the state is finalized, but my sources tell me it shouldn't be too much longer and you'll hear from them."

"Ian, I don't know what to say. Katie and I have nothing of our own." Her eyes teared. "This will help me out so much, I can't tell you. If it wasn't for living with Woody, I wouldn't be able to make it on my own."

"If you hold out, the state may make you a better offer than they would the others. That's providing a company interested in moving in doesn't make you an offer first."

"If Mom and Dad had held on, they'd have been so much better off, financially that is. Hmm, how sad." He noted the far-off look in her eyes.

Ian couldn't find any sympathy for them.

Colleen eyed him with a sideways glance. "You know, Ian, you're more of a softy than I'd have taken you for."

Ian gave her a blank look.

"Not used to charitable acts, are you?" She was making fun of him now, and he had to fight the urge to smile back at her. "Come on, Ian, lighten up." She elbowed him in the side.

He gave a nonchalant shrug. "I simply don't need it. That's all there is too it. Don't make it something it's not, Colleen." Her attempt at lightheartedness made him uncomfortable. "I probably should be going."

"First, you're going to lunch with your sister and your niece. My treat. I get a discount at the truck stop."

Ian didn't know how to respond. His first response was to beg off, but then he saw Katie Rose grinning as she came toddling toward him with an old vase Gladdy had always kept full of fake roses.

"Let me take you to a proper restaurant, my treat."

"What's wrong, the truck stop not good enough for a big shot like you?" She took a pack of cigarettes out of her tattered purse.

"Okay, the truck stop it is." His little sister wanted to spend time with him. For the first time in a very long time, he was experiencing a normal family activity, born out of an absurdly abnormal tragedy. He wished the bitterness he felt would go away, but it wasn't, and he suspected it never would.

Colleen set the cigarettes down, took the vase from Katie and brought the little girl up to her hip. Ian studied the two of them for a moment as Colleen bounced her daughter. For some reason he couldn't quite fathom, he thought of Lucy.

Chapter Eleven

So many emotions ran through Ian as he drove along Interstate 94 on his way back to Madison that night. He'd actually hated to leave Colleen and Katie that evening. He could have done without Woody, but Colleen seemed taken with him. He was nearly halfway to Madison when the cell phone vibrated in his pocket.

"Ian?" The connection seemed bad.

"Who is this?"

"It's Colleen. I'm sorry." The voice was slurred and tinged with tears.

"Colleen? Sorry? What's..."

"I...I need help, Ian. Oh, God, I'm sorry."

"Where are you?" He immediately pulled his car to the slow lane.

"At my apartment." In the back he could hear a man's voice. He couldn't make out what he was saying, and then the voice seemed nearer and sobs racked Colleen's voice.

It was Woody. He said, "Get off the damned phone before I strangle you with it, and shut that kid up." Katie's cries could be heard in the background.

"Colleen..." He was frantic. "I need an address."

She screamed the address through the phone before it went dead. And Ian's heart dropped.

As though a man possessed, Ian drove his car into the median and with a spray of gravel, entered the lane that would take him back to Milwaukee. The next fifty miles were a blur of headlights and road signs. He exited into the unsavory neighborhood his sister called home and screeched to a halt in front of her apartment building.

Fueled by fear and rage, he bolted up the dilapidated stairs to the apartment Colleen and Katie shared with Woody. Without bothering to see if the door was locked or not, he raised a foot and sent the door flying back with a jolt. Katie was in her playpen, screaming, with tears running down her cheeks. Woody came barreling down the hall toward him in a black T-shirt, his long hair flying behind him, his tattooed arms clenched, ready for a fight.

"Who the hell do you think you are?"

"Your worst nightmare."

Woody came at him, fists ready, eyes blurred by drugs or alcohol. Ian didn't know which, didn't care. As he swung on Ian, he tripped on one of Katie's stuffed animals. Before he could right himself, Ian connected a fist to his jaw and sent him flying backward into the kitchen table. Dishes, toys, and dirty laundry went flying everywhere. Colleen came running down the hall, her face bruised, clothes torn.

Ian grabbed her by the wrist just as the man pulled himself up from the heap and came at them both.

"Woody, no," Colleen yelled as he swung an arm in her direction, tearing her from Ian's grasp and throwing her against the wall. A framed picture crashed to the floor as Colleen sunk down beside it.

Woody swung and connected with the right side of Ian's head. It felt like his head exploded and the force sent him hurling into the wall with his right shoulder. As he struggled to pull himself up, Woody advanced on him. As he braced himself for the onslaught, the goon was stopped by a frying pan to the face. Woody went down hard, blood spurting from his nose. Colleen stood over him, the pan dropped to the floor. She extended a hand to her brother.

"You okay?" Colleen asked as she went to pick up a screaming Katie.

Ian rubbed the side of his head. "I'm fine. What did he do to you?" A bluish smudge was apparent on the side of her face.

Makeup smeared her face as tears ran. "I've seen him mad before, but this was different. I don't know what he was on, but it scared me so bad. I thought he was going to kill me." Katie screamed once again, gasping for air between sobs. "I told him we were leaving to live at Mom and Dad's house, and he went berserk. I just want a normal life for my little girl, Ian. Is that so much to ask?"

Ian crossed the room and patted Katie's back to help calm her. "There, there." A new thought occurred to him.

"Did he harm Katie?"

"Oh, no, she was asleep until all hell broke loose." Colleen kissed her daughter's cheek. "Oh, my little baby, I'm sorry you're stuck with a momma like me."

Woody groaned from the floor and brought a hand up to his face.

"There's no time to feel sorry for yourself, Colleen. It's time to get yourself together and get out of here." Colleen handed him the baby.

"She needs her blanket and I have a few more things to grab." Colleen pulled a dirty, tattered yellow blanket from the playpen, handed it to Katie, and ran to the bedroom. With his free hand Ian squatted to pick up the frying pan and stood over Woody, bouncing Katie on his hip.

Katie hugged the blanket to her with all her might as her sobs subsided. It wasn't long before her little body was still and slack in his arms in slumber. Her peaceful face betrayed the life he was certain lay ahead if he failed to intervene in their lives.

Things had to change. The baby in his arms would not meet the same broken childhood he'd known, not if he could help it. It was time to pull what was left of his family together.

****

The Barlow home loomed before Lucy, its once-inviting face now a sad box that housed an unhappy family, or part of one. It had been nearly two weeks since Ellie's marriage had fallen apart. Still, a cloak of uneasiness clung to the otherwise well-manicured exterior of the home. It was Ellie's foreboding phone call that had summoned Lucy here this cool summer's evening.

"Can you come? I need you," Ellie had said, a mixture of desperation and depression that caused Lucy to abandon the jog she was about to take.

Now she stood on the curb trying to gauge what she would find on the other side of the paneled oak door.

Lucy's first timid knock was unanswered. The raw edge of panic ripped through her fueled by the haunting emotion of Ellie's voice. She knocked again, more loudly this time.

Still no answer. She rose on tiptoes and peered

through the row of small windows along the top of the door. A narrow slash of light zigzagged across the stairs in the foyer.

Nervously she tried the door, found it open, and stuck her head inside.

"El, you here?" The lilting voice of Martina McBride flowed from the bedroom at the top of the stairs. Otherwise, the house was dark, eerily so.

A shuffling noise from upstairs, then, "I'm up here. Come on up."

Lucy followed Ellie's voice into the master bedroom, fully expecting to find her sister in a deserved pool of pity the size of Lake Superior. Instead Ellie was standing in front of a full-length mirror fluffing her blond hair and looking like a million bucks.

"Are you okay?"

Ellie ran her hands across her blue jean-clad tummy and admired herself in the full-length mirror as Lucy entered the room.

"Better than ever."

Lucy knew better, but her instincts told her to tread carefully, especially once she surveyed the condition of the bedroom. The normally tastefully chic bedroom decorated in hues of sage green looked like a clothing bomb had gone off.

"Wow, look at you. What's going on? You scared the shit out of me with that phone call."

"I know. I apologize for that, but you know, Martina started singing about 'Independence Day' and 'Angel's Wings' and I guess it was catching." Ellie slipped a silver watch over her left hand. The right was adorned with a collection of bangles. A wide pewter buckle held the black belt in her jeans. She wore a white shirt and purple velour suit jacket. Silver earrings dangled from her ear lobes, and Lucy noticed a bit more makeup on her face than usual. Her blond hair was arranged in a sleek style around her face leading to graceful wisps at her shoulders. Her sister was a knockout.

"You said you needed me. Has Randy done something?" As though he hadn't done enough already.

Ellie shrugged. "A momentary bit of self-pity got the best of me. Don't worry, I'm fine."

"The room looks like a cyclone blew through. And you are stunning. Care to share?" Lucy took a step toward her ready to lend a comforting embrace.

Ellie turned to face her. "Nothing's going on except that my husband just left me for someone else, and I've decided it's time for 'out with the old, in with the new.'" Lucy didn't miss the stance of strength and defiance Ellie was trying desperately to convey before she turned back to the mirror. "You know, I haven't fit into these jeans in over a year. A "Marriage-on-the-Rocks" diet isn't one I'd recommend. But hell, it works."

"Oh, Ellie..." Lucy felt tears well as she went forward, arms open wide. "I'm so sorry. I don't know what to say." Ellie gave her a quick squeeze, then stepped back and quickly turned her attention once again to the mirror.

"I'm not wallowing in this. I refuse." Ellie pushed back tears with freshly painted fingernails while Lucy wiped her own tears with the palms of her hands. "Darn, now I have to redo my makeup." Lucy watched as she disappeared into the bathroom.

Suddenly the stillness of the house alarmed her. "Where's Abby?"

"She's spending the night with her daddy at an inn over in Woodruff. He took tomorrow off to take her to the water park. Not wasting any time buying his daughter's loyalty and affection, is he? Yep, Randy was never one to waste time. Why, this afternoon as I was leaving the shop I saw his vehicle at the Bluebird and his girlfriend leaving his room."

"No." Now she understood the change in Ellie.

"Yes." She bit her lip, then continued, "When he called to ask to take Abby I confronted him with it, and he said he'd called her there to break it off with her once and for all. I've heard that before. I don't know that I can believe him or not, but it doesn't really matter. I refuse to be treated this way. He's scum and I don't need him."

"You certainly don't, El." Lucy studied the picture of strength before her in the bathroom mirror powdering her face. She moved so that her face was next to her sister's in the mirror. As different as they were on the outside, inside they were one, carrying with them the same trove of memories and experiences that childhood had offered them. The mirror provided a portrait of two bodies, truly one heart.

"I'm doing my best not to let him see me crumble." Ellie's voice couldn't hide the bitterness. "I'm not, you know, going to crumble. I'll show him." Her hand bumped a decorative rose-hued jar and sent it tumbling into the sink. "Shoot."

"What are you planning?" She placed a well-meaning hand on Ellie's shoulder to be sure she had her sister's complete attention. Ellie's eyes joined with hers in the mirror. "You need to go slow here. This has been a major shock for you, and you cannot go off and do something foolish just to get back at him. Take the time to work through your feelings before you take action."

"Oh, don't look so scared. It's not like I plan to lynch him by the 'you-know-whats' or anything. And I don't have time to seek out the piece of trash he's been sleeping with to exact my revenge. I don't believe him for one minute. No, I'm going to have some fun, for once."

"You are?" Lucy was not only confused, she was a bit frightened by the steely performance.

"Yes, I am. Two can play this game. I'm going out on the town and heaven help the men that get in my way."

"Careful, you don't need any more trouble than you've got at the moment. Abby needs at least one sane parent."

"You don't have to tell me that. I just want some fun. I need a distraction. I refuse to allow him the satisfaction of my dissolving into a heap because he left me." Ellen turned toward her sister. "You need to come with me. You could use a good time as well. Let's burn up the town."

"Me?" Sisterly loyalty could be so scary at times.

"Yes, *you*." Ellie turned back to the mirror and began to freshen her lipstick.

"I don't think I'm really up to it." Of course, she wasn't going to let her sister enter the uncharted waters of separation all alone, much less the bar scene, during peak tourist season. "Maybe a movie would be good."

"Movie? No, I want diversion, distraction, whatever. I'm getting out of this house, and I want music and people and fun."

Her sister was primping with a vengeance. "Take it

easy on that stuff," Lucy said after the third trip the lipstick made over her lips. "You don't want to look like Big-Hair Belinda down at the Hairhouse."

The look Ellie leveled on her from the mirror was near to deadly. "You're comparing me to Belinda Ratzenberg?"

Back paddle, Lucy. "No, no, you're beautiful, but..." She waved a palm at Ellie and all the clothes strewn about the room. "This...isn't you." To her relief, Ellie didn't throttle her.

Ellie's eyes were so intent upon Lucy that she dropped her lipstick onto the bathroom floor. "Damn." She picked it up and dabbed at the slash of frosty pink on the white floor with a Kleenex. She stood and viewed the smooshed top of the tube. "This was my favorite one." Frustration blushed in her throat as she sent the tube flying into the corner wastebasket.

Ellie blew out a puff of air before her expression softened. "Time to live a little. Indulge me, okay? I need to act out a little or I'll go crazy here by myself, and we could both use a good men-cleansing."

"Okay, I'm game, but where will we go? I haven't been out in ages."

"Now that surprises me, you being single and all. I'll admit I thought I was going to see a whole new Lucy emerge after you bedded Mr. Flynn. You still seeing him?" She spritzed perfume into her cleavage. The flowery scent wafted about the room.

Lucy groaned. The last thing she cared to discuss right now was Ian Flynn. That train wreck was better left in a dying heap by the side of the track.

Ellen's shoulders slumped as the defiance she'd been sporting waned and was replaced by concern. "What's happened with him? Have you seen him since that night you, well, you shagged him?" She moved past Lucy and into the bedroom.

"Don't go there, trust me." Lucy followed her out of the bathroom.

"Okay, now you have to tell me." Ellie searched for something in her jewelry box.

A weary sigh slipped from Lucy. How could she put into words the turmoil churning within her? She and Ian had shared amazing sex together, twice, but that was all. Oh, yes, they did save the life of one little boy. They'd comforted each other, savored each other, shared bits and pieces of their lives, but that was all. And now he was gone.

"There's nothing to tell, nothing at all. He's gone, went to Madison for the rest of the summer." Silently she prayed Ellie would leave well enough alone. "I haven't seen him since, don't plan to, ever."

Ellie's eyes narrowed as though she were targeting Lucy, then widened.

"Oh my God, you're in love with him, aren't you?"

"What, where do you get that?" Lucy put on her best "I'm stunned" expression, not feeling quite convincing enough. Older sisters could be such know-it-alls sometimes.

Ellie pointed toward the mirror. "Look at your face, Lucy. You never could keep your feelings to yourself. Go ahead, look. It's written all over your face."

Lucy turned, but failed to see anything out of the ordinary, other than the fact that she could use a little more sleep. She held her palms up and shrugged her shoulders. "You're seeing things. Besides, how could I fall in love with someone I barely know?"

"Happens all the time. Attraction is a strange creature."

"Anyway, he's gone, left just like that." She snapped her fingers for effect. "He obviously wasn't so taken with me. I guess a redneck from the sticks doesn't hold the same appeal as the slick women he meets in the city."

The smile slid from Ellie's face and a far-off stare clouded her eyes. "Happens all the time. Look at Randy and me."

Lucy turned to face her. "You don't think he's in love with this...with her?"

"He promised me it's over, that it was a mistake, and he's very sorry. Big deal. I don't want to hear it." Ellie became agitated, and Lucy was sorry she'd asked. "Come on, let's rip up this town a little and forget about these losers we've attached ourselves too. Men. Who needs them?" As Ellie headed for the bedroom door, she picked up a tapestry pillow lying on the floor and hurled it across the room.

Lucy instinctively ducked as it whooshed past her head. "Hey." The pillow struck a watercolor print of a field of red poppies and turned it crooked.

Ellie glanced back over her shoulder. "Sorry, Luce."

"I've never seen you like this. You've always been so calm."

She shrugged one shoulder and said, "Look where calm has gotten me. Enough is enough. We're going out on the town. Let's go."

****

Stud and Sylvie's Par-A-Dice sat just outside the city limits along a rolling stretch of Biermann Road. The parking lot that surrounded the worn, white facade was nearly full. Multi-colored lights dangled from the edge of the porch that seemed to barely hang onto the main structure. The thump of the jukebox greeted them as they climbed the steps.

The door opened, filling the night air with raucous rock and roll, cigarette smoke, laughter and Tim Custer spilled out of the bar. A burly biker dude, he was dressed in leather and a ripped T-shirt with the imprint of Black Sabbath splashed across his chest. Long, straggly hair hung onto his shoulders from his balding head where it blended with the beard covering his neck. He'd been a classmate and most definitely did not match the scrawny boy Lucy remembered.

"Woo hoo." Tim ogled them, raising his tattooed arms and swinging his hips. "Laaaadies, let's boogie."

"Not on your life, Timmy." Lucy said as she tightened her grip on Ellie, who immediately shrugged her off and sidled up to this gargantuan.

"Come back in three drinks and we'll see," Ellie drawled as she squeezed past him into the smoke-filled interior. *What had happened to the sister I knew and loved?* The biker came through the door toward Lucy, a front tooth missing from the dopey smile he sent her way, his leather vest much too small to cover the T-shirt stretched across a generous beer-gut.

In a gruff baritone he said, "You could take a lesson from her. Loosen up, honey."

Lucy raised her eyes to his level. "Screw you." She

left him standing alone on the porch.

As she entered the tavern, he called behind her, "I'm ready when you are." *Poor choice of words, Luce.*

The place was definitely hopping tonight, not that Lucy frequented the establishment all that often. Through the haze of cigarette smoke and the aura of neon, she scanned the throng for her sister. Ellie had already found her way to the bar and was attempting to gain Sylvia's attention. Lucy pushed her way toward the bar.

"Hiya, Lucy." Deb, a teller from her bank, came toward her. This was not good. If she held any hope for catching up with Ellie, ditching Deb was a must. The woman simply didn't know how to say hello and leave it at that.

"Yeah, hi, Deb." Lucy continued to push on, but Deb stopped her with a hand on her arm.

"Hey, how've you been? I heard about you and Shooter." Lucy doubted the woman was concerned. She was simply looking for water-cooler gossip for Monday morning.

"I'm great." With an eye to the bar, she saw that Ellie had yet to get the bartender's attention.

"I heard he dumped you for someone else. That's too bad." The woman's need for salacious gossip was apparent all over her face.

"You know what? The last thing I want to talk about is men. I have to find Ellie." Lucy simply walked away.

As she joined Ellie at the bar, a sleazy looking drunk known as Romey swung his drink in their direction and nearly spun himself from his barstool.

"Well, looky here," he slurred, batted heavy eyelids, and forked a cigarette with two dirty fingers. "We got us some lookers. You ladies need a seat? I got one here." He patted the leather-padded stool next to him.

"No thanks." Lucy smiled at the old man.

He leaned toward them, holding the hand with the cigarette by his mouth as though he were going to share a deeply guarded secret with them. "The beer is piss-warm here tonight. I gotta go home now." He gulped the last of his beer and swung from his perch. "The little lady is waitin' for me." He smoothed his shirt with unsteady hands.

"Romey, you're not driving, are you? Because if you are, I'll give you a ride," Lucy whispered so as not to embarrass him.

"Nope, Sylvie called the taxi ta come ta git me." The short stick of a man balanced precariously on his booted feet. "Learned my lesson with that, still haven't got my license back."

"That's a good thing." The two women stepped back to allow him wide berth to take his leave.

Squinting as though he couldn't see through the fog of drunkenness, he brought his face closer to Lucy's and she tucked her chin in to avoid his beer breath. "Wish I could stay and wine and dine you two fine ladies, buts I gotsta go." He crinkled up the right side of his face as he worked up a wink. "Bysie, bye." And with that, he swaggered off into the crowd.

The two assumed places at the bar and Ellie said, "If that's what I've got to look forward to, celibacy looks pretty good."

"You're too young and you look too good to talk like that." Lucy gained Stud's attention and ordered a Miller. Ellie, to her surprise, ordered a tequila sunrise.

"Tequila. El, you better watch it. Tequila hangovers will kill you."

She was eyeing her drink like a kid with Kool-Aid. "I haven't had one of these since before I married Creepface." She took a sip. "Hells bells, that's good." And proceeded to down the drink before Lucy finished half of hers and promptly ordered another.

What have I gotten myself into?

Some of the bar patrons began dancing in the middle of the room to "Mony, Mony." Two men approached dressed in baseball jerseys, more than likely from the softball tournament held that afternoon at the city field. Lucy spied them out of the corner of her eye. They were good-looking with a demeanor that screamed "jock."

"Oh no." Intuition told her what was coming. Her instinct to flee was kicking in big-time.

The taller of the two, his eyes squarely upon Ellie, asked with a slur to his voice, "How 'bouts a dance?" He looked nice and he also looked to be well on his way to inebriated.

Lucy was quick to answer him. "Oh, I don't think..."
"I'd love to."
"Ellie...what happened to declaring war on men?"

Ellie never looked back. Before Lucy could utter more of a protest, her sister was shimmying shamelessly in the middle of the dance floor with the jock. A tap on her shoulder sent a sick feeling through her. Turning, she mustered a weak smile for Jock Number Two.

"How about it? Want to kick up your heels?" His brown eyes seemed warm, his smile sincere and the dimple in his chin undeniably attractive.

What the hell. If you can beat 'em, dance. Besides, she'd be able to keep a closer eye on the whirling dervish out there that had, at one time, resembled her sister.

"Sure." He gave her a start by grabbing her hand and leading her to the dance floor. Lucy had to admit it felt good to be out and far too long since she'd had fun. She hadn't danced in what seemed like forever, although it was tough to keep her attention on the beat and an eye on her sister at the same time. To his credit, Jock Number Two could actually move.

He had a nice little swing to his hips, and when he leaned in nearer, his smile threatened to break the concentration it was taking to dance and watch her sister. Ellie's partner was thoroughly enjoying her exuberant gyrations.

The song ended and the calming strum of a guitar filled the bar as a slower tune began.

"Thanks." Lucy flashed him a smile and began to back away, her attention briefly turned toward her sister. "Ellie?"

Lucy watched, feeling her jaw slacken in surprise as Ellie embraced Jock Number One, and they began to sway to the music. A large hand took one of hers. Lucy snapped her mouth shut and turned her attention to her partner.

"Up for another one?" His thumb was doing circles on the top of her hand.

"I...I suppose." *Damn that Ellie. I hope she knows what she's doing.* She loosely placed her arms over his broad shoulders and purposely kept her head from resting upon any part of him. He brushed his chin against her hair and she felt herself bristle.

He placed his mouth against her ear and whispered. "Loosen up a little, enjoy." Hadn't she heard that already once tonight? She suddenly had a picture of her dressed as a mousy librarian lost in a sea of hedonism. It was ridiculous, she knew. She certainly wasn't against having a good time. She'd had many a good time in this very bar. Maybe she was being a bit too responsible, but someone had to be.

As the song ended, Ellie announced she needed another drink and pushed her way back to the bar.

Ellie gained Stud's attention, and the balding, rotund man made his way to the bar, wiping as he came.

"Another sunrise for me and a beer for Lucy."

"No thanks, I'll have a Pepsi."

"Soda? Oh, come on." Ellie looked absolutely crestfallen, in a drunken sort of way.

"Pepsi. One of us has to drive."

"I'd be more than happy to give you ladies a ride," Jock Number One piped up.

"No thanks, I have to get up early anyway," she said to a sorry set of blurry eyes.

"Ohhh, Lucy, you're susha party-pooper." Ellie promptly slammed her third drink. "I haven't had this mush fun in, oh, who knows." She waved a dismissive hand.

"Someone has to keep a clear head." Leaning nearer to Ellie, she whispered, "You're getting too drunk, Ellie. You're not used to this."

"Well, time to build my tol...toler...whatever." With that, she punched a fist into the smoky air and let forth with, "Woo-hoo. I love this music." She began swaying from side to side and patting the bar with her hands in time to the beat.

Lucy glanced at her watch. *Crap, only eleven thirty and the band played until one.*

Jock Number One sidled up alongside Ellie's swaying form and whispered something in her ear. The two of them giggled and danced their way back to the throng on the dance floor.

Lucy watched them go with a withered feeling. This was going to be a long night. Turning toward the bar, Jock Number Two was looking directly at her with eyes she couldn't quite read.

He leaned a brawny arm upon the bar and seemed to be studying her. "You know..." He came nearer. "I don't even know your name." His voice was deep, steady.

"It's Lucy, Lucy Mitchell." She'd been so fixed upon her sister that she hadn't paid much attention to this man she'd been dancing with. He was a good head taller than she, although she was seated on a barstool. Sandy hair fell across his forehead and curled at the back of his neck. His jersey stretched quite nicely across broad shoulders. There was an air of confidence about him that was admittedly sexy.

"Dan Webster." He put a hand in her direction, his lips curving on one side revealing a dimple in his cheek.

Cautiously, she took his hand. She hadn't noticed him drinking as much as his partner, and he was obviously not as drunk as the two on the dance floor.

Dan cocked his head in the direction of the dancers. "I hope Troy behaves himself. He's quite the ladies man."

"And you're not?" The words were out before she could stop them.

He seemed a bit taken aback at first, then amused. "I'm too choosey."

Smooth, real smooth, this one. Lucy nodded, amused. "Me too."

A wide smile spread across Dan's face. "There you have it, something in common."

Lucy felt her guard drop. She liked this jock named Dan, at the moment anyway, and felt the glow of a smile.

"What's the story with your sister?" He waved his drink in Ellie's direction.

"How did you know she's my sister?"

"Same nose," he said matter-of-factly. "Woman scorned?"

Was this guy psychic? "What makes you think that?"

He pushed a shoulder up in a shrug. "She's trying too hard to have a good time."

Lucy turned to see her sister and Troy shimmying shamelessly. "She's got some issues at the moment."

"She seems nice, so does her sister." He had the nicest eyes.

This Dan seemed nice as well, but there was

something missing. She couldn't quite put her finger on it.

"How did you fare in the tournament today?"

Dan chuckled. "Changing the subject on me, are you? Since you asked, we won."

"Congratulations. I take you're not from around here." She glanced Ellie's way.

"Our team's from Plover, down by Stevens Point. We heard about the tournament and, well, thought it was a good opportunity to get out of town."

And likely party without wives finding out. Lucy silently chided herself for her cynical frame of mind. Still, her gaze surreptitiously slipped to check for a wedding ring. No ring.

Dan startled her by taking her hand in his. "Come on, let's dance." He led Lucy to the dance floor.

It felt good to dance with Dan. He carried himself well. The last number was a slow one, and he ran his hands up and down her back. Lucy found herself pulling him closer, close enough that she could feel he was definitely interested in more than dancing.

Being in the arms of a charming, handsome man such as Dan, who was clearly attracted to her, would normally have been a thrill. Not tonight. She'd been dumped by two men in the span of, well, too recently, and Dan simply couldn't fill the void within her heart.

The two returned to the bar to discover that Ellie and Troy were nowhere in sight.

"Where do you suppose Troy and Ellie have gone?" Lucy tried not to panic. Ellie was a grown woman after all.

"Who knows? They're probably out doing what we should be doing right now." He pushed himself back between her legs as she sat on a barstool. He leaned toward her with his lips. She leaned away from him and pushed him from between her legs.

"You aren't one of those prissy chicks are you?" He squeezed her thigh. The bubble that had carried Dan this far burst in an explosion of reality.

"You mean, do I put out?"

He seemed genuinely surprised by her question. "Kind of direct, aren't you?" Then he smiled and traced a finger along her jaw.

"I hate people that beat around the bush, don't you?" She purposely tried to sound seductive. "And I don't like strings. There'd be no strings attached to you would there? I mean I wouldn't want your wife to find out and spoil things."

"What my wife doesn't know doesn't hurt her."

Lucy promptly poured her Pepsi down the front of his pants.

"Son-of-a..." Dan jumped back and threw his hands in the air, nearly loosing his glass of beer in the process. "What the hell was that?"

"Oops, I'm sorry." She clucked a few times and shook her head. "I hope your wife can get that out. Looks nasty."

Dan glared at her, slammed his beer down on the bar, and took off for the bathroom. Stud caught Lucy's eye and winked.

Lucy watched Dan go and made her escape as soon as the door labeled 'Bucks' closed behind him. She had to find Ellie before she did something she'd regret.

The parking lot was loaded with vehicles, but only a few people. Lucy's eyes scanned the entire lot, with no sign of Ellie or Troy.

"Ellie," she yelled. No response, except the stares of various small groups huddled by the cars. She called again. This time she heard, "Over here."

"Where are you?" The parking lot was nearly full.

"Here." A hand rose out of the window of a car parked toward the back of the lot.

Lucy followed the hand and found her sister in the passenger seat of a red TransAm, tears streaming down her face, and Troy's large body slumped over her.

"Ellie?"

"Luce, you have to help me." A sob escaped Ellie. "I think he passed out. Either that or he's dead, I can't tell which. He kissed me and then just slumped over on top of me." She pushed at the generous girth on top of her.

Lucy opened the car door and checked Troy's pulse.

"He's still alive. He's passed out is all."

"I've been trying to get him off me, but I can't. He's a big guy. I didn't know what I was going to do."

"Open the door." Lucy attempted to slide in next to her with no luck. She pushed and pulled at him while tears ran down Ellie's cheeks. "Good grief, he didn't look this big in the bar." She anchored her hands under his armpits and pulled. "This is no good, El. I'm going to pull up on him. Try to slide out from under." Across Ellie, Lucy put her hands under Troy's shoulders and pushed up.

"Wait, my purse is caught." Ellie gave a yank and the purse appeared. "Okay, now push."

It was just enough that Ellie could wedge her body from under him. The two women poured from the car and sat on the gravel, their backs against the door of the car.

"If this is the kind of thing a single girl has to put up with to date, I don't want any part of it." Ellie's chin quivered and more tears flowed as she dug a tissue out of her purse.

"It's not that bad. Look at me, free as a bird and lovin' every minute of it. Every once in a while you run into a good one and then you wonder what's wrong with him that he's not taken." Lucy shrugged her shoulders and thought of Ian. Ellie wiped the tears from under her eyes and blew into the tissue.

"I...I don't know how you stand it. I didn't see one good specimen in the bunch, except Dan. He seemed nice."

"Yeah, nice."

"Okay, what?" Ellie pushed the hair back from her face.

"Well, he...oh...he was a tad too horny for a married guy." Might as well come clean. "And he wasn't Ian." It was a bittersweet confession. She'd lost her heart to a man that threw her aside as easily as an uneaten sandwich.

Ellie's mouth formed a perfect *O* before she broke into a grin. "I knew it. I knew you really liked him." She sniffled, Lucy winced. "We're a pair, you and I. Randy's probably so happy to be rid of me."

Tears began again, and this time Lucy joined her.

Lucy slid an arm around her shoulders. "Come on now. This is the alcohol talking." Ellie continued to cry. "El, this is his failing, not yours."

"It takes two. Don't you watch Oprah?"

"No. Give me that tissue." Ellie waved the damp tissue at Lucy. "On second thought, don't."

"Sorry, it's the only one I've got." Ellie dabbed at the

last of her tears.

"Look at it this way. Your first date, and you left the guy unconscious." She gave her sister the thumbs-up. "Way to go, sis."

Ellie gave Lucy a sideways glance, swiped at her nose one last time, and began to giggle. Lucy joined her and the two sat against the car, gravel under their butts, with peals of laughter filling the night air, that is, until a shadow slanted over them.

Looking up, shielding her eyes against the glare of the lights dotting the parking lot, Lucy saw the silhouette of Shooter Lushinski

He stood over them, hands stretched out to each. "Ladies, I'm hauling your sorry butts home."

Chapter Twelve

Shooter angled his Chevy 4x4 in the driveway, and Ellie slid from the passenger seat. "Well, Shooter, it's been interesting."

Shooter wrapped an arm around Lucy before she could slide over, a mischievous smile upon his face. "Always is, El, always is." Lucy jerked her shoulder, but Shooter simply tightened his grip. She tried to communicate a "don't leave me" to her sister, who simply gave her an uneven smile and attempted a wink.

She decided on the direct approach. "Ellie, you're not leaving me with him, are you?" It was actually more of a joke than anything. That would be the day she'd be afraid of being left with Shooter.

When he put his mouth next to her ear, she felt the warmth of his breath on her neck, and increased the pressure of his arm more tightly around her shoulders. "Honey, I'm not into threesomes, even though Ellie's looking rather hot tonight. But I suppose I could be convinced if you ladies just gotta have me. Far be it from me to disappoint two such luscious babes."

Lucy hung her head and laughed. Some things never change.

Ellie steadied herself on the truck door. "Shooter, I just left a guy unconscious, you better run while you can." She giggled, hiccupped, and giggled again. "Oh God, I'm going to be sick tomorrow. Lucy, you better check on me in the morning. Heck, I think I'm going to be sick right now. I'm a little rusty at this stuff." She burped once and clutched her stomach.

"I'll see you in. Better yet, I'll stay over and take Abby's room." She began to scoot across the seat, extracting her shoulder from Shooter.

"Wait, hey, can I come?"

Lucy swung her head in his direction, her body perched on the edge of the seat, and her heart skipped just a tad. He was still the handsome boy she fell in love with in high school. His oval face still held the same dimpled smile, his eyes the same glint of naughtiness, all framed by a mass of sandy curls. A memory of the two of them in his pickup, he dropping her off after a party at the gravel pit at Betsey Creek, the truck reeking of beer and hormones on overload. She needed to get out now.

"No." And out she jumped.

"Lucy, I really don't think I need a babysitter." Ellie looked a bit green as she swayed to and fro in the light of the streetlamp.

"Yes, you do, and no," she turned to Shooter, "you cannot stay."

Shooter grinned a crooked smile and followed her across the seat and out the door. "Aw, come on, Luce. Here I rescue you two lovely broads and this is the thanks I get?"

"Thank you, now good night." Lucy turned from him as Ellie promptly puked into the spirea bush along the walk. "Oh, crap, Ellie I'll be right there." Lucy crossed the driveway with Shooter close behind.

Ellie ripped off a hosta leaf and wiped her mouth. "The neighbors are going to love this one. You know witchy, old Jean across the street has her telescope on me. I'd lay money on it." She spit into the spirea.

Shooter chimed in with, "Want me to moon her?"

"Oh, that's all I need." Ellie tucked the leaf under the plant and nearly toppled over in the process. "Oops."

"Shut up, Shooter. Come on, El, let's get you inside." Lucy steadied her sister as she righted herself and started for the door.

Shooter grabbed Lucy by the arm. "Are you sure I shouldn't stay? She looks awful. I'd feel real bad if she took a turn for the worse." Shooter gave her his best "yes, I am really, really sincere" look.

"Cut the crap, Shooter. You couldn't get within two feet of puke and you know it. Thanks for the ride, although I didn't think it was necessary. Now, go. I can handle this." Ellie was already in the house.

"Wait, Lucy, I..." He shoved his hands in the pockets of his jeans and seemed to be searching for the right words. "Well, I..."

"What? I have to get in there before she spews all over the place." In other circumstances she'd gladly spend time catching up with him, but this was not the time, nor the place. "Why don't you call me sometime? I'd love to hear all about your new love, but I can't right now."

"That's just it, it didn't work and I, well I purposely went to Stud and Sylvie's to find you tonight. I..." He toed the pavement as though he were nervous, which for Shooter was next to never.

She didn't have time for this. "You...what?" She spread her hands out before her. She wasn't sure if she was anxious or simply frustrated with him.

"I really needed to see you tonight."

This was a no-brainer. "No. Been there, done that. Shooter, you can't give me what I need." The tables had turned. Lucy hadn't been sure when it happened, but it had. She needed more. She could no more go back to the casual couple they'd been than she could deny her love for her sister. A sister who needed her at the moment.

"What do you want?" His face was suddenly serious.

She couldn't readily voice an answer to his question, but her heart knew the answer.

"Luuuuccccyyyy," Ellie wailed.

"Thanks for the ride." She kissed his cheek. "See ya."

****

Ian felt his chest constrict as he stood in the doorway of his guest bedroom watching the tiny form of his niece asleep on the bed of blankets on the carpeted floor. He'd never been so close to a little person before, and he found her fascinating. How could a human being be as innocent as this little one? What circumstances in her life would destroy that innocence? He knew all too well the road her life could follow if someone didn't take a stand.

She had one pudgy hand in a fist by her open mouth, the other wound into the folds of her blanket. Ian quietly took a step forward. Her feet were so tiny, her toes even tinier. Curls crowned her head and her chest rose ever so slightly with each breath.

Ian angled his head to one side and bent slightly to get a better view of her face. Eyelashes brushed rosy cheeks. Katie stirred slightly, pursing her lips like an old woman, and then relaxing again in sweet slumber. Ian wondered what she must be dreaming.

The spill of light from the door behind him grew as Colleen pushed it open and crept in.

Ian turned to see a smirk on her face.

"Katie-watching, are you? It's one of my favorite things to do," she whispered.

Ian had to smile at that and knew the constriction in his chest wasn't anxiety over having his sister and her baby invade his home, it was love, pure and simple. So simple and so pure, in fact, he was forced to swallow the lump that had formed in his throat before he could answer her.

"Yes, she's quite something."

"That she is." He watched as Colleen's eyes swept lovingly over her child. "I hope you're hungry."

"Hungry? Why, yes, I am."

A bright grin lit her features. "Good. Follow me."

Ian followed his sister to the stark, stainless steel kitchen in his high-rise apartment overlooking the capitol building. Colleen had prepared what appeared to be a sumptuous late-night breakfast for them both.

"Where did you learn to cook like this?" he asked as he reveled in the ham, mushroom, onion, green pepper and egg concoction smothered in a white sauce. "This is fabulous, Colleen."

"Chuck, the cook at the truck stop, is real talented. He was a chef at one of those fancy Italian places downtown, but then his drinking got the best of him and he lost his job. Their loss, our gain. He still struggles with the bottle now and then, but he's a hell of a cook. I'd stick around sometimes and he'd teach me some of his tricks."

They made small talk while finishing the meal. When they were done, Ian helped her clean up. Afterward, they took a cup of coffee and sat out on his balcony.

"How'd you afford a place like this anyway? You know, it's nice and all, but..." She made a face, squiggling up her nose.

"But what?" Even her coffee was wonderful.

"Well, it's so cold. Needs a woman's touch something fierce." Colleen kicked back in her chair and braced a foot on the rail of the balcony.

"You think so?" It amused him to receive advice from

his little sister.

"I know so." She took a sip of her coffee. "The view kicks butt, I'll give you that. Damn, I forgot my cigarettes. You got any?"

"No. That's something you need to stop right now. It's a nasty habit and too expensive for someone in your shoes."

"Yeah, I've been meaning to quit."

"No time like the present."

"Okay, okay. I'm done. Are you happy?" She sipped, he grinned. "If I go schizo on you in the middle of the night you know why."

Ian laughed. "I'll take my chances."

They spent a quiet moment sipping coffee and taking in the view of the city.

"Colleen, we need to do something about your living arrangements." Ever since they'd arrived at his apartment, Ian's brain had been reeling with options for them.

"Yeah, I know, but we can talk about that tomorrow. I'm beat, and right now I just don't know what we're going to do. Woody's going to be out for blood after what I did to him tonight." Colleen angled her head his way and sent him a ragged smile. "By the way, thanks for your help."

"Thank God you didn't marry him. At the least you should be entitled to child support for Katie. Hopefully he'll pay up and stay out of your lives." Ian ran a hand through his hair. It had been a hell of a day.

"Oh, Woody's not her father," Colleen said matter-of-factly.

Ian realized he'd been generalizing regarding his sister's life. "If it's not Woody, then who?"

Colleen shrugged. "I'm not real sure. I've got a few ideas, but I never followed up on any of them."

Ian nearly spit out his coffee. "How the hell could you not know the paternity of your own child?" He suddenly had the feeling he'd just jumped right back into the frying pan with both feet.

Colleen's face sobered. She sat up straight and cradled the cup in her hands. She kept her eyes downcast. "I'm pretty sure who it is, but I don't want him to know." She looked to Ian with a dead-serious gaze. "He's a loser, worse than Woody."

"Worse than Woody?" That was certainly disturbing.

"I haven't seen him in forever and don't want to. You have to understand, I was a party-girl, loved my tequila and my pot, but then I found out I was pregnant." She looked to him with tearful eyes. "Ian, it changed me. I wasn't going to be that loser anymore. Of course, I suppose in your eyes, working in a truck stop and living with Woody looks like being a loser, but I'm trying. I haven't been high or drunk since I became pregnant. I'm damn proud of that. Almost as proud of the fact that I went back to school last year and got my GED. My daughter isn't going to have a high-school dropout for a mom or be raised in a bar. I'm not my mother, if that's what you were thinking. I was using Woody for the cheap living arrangement so I could put some money away to go to school."

Ian felt a sick stab of guilt at having been absent from her life. "I wish you would have called me. I'd have helped."

"I didn't want to embarrass you."

Colleen's words stung. His heart ached for her. "I'm sorry." There was nothing more he could say.

"It's okay. You came through when I needed you most." He watched as a satisfied grin spread across Colleen's face. "You know, we didn't have it so good, you and I, but at least we both pulled ourselves out of the kind of life our parents had."

Ian set down his coffee cup and stared out at the city lights. Colleen did the same. It was an amiable silence between them now. His sister was one hell of a woman. He silently vowed to make it his mission to give them a better life. The baby sleeping down the hall would not know another night of fear if her uncle had anything to say about it. Of all the scenarios he regarded for his sister and her child, his thoughts always returned to Lucy and the camp.

"Colleen, I'm thinking we should get to bed. Tomorrow is going to be a busy day. We're going to take a trip." He took her cup.

Colleen's brows knit together as she asked, "A trip? I'm supposed to work the dinner shift. I'm not going anywhere. I need the money now that I'm through with Woody. Besides, all of our stuff is still at the apartment and Woody will probably have it locked tighter than Fort Knox. He's such an asshole."

"You're not going back there, ever. I'll buy you and Katie all the clothes and baby things you'll need. I won't have you dealing with the likes of Woody again, you can trust me on that. And you had better call Chuck, because you won't be in, not ever. We're going north. I take it you've never been to summer camp."

"Summer camp? I'm a little old for summer camp and Katie's way too young, although I'd love to send her someday. That's a weird question. Have you lost it?" She pursed her lips in a disapproving expression and backhanded the air between them. "Crap, you were supposed to be the sane member of the family."

Ian chuckled, relief flooding him. "Thought you knew me, huh? There is someone up north that I think can help all three of us. In fact, I know she can." It was so clear to him what he needed to do. Now all he had to do was convince Lucy.

****

Lucy, clad only in an oversize nightshirt and fleece shorts she'd borrowed from her sister, sat in the wicker chair in Ellie's screen porch, legs crossed and cradling a coffee cup in her hands, staring out at the Sunday morning sun dancing on the tiger lilies along the edge of the Barlow's lawn. It had been a restless night with Ellie running to the bathroom every few hours. Thankful she hadn't drunk much the night before, Lucy listened for any sound of her sister. It wasn't long, in the silence of the house, before her thoughts turned to Ian.

Just the mere thought of Ian caused her blood to race and warm prickles to play upon her skin. She'd tried to keep busy these last few weeks, pretending she wasn't hurt by his abrupt dismissal, but she couldn't. The way he'd treated her stung and as much as she'd steeled herself against an involvement with him that held any true meaning, any true emotion, she'd failed miserably. He'd gotten to her. Somehow his cool demeanor had pierced the armor of her heart, and she couldn't get him out.

The ring of the telephone interrupted the struggle with her heart. Quickly she set her coffee cup on the side table and raced to answer it before Ellie woke.

"Hello, Barlow's."

"Lucy? What are you doing there this early? Don't you have to work today?" Mother.

"Hello, Mom. I have today off. Ellie's still in bed. Do you need me to get her?" This was the last thing she needed.

"Is everything all right? She's always been my early bird."

"Everything is fine," Lucy lied.

"Well, I know it's not. I could tell by the sound of her voice the other day. I want to know what's happening and, Lucy, don't you dare sugarcoat it for me. You two have always protected each other. I want to help if I can."

Oh well, Ellie was probably going to kill her for this. "She and Randy are having a tough time of it lately."

"I knew it. I was always afraid you girls would experience what I went through. I'm so grateful I found Steve, I just want you girls to be happy too. But I don't want you to take as long as I did to find happiness."

"We'll be fine."

"I know you will, but I want you to learn from my mistakes."

"What mistakes?" Lucy's head hurt and she was not in the mood to revisit the past.

"Let's face it, you girls were on your own a lot. I wasn't exactly Mother of the Year. I regret that so much."

Lucy groaned inwardly. "Don't do this. It's not necessary."

"Yes, it is. You listen to me, Lucy. You've closed yourself off from relationships, and I feel responsible."

"You shouldn't. It was dear old Dad that screwed things up." Lucy felt her flight response kicking in. Their divorce was never a subject of conversation.

"No, it wasn't," her mother said flatly.

Lucy massaged the bridge of her nose. "What do you mean? He left us. End of story."

"Far from it. I pushed him out."

"He left with Ellie's teacher, Mom. Have you forgotten?"

"You were so young. Lucy, I was not a good wife by any means. Your father bored me to tears so I began spending time at the bars and I'm ashamed to say I had an affair."

"What?" One more revelation in this family and Lucy'd run for sure.

"He found out and couldn't forgive me. He met Ellie's teacher at church and, well, the rest is history. You never allowed him back into your life. That was wrong, and I shouldn't have allowed it to happen. Other than his running off with Miss Dyrkaz, he was a good man. You need to learn to forgive."

The sound of the French doors opening brought Lucy's thoughts to the present. Ellie came plodding through barefoot and in her pajamas. Her hair was in a shambles, and she had bags the size of Wisconsin under her eyes and a pallor to her skin that reminded Lucy of curdled milk.

Lucy pointed to the phone in her hand and mouthed "'Mom." Ellie shook her head no.

"Lucy? What's wrong?"

"Oh, nothing, except that I just found out I've based my life on a lie." The heat of anger spread through her like wildfire. "Has Ellie known this?" Ellie's eyes rounded.

"I don't know, but I want you to find someone to love like your father and I have. I've forgiven and I hope that he has too. We're not bad people, just not meant to be together. Let him into your life, Lucy. You'll be better for it."

"I'll think about it." Now she was the one feeling nauseated.

"Please do, Lucy. Love you."

"Bye, Mom." Lucy placed the receiver back in its holder and faced her sister.

"Morning." Ellie grumbled and ambled to the wicker rocking chair in the corner. She gently eased her body into it and tipped her head to rest on the back of the chair.

In a gravelly voice she asked, "What was that about?"

"Nothing important, I'll tell you later." Lucy needed time to process this new information. For now, she tucked it away.

Oh, it was sad to see her sister suffering, but it

served her right for partying her ass off without easing into a tolerance for nightlife in a more gentle fashion. "Tough night, huh?"

"Yup." Ellie drew in a deep breath of the cool morning air, and then puffed it out with an exhausted sigh. "I don't ever want to do that again. I mean it, never."

"Can I get you something? Maybe some dry toast and tea?" Lucy stood, set her cup aside, and stretched her weary muscles.

"No...well, I guess. Tea and toast should settle things down a bit."

Lucy went in to the kitchen and began preparing Ellie's breakfast when the front door sounded. She turned to see Abby come through the door followed by her father carrying a backpack and a teddy bear. Dealing with her two-timing brother-in-law was not what she'd had in mind for a relaxing Sunday morning, although Abby was a nice bonus. And for her niece's sake she'd be nice. She'd try, anyway.

"Abster, how was 'The Waters'?" She filled the teapot and set it on the burner.

"Fine, but my mom wasn't there." The little girl went directly to the refrigerator. "I want a Popsicle."

Randy set her things down at the end of the cupboard. "Not now, Sweetstuff. You just had breakfast."

"Mommy lets me." Her eyes were round with innocence.

"No, Mommy doesn't." Randy looked to Lucy. His eyes seemed to be questioning Lucy's presence and Ellie's absence. Lucy angled her head in the direction of the porch and then turned her back to him. "Abby, let's go say hello to Mommy, and then you can watch cartoons for a while, so I can talk to Mommy and Auntie Lucy."

Oh great. She was stuck in a vortex sucking her into the middle of this sorry situation. Waiting until Abby exited to the porch, she leaned nearer Randy. Speaking in a hushed tone, she said, "Excuse me, but I don't really care to hear anything a schmuck like you has to say, Randy. I hope you know how you have totally screwed up a perfectly good family."

Randy lowered his face to her level. "No one knows better than me. I can assure you of that. Now come with me, I have some things to say."

"No way." Lucy was not about to allow him to control this situation.

"Give me a chance, that's all I ask." And with that he snapped the burner off, gripped her elbow, and steered her onto the porch. Just like a man to resort to brute force when intelligence and common sense failed.

Lucy broke away from him as Abby ran between them on her way back from the porch. The television came to life as Ellie, on seeing Randy following Lucy, pushed herself up in the rocker and attempted to smooth her hair without much luck. Lucy sank into a wicker chair and waited for the unpleasantness to begin. Randy stood before them looking tanned in his khaki shorts and sage polo shirt and sandals and more than a bit nervous, which made Lucy feel a bit better.

"Ellie, honey, what happened? Are you sick?" He knelt before Ellie, resting his hands on the arms of the rocker. Lucy groaned at his attempt at concern and sent a glare of annoyance at Randy. Ellie stiffened at the closeness of his proximity, as did Lucy, watching for any unkind touch on his part. She'd gladly rip him to shreds in defense of her sister.

Ellie didn't appear to be fooled for a moment. "Don't 'Ellie honey' me. Just keep your distance."

"Can I get you something? Do you think it's the flu?" The concern in his voice was nearly believable.

Lucy couldn't keep her mouth shut. "It's not the flu, she's hung over." Randy's eyes nearly bugged out of his head as he swung his gaze between the two of them. Lucy couldn't help but rub it in, really she couldn't. "Yes, that's right. Your wife is hung over. We went out on the town and had a great time. We danced and drank the night away. She's finally getting out and having a little fun. Something that's been sorely missing from her life thanks to you."

Ellie cradled her head in both hands and groaned. "Thanks, Lucy, just thanks a lot."

Randy stood. "You drank too much? That's not like you at all, but"—he turned his eyes on Lucy—"it's just what I'd expect from you. Don't you dare corrupt Ellie."

When Lucy grabbed the arms of the chair and

pretended to come at him, Randy flinched. "And I, I mean we, didn't expect you to go nosing around Miss Big-Hair." She flung a hand over her head to dramatize. "Be very careful when you're throwing around the insults, because at the moment, none of us have ever screwed up as badly as you."

Randy's demeanor suddenly changed. "You're right." He sank into a chair in the corner of the porch, bit the inside of his lip, and suddenly looked exhausted.

Ellie spoke up. "I don't want any fighting this morning. I don't have the stomach for it, so if you two could please stop, I'd appreciate it."

Both mumbled, "Sorry." Truly, Lucy did not want to add any rancor to the situation for Ellie's sake.

"Now." Ellie straightened her shoulders and took a deep breath. "Did you and Abby have a good time?"

Randy shrugged. "Not really."

Ellie leveled a disbelieving look upon him. "How can you go wrong with a water park and a six-year-old?" She shook her head, and then winced. "Honestly, a water park. Short of the water being turned off, I can't imagine it being a bust."

"She missed her mother. We both did." He leaned his elbows on his knees and hung his head.

"Oh, come on." Lucy just couldn't seem to keep her mouth shut.

Ellie gave her a pleading look. "Please, Lucy."

Randy was clearly annoyed. "You know, Lucy, I wanted you to be here because you've always been family to me, but I've changed my mind. Don't you have somewhere you need to be?"

Lucy stood before them. "You know, I do. Ellie, are you okay with him here?"

"We're fine. Where are you going?"

"To open my graduation gift." She turned to leave.

"Your what?"

"I'll explain later."

****

Back at her house, Lucy took the small, neatly wrapped box from the shelf in her closet. She blew the dust off the top as she took it into the living room. She sat for a few moments and stared at the silver box and burgundy bow in her hand as the sounds of Butternut Creek filtered in from the street. Why had she kept it this long? Any other gift he'd sent her was given to the Christian Mission.

Carefully she loosened the paper and slid it off, letting it fall to the floor. She opened the white gift box and extracted the blue box inside. Opening the lid, she found a gold chain with a charm in the shape of a giraffe.

Tears immediately stung her eyes as memories unfolded. Her favorite childhood toy had been an ugly, yellow giraffe. She'd carried it with her everywhere until she'd entered kindergarten. He'd remembered.

Wiping the tears from her eyes, she reached for the phone book and, after finding the number, dialed. The voice on the other end felt like a comfortable blanket thrown over her shoulders.

"Dad, it's Lucy." She'd never known forgiveness could taste so sweet.

****

A maelstrom of emotion assailed Ian as he parked the rented minivan in front of Lucy's house. First of all, to be driving a minivan loaded with baby items, an actual baby, and his sister was incredible enough to comprehend. Now he was about to confront Lucy with his family and plead his case.

He cut the motor and angled his head to get a better view. Toty was in the yard; the windows and the front door were open. She had to be here.

Colleen stirred in the bucket seat across from him. She stretched and began to yawn, but Ian stopped her with a motion of his head toward the backseat. They both turned to see Katie, head crooked to the side and sound asleep in her car seat, chubby arms wrapped loosely around a brand new teddy bear. A wreath of curls spilled around the face, so serene in slumber. They smiled at each other as they turned back toward the front.

"This the place?" Colleen seemed to be studying the house and the neighborhood. "Looks nice. Kind of Norman Rockwell-looking, you know what I mean?"

Ian smiled at her attempt at description. "It is. There isn't much that rocks this little town." Except a developer threatening to ruin it all, he thought ruefully.

"You sure this friend of yours will help us?" Colleen eyed him suspiciously.

That was the question of the day. "She will." He wished he felt as confident.

Ian left Colleen and Katie in the van while he crossed the yard. No need to wake the child just yet. His footsteps creaked across the porch. He could see inside through the screen door. Country music blared from somewhere inside along with the whirr of a vacuum cleaner.

He knocked once. No response except the voice of some country singer telling him "my give a damn's busted." Not a good sign.

He knocked harder. Still nothing.

He opened the screen door and slipped inside. She was not in the living room or the dining room. The kitchen was empty as well. He found her in the bedroom, the room they'd shared that one torrid night, pushing the vacuum and swinging her backside to the beat of the music. The sight caused a thrum of appreciation to warm his loins and spread through him like wildfire. The sight of the bed and the memories it evoked brought a flood of sensory recognition. The taste of her, the scent, the feel of her body against his. He had to fight the urge to step behind her, place both hands on her derriere, and teach her to enjoy the rhythm in a whole new way.

Unfortunately, there was no time for that sweet possibility. There were more important issues at hand than the effect she had on him and the glory the satisfaction of that fantasy would bring.

"Lucy," he said over the noise, then promptly jumped back as she shrieked and bolted from the shock of his voice behind her. The vacuum hit the underside of the dresser with such force that an old lamp with an elaborate glass base came toppling off. Lucy dove to catch it, and Ian dove to catch her when she lost her balance. Together, they landed on the bed.

Absolute venom was the only description for the look she gave him. She elbowed him in the ribs, jumped off the bed and wrestled the lamp out of his hands. She stood before him with the lamp on her hip, and for a brief moment he was concerned she might pitch it at him.

"Ian, what the hell..." Her breasts rose and fell with

each deep breath she took. Graceful wisps of hair strayed from her ponytail as fire danced in her eyes, and her face took on a gorgeous shade of red. Ian enjoyed her attempt to appear unshaken at the sight of him. It was rare, he guessed, that Lucy Mitchell was taken by surprise. She placed the lamp on the floor and bent over the vacuum. He watched as she yanked it out from under the dresser and snapped the motor off.

"Do you know that you scared the living hell out of me?" She angled her head and gaped at him. "What happened to you?"

Ian touched the swelling under his right eye. "I ran into a door." He pushed himself up from the bed and stood before her, trying not to laugh for the look on her face. "Sorry, I didn't mean to startle you."

She looked so good to him in her torn and stained Wisconsin Badgers sweatshirt and fleece shorts. She must have mowed the lawn, because she smelled wonderfully of fresh-cut grass.

"Sorry? That's all you have to say?" Her brows completed a v over her fiery eyes. "You broke into my house, I'm calling the cops."

"Calm down. I wouldn't call it breaking in. The door was open."

"We may be more lax here than in the city, but you don't go entering people's homes without knocking. That's just plain rude." She looked so cute with her nostrils flaring, the steely set of her jaw, and the pretty little pout to her lips. He simply couldn't help himself. He kissed her. And she slapped him.

"What the hell was that for?" Christ, she had some power behind that slap. The whole side of his face stung. He flexed his jaw in response.

"For breaking into my house and then thinking you could kiss me. Typical male thought process. Did you really think you could just lay a kiss on me and everything will be just fine? I'm not that easy." She pushed him and he lost his balance and fell back onto the bed.

With a finger pointed toward the front door, she said, "Leave, Ian. I don't want you here and I have nothing to say to you."

This was getting to be exhausting. Not only did he get up at the crack of dawn to find a rental van, he also had to take his sister and Katie shopping for clothes and all the baby paraphernalia they needed. He'd spent nearly six hours on the road, and now the woman he loved was repeatedly accosting him. Yes, loved. That was becoming clearer to him with every moment that passed since he'd left her. The hostility he'd been met with was completely unclear. Sure, he'd surprised her and she obviously didn't like surprises, but most people would be over that by now.

"Lucy." He reached for her arm, but she avoided him. "Where is this animosity coming from?"

"Animosity?" If looks could kill, he'd be drawn, quartered, and ground into pieces. "Cut the big words. How about pissed off?" When he didn't answer her right away, she nodded as though trying to make a small child understand. "Yes, Ian, "pissed off" is the correct description."

"Okay, I give. Why are you pissed off at me?" He crossed the room and stood before her.

"For leaving." Suddenly her eyes lost that hawklike quality of a "pissed-off woman" and she allowed a hint of vulnerability to appear.

"Leaving?" He had all he could do to hide the smile that wanted to break across his face. Lucy Mitchell cared for him. She missed him. As quickly as the brief show of vulnerability broke through, it was gone.

"Yes. You left the morning after our night together by the lake without so much as a goodbye, thanks for the roll under the pines, nothing." She threw the words at him with such force, he was uncertain how to respond, but slowly he understood. In the rush to reach the scene of his parents' demise, he hadn't said goodbye, hadn't told anyone the circumstances, and he knew he'd left her feeling abandoned. Not a good move considering his current circumstance. Even Ian Flynn, famous for remaining aloof, unaffected and his heart impenetrable, understood her anger and her hurt.

"Lucy, let me explain."

To his surprise, she gave him a shove backwards and advanced on him pointing a finger in his chest. "I'll bet you can explain, no let me do it for you. You thought you'd get a final, shall we say, lay of the land, before getting the hell out of here and going back to your cushy life in the city. Tell me, Ian, did you laugh all the way back? You got yourself some backwoods action and then left. To hell with the upheaval you caused in my life. To hell with me."

He grabbed her by the wrist and hauled her to his chest. "Lucy, you don't know what you do to me. I apologize for leaving so abruptly, but I thought of you constantly."

"I'll bet you did." She pushed at him with her free hand, which he promptly grabbed. He brought both of her hands behind her back holding her against him. His face was just above hers.

"I need you, Lucy." He could feel her breasts against him, the rise and fall of her breathing and he felt himself stir in response. All he wanted was to sink into her, let her engulf him, feel the comfort of her arms, her mouth on his, drown in the essence of her.

The feel of her against him and the sweet smell of that grass was too much. He'd missed her too much. He wanted comfort and he wanted that comfort to come from Lucy. So he kissed her again, hard this time.

She pulled her mouth from him and struggled once again. "Ian, I'm so angry with you."

"Be angry, be happy, be smelly, I don't care. Just be with me." With that, he gained her full attention.

"Smelly?" Her body relaxed and her eyes questioned.

"Just go with it, I'm trying to be romantic here."

"Well, you're sucking at it, and I refuse to be so casually thrown aside."

She could throw any insult at him, and it wouldn't matter. His heart was soaring with the nearness of her. He could no more stop the next words from leaving his mouth than he could prevent his heart from beating.

"I love you, Lucy. I do." It felt so good to say those words. He didn't wait for her response. He lowered his mouth to hers.

Chapter Thirteen

Lucy allowed Ian to kiss her simply because she was too shocked to respond otherwise. *He loved her.* What kind of bull was this? She didn't believe him for one solitary minute.

She did have to admit it felt good to have him back in her arms. Oh hell, who was she kidding? It was glorious, intoxicating. She closed her eyes, her knees went weak, and she pressed against him.

Against her mouth, in a whisper he said, "God, I've missed you, Lucy." He released her hands, and she moved her palms up the sides of his arms, feeling the swell of muscle there before curving to cup the back of his head.

His hands caressed her back, pressing her against him.

Her brain was dizzy and her heart reeling. How can this possibly be? She opened her eyes slightly, and, yes, Ian was kissing her with all the intensity of someone actually in love. She loved him too.

Suddenly something small, warm, and moist clutched her leg. Lucy gasped.

Ian's eyes widened. "What?"

"What's that?" Lucy whispered as she cautiously looked down into the wide eyes of a cherub, complete with curls and rosy cheeks. Now she knew she was dreaming. Ian broke into a chuckle that shook his chest. The baby looked up at them with an angelic smile and dimpled cheeks.

Lucy tore her eyes from the baby to Ian. Somehow he didn't seem all that surprised. Lucy studied him a moment.

"Hi, sweets." Ian grinned down at the child, to which she made a happy, garbling sound and clutched Lucy's leg more snuggly.

Lucy slanted her eyes toward him. "You've been busy while you were gone." *Let's see him explain this.*

Before he could answer, a female voice interrupted. "So this is what's taking you so long." Lucy angled her head. There in the doorway of the bedroom stood a young woman with an amused grin on her face. The woman certainly didn't look like Ian's type, although Lucy thought wryly, she probably wasn't his type either.

What kind of twisted situation was this? Ian shows up on her doorstep, confesses his undying love, and then presents her with a wife and baby? This was just too weird.

Ian continued to hold her in his arms. She angled her head nearer his. "Talk fast, Ian, because you may not live beyond this room."

Ian touched his lips to her cheek. "Lucy, I want you to meet my sister."

No way could this be Ian's sister. She didn't resemble him one bit.

"Sorry Katie interrupted you." The female came forward, picked up the child and bounced her on one hip. One side of her mouth drew up in a smile. "Go ahead, finish what you started. We'll just wait outside." She winked at Ian.

Lucy shifted her eyes in his direction. There was a resemblance in the eyes now that she studied them closer. This was so confusing.

Ian kept an arm circled around her as he spoke. Lucy continued to study the intruders. "Lucy, I'd like you to meet my sister Colleen and her daughter, Katie Rose." At the sound of her name, the child pointed a drooly finger his way and said, "Uncky."

Colleen kept her eyes on the child. "I think that's Katie's version of 'Uncle Ian.'" The child tilted her curly head into her mother's shoulder and smiled up at them. It was a look of pure innocence, and Lucy couldn't resist smiling back at her.

"She's beautiful." Lucy touched a finger to Katie's chubby arm. The child's mouth curved to a wide smile revealing tiny, white pegs of teeth as she circled Lucy's finger with her wet hand. The light in the child's blue eyes seemed to spread about the room and engulf them all, wrapping them securely in the purity of her innocence.

Katie opened her mouth, stuck out her tongue and promptly blew out her cheeks and sent a spray of spit accompanied by a farting sound ending the rapture. Lucy wiped her face with the palm of her hand while the little girl giggled freely.

"Katie Rose," Colleen chided. "I'm sorry. She's just learned to do that and thinks she's pretty funny."

"That's okay." Lucy looked to Ian, who was stifling a grin.

Colleen wiped Katie's mouth with a tissue from her pocket. "I haven't decided yet if that's disgusting or cute. I'm kinda new at this motherhood stuff."

Ian placed a hand on Colleen's arm. "Can you give Lucy and me a few minutes?"

Lucy wasn't sure she trusted her heart to be alone with Ian so soon after his profession of love for her. "You can sit on the porch if you like," she said to Colleen. "I can offer you some iced tea or water."

"That would be great. Thanks. But finish what you started." She chuckled as they left the room.

"I'll be back," Lucy said to Ian.

She settled both Colleen and Katie on the front porch, Colleen with her glass of iced tea and a cup of milk and a cracker for Katie. She found a stuffed dog Abby had left and took it to Katie before heading back to find Ian. He was sitting in the backyard on an Adirondack chair she'd rescued from a garage sale. He smiled when he saw her coming.

"Ian, you've got some explaining to do." She stood before him, hands on her hips.

Ian's face became serious. "I need your help."

"With all your high-powered friends, you need my help. I can't see it." Red flags were popping up all over the place.

"Colleen has gotten herself in a bad situation with a man, and I'm trying to help her out of it. She's my sister, Katie's my niece. I couldn't very well leave them in the dire straits where I found them."

"What do you expect me to do? Don't get me wrong, that's a beautiful little girl and your sister seems nice, but I don't know what I can do for them." Her heart was sinking with each moment. He needed a favor. Did he profess his love for favors often?

Ian raked a hand through his dark hair, and for the first time, Lucy saw exhaustion in his eyes.

"Really, Ian, I don't know what I can do. I don't know that I'm the right person for this."

"Don't you see?" His voice was tinged with anger, or was it desperation? "You're the perfect person to help them."

"Me?" Lucy spread her arms. She didn't have much to offer, not compared to the life he led.

"Lucy, you provide safety and happiness every day for the kids of the camp. It's the kind of existence I want for Katie. I want her to feel safe, to run barefoot under the pines, learn to swim in a lake, feel the sun upon her little face and know she's loved. Those simple things every child should have, I want for her." He turned away from her for a moment, and she felt certain he was trying to gain control of his emotions.

"The question remains, what do you want from me?"

"Could they stay with you for a while?"

"With me? Oh, I don't..."

"You have more bedrooms upstairs, don't you? They won't be a financial burden, I'll see to that. Also, I spoke with Lida on my way up, and she's willing to give Colleen a job in the kitchen."

"Lida knows about this?" It was a conspiracy.

"Yes, and she's grateful for the help. Colleen's a wonderful cook."

"Who will take care of Katie?" Summer was coming to a close, and before long she'd be readying herself for the school year ahead.

"Lida said she could hook them up with the day care run by her church. Please say yes, Lucy. This will mean a whole new life for them. I promise. She needs to get out of the city for awhile, away from her boyfriend. It's only until she can catch her breath."

Lucy considered his request. "Where are you going to be in all this?" she asked, determined not to be ruled by her heart.

"I'm sorry, but I'm leaving right away. I have meetings to attend in Madison tomorrow. These are some of the most important meetings of my life. I'm asking you to trust me."

Lucy dismissed his last statement. Now her role in this was becoming all too clear. She was going to bale him out with his family while he jaunted off to his life in the city.

"Do I look that stupid to you?" Tight knots of anger worked through her.

"I don't understand..."

"You heard me. You kiss me, profess your love, then leave me your sister and her baby to care for. I'm no one's doormat. Especially not yours." Her stomach clutched and tears threatened. "I mean it, Ian. Is this the real reason you came back?"

"Of course not. Trust me, Lucy. I do love you. I love you more than you know. I'm trying to fix the future for all of us. I promise." He stood before her and placed hands on both her arms, pulled her to him, and kissed her forehead. "I'll be back as soon as I can." She watched as he reached into his wallet and stuffed a fistful of money into her hands. She looked down to see a wad of hundreds.

"What's this, a payoff?" How much more insulting could he be? She balled her fist and thought of throwing it back in his face.

"No, it's money to help with groceries and whatever Colleen and Katie need."

Lucy looked at the bills in her hand. "They must be big eaters." She closed her hand over the bills and pushed them back at him. "Don't give it to me. If this is for Colleen, then give it to her."

"Just keep it." He ignored her hand. "I have to leave now or I'll never make it back by morning."

As hurt as she was, she still worried about him. "You can't drive all the way back today, it's not safe." Stupid man.

Her answer was a brief brush of his lips on hers. "Goodbye, Lucy. I'll be back as soon as I can." And with that, he turned and left her standing alone, feeling completely confused, used; and the knot welling in her throat threatened to burst at any provocation.

From the front of the house, she listened as he said goodbye to his sister and niece. When she heard the bang of the screen door, she plodded to the porch. Colleen was

Moonlight Bay

holding Katie on her lap, coaxing the little one to wave bye-bye to her uncle. As she approached, Colleen smiled her way. Lucy reached the open door just as a minivan disappeared down the treelined street.

"Thanks, Lucy." Colleen smiled at her.

Lucy continued to stare at the empty street. "I haven't done anything."

"You've given us a chance, and I won't make you sorry. I promise." Lucy had heard those words only moments before.

Katie began a singsong of sounds and began to clap. "She's singing us a song," Colleen explained. "Yay, Katie." She bounced the baby enthusiastically while Katie clapped chubby hands together and squealed with glee.

Lucy couldn't help but smile at the two of them. She may have just been dumped by Colleen's brother, but she would do whatever she could to help Katie and her mother. If she had anything to say about it, someone here was getting a better shake out of life. Too bad it wasn't her.

****

The next few days passed companionably as Lucy and Colleen developed a friendship. Incorporating a child into her home was enjoyable, and for the first time, Lucy felt as though her house became a real home, not just a place to eat and sleep. Katie was a joy and Lucy found herself drawn to simply watching every move the toddler made. Seeing the world through the innocence of a child was rejuvenating.

Colleen proved herself a capable, energetic worker with a real talent for the kitchen. Within a few days, she found many ways to lighten Lida's load, and Lida, overjoyed at having company in her kitchen, allowed Colleen the freedom to experiment with some of the recipes that had long been staples of the camp.

Evenings found Lucy and Colleen cross-legged in the grass behind Lucy's house, sharing conversation along with a glass of iced tea or lemonade while they watched Katie explore.

On this particular evening, they were joined in the backyard by Ellie and Abby. The women sat on a quilt spread on the grass. Ellie had brought a bottle of Door

Peninsula Plum Wine and fluted glasses along with Brie and crackers. While they sipped and ate, Abby followed Katie around the yard, picking dandelions and chasing butterflies as the early evening sunshine streaked across the yard.

"Look, Mommy," Abby called, "she wants to eat the dandelion."

"Oh no," Colleen said, "she can't have that." She began to rise but was waved back by Ellie.

"Abby, just take it gently away from her." Ellie sipped and watched lovingly as Abby's little hand closed over Katie's chubby one. Katie relinquished the flower easily enough, and giggled, thinking it a game between them.

Abby was enjoying her role as substitute big sister. "See." She held the flower up. "I got it from her."

"Good job, Ab," Lucy said. Katie waddled across the yard, a large dandelion in her sights. Abby sighed heavily, threw the dandelion away, and followed, shaking her head as she went. The women shared a smile at Abby's self-importance as Katie's caretaker.

"She really is a cutie, Colleen. Such a happy baby. It's easy to see you've done a good job with her." Ellie stretched her toes into the cool of the grass.

Colleen finished her wine. "I almost screwed everything up because of the ass...excuse me, jerk, I lived with. Thanks to Ian, we're on the right track now."

"Sorry," Lucy ventured, "but I have a tough time seeing him as the attentive big brother."

"Lucy." Ellie leveled a warning on her. "Be nice."

"Just an honest observation." Lucy swirled her wine.

Colleen grinned. "And you'd be right about that. I hardly knew who my brother was until the last few weeks. Too bad it took the shooting to bring us together." Colleen smiled and waved at her daughter as Katie danced a dandelion up and down at them.

"What?" Lucy and Ellie nearly spilled their wine as they simultaneously jumped at the mention of a shooting. "What shooting? What happened?" Lucy asked.

The smile slid from Colleen's face. "You don't know?"

Both of them shook their heads.

Colleen narrowed her gaze upon Lucy. "After the lip-lock I witnessed between you two, I'd have thought he told you everything."

Lucy felt her face color at that. "Ian doesn't share much of himself with me. I've just been along for the ride, so to speak. In fact, I didn't think I'd see him ever again, and then he shows up in my house without so much as a word. I've stopped trying to figure him out. Life's a lot easier that way."

"I can see that. He's not exactly an open book."

Ellie recovered enough to ask, "What happened?"

Colleen was introspective a moment. "My mother shot my father and then killed herself."

Lucy felt as though the lawn had just opened and swallowed her whole. As the words began to register in her brain, flashes of horrible scenes unfolded before her. Whatever the circumstances, it was a tragic legacy for a family to bear. Ian, so reserved, so self-assured. What was he feeling inside? A shock of this magnitude would most certainly have a jarring affect to the very core of a person's soul.

As she listened to Colleen's heart-wrenching story, she could only think of Ian and Colleen, her newly found friend, and little Katie. Would she ever have to bear the sting of this terrible thing?

By the time Colleen had finished, all three were wiping tears from their eyes. Ellie knelt beside Colleen and hugged her as Abby came and stood before them. Katie was bending over a butterfly.

"How come Katie's mom is crying? Is she sick or something?" Abby's brows came together, and she scrunched up her nose.

"No, sweetie. She told us a sad story, but it's okay." Ellie patted her arm. "Go play now." To Colleen she said, "You and Katie will be fine. You're with us, and we'll see to it you both have a good chance here."

"How did Ian react to all this?" Lucy hated to pry, but she had to ask. As angry as she was with him, she was curious whether he was able to let his guard down in the face of tragedy. "I mean, he doesn't strike me as, well," she said, feeling stupid for asking. "He just doesn't seem like he'd be comforting. I'm sorry, I don't mean to..."

Colleen dabbed her eyes with the bottom hem of her

shirt. "It's okay, I know what you mean. It's funny, but he's been there for me every step of the way. I was a freakin' mess with all this. Dealing with cops and the dude at the funeral home and taking care of their bills and all. I didn't know which way to turn first, and then Ian showed up. He took over." She dipped her head. "I know that doesn't surprise you, but he took care of everything. Even though we didn't have it so good as kids, he gave them a proper funeral, paid for everything, even signed the house over to Katie and me. We listed it for sale. I couldn't really see raising my daughter where her grandparents, well, you know."

Lucy and Ellie nodded sympathetically.

"Anyway, I really need the money. Of course, every time I go to spend a penny, Ian's there with all his money. He's really loaded. Anyway I think I'll use the money to buy a house here." She took a sip of her wine.

"That's wonderful," Ellie said. "We love having you here."

"I think this would be a good little town to raise Katie. The people seem real nice, and I like my job a lot. It's so cool to be around all those kids. Ian wants me to go to school this winter. He says you have a technical college close by. Says he'll pay for it if I go. I'd really like to be a chef some day. Anyway, I guess a girl can't pass up an opportunity like that."

There was so much more to this man than Lucy realized. Lo and behold, there was a generous heart beating inside that muscular chest. A warm prickle spread in her belly as she thought of him and wondered where he was this beautiful evening.

"Looks like all that's missin' here is a good man to entertain all these women." The slow, smooth voice from behind drew their heads around. "I'm thinkin' I showed up just in time." Shooter was leaning against the porch rail, his muscled arms supporting the bulk of his weight as he leaned over the rail.

Lucy turned to look at the other two. "Look what the cat dragged in."

"Hey, Shooter." Ellie waved his way, to which Shooter gave her a wink. "It's been a while."

"I hate to barge in on you, ladies." He sauntered off

the porch and crossed the grass. "But I've got something for Luce."

"It's my lucky day." Lucy wasn't all that unhappy to see him, but now it was something akin to seeing an old friend. A dear old friend. "This is my ex-boyfriend, Shooter."

"And who might this be?" Shooter's eyes warmed at the sight of Colleen.

Lucy pulled her legs beneath her and gestured toward Colleen, amused at the light in his eyes. "Colleen, this is Shooter Lushinski. Shooter, this is Colleen Flynn, and over there is her daughter Katie Rose."

"Shooter, hmm, I like that." Colleen grinned up at him, and a blush kissed her dimpled cheeks.

"Nice eyes." Shooter winked at her. "Cute kid."

Lucy rolled her eyes. "Ugh...you're so smooth, Shooter."

"What?" He pretended to be insulted before he bent to take Colleen's hand, which he shook in a leisurely way.

Ellie giggled. "You always were something, Shooter. I just don't quite know what."

"El, I'll take that as a compliment."

"To what do we owe the pleasure of your company?" Lucy asked. "Or are you just cruising for chicks?"

"I found your Toby Keith CD in my truck. You want it back?" He couldn't seem to take his eyes off Colleen.

"Of course, I want my Toby back."

"Good. I left it on your hall table. Hey, Colleen..." He sat beside her on the quilt.

Lucy found this thoroughly amusing. "Would you like a glass of wine?" She held her glass high.

"No, I, well..." He angled his head to get a view of her left hand. "Are you married?"

Colleen giggled. "No." She wiggled her fingers before him to prove the absence of a ring.

Shooter rubbed his palms on his jeans. "Here's the thing. I've got this wedding to go to next Saturday. Would you like to go with me?"

Colleen took a sip of her wine. "Sure."

Shooter broke out in a smile that stretched from ear to ear. "Great. If I can have your number, I'll call you."

"I'm staying right here, with Lucy."

"Really?" Shooter's eyes questioned Lucy, but before she could answer, Katie toddled up before them, pointing toward the house and repeating "Uncky."

****

"Uncky." Ian's heart melted at Katie's announcement of his arrival. He waved at the little girl who gave him a wide smile and bent to pick a dandelion.

"Ian, you're back." Colleen called to him. "My brother," she explained to her admirer, as Ellie waved a hand in welcome.

Lucy's head turned slowly, her eyes widened slightly. "Ian." A slow smile lit her face. Then she saw Jonah step around him. "Jonah, what are you doing here?"

Jonah hitched a thumb toward Ian. "He finally gave me a ride in his car. It was pretty cool." The grin on his freckled face was all the thanks Ian required.

"He snuck out with permission this time. Lida said he could come with me." God, it felt so good to speak with her. His heart was so full that he feared it wouldn't be able to hold the depth of love he felt.

Ian descended the stairs to the lawn. His heart soared with every step toward her. He had to do this right. He needed to slow down.

"Ellie, good to see you." He stopped at the edge of the quilt and nodded to Lucy's sister.

"Hello, Ian. Good to see you too." She smiled gleefully at Lucy. Lucy looked demurely away from them. An expression Ian had never seen from her.

"I hope your life is going well these days, Ellie." This small talk was killing him.

"It is. Randy and I are still separated, but we're working it out with the help of a counselor."

"Wonderful." He wiped his clammy palms on his shorts. Time to meet his future. He tapped Lucy on the top of her head.

Slowly she raised her eyes to him.

"Hi."

"Hi," she answered.

He knelt beside her. "I have something I want to tell you."

Lucy set her glass on the grass and pushed her body around to face him. He so wanted to gather her in his arms.

"Lucy, I'm going to come right out and say this. I'm retiring, in a sense. I've sold my company to WisFirst, out of Green Bay, and bought the camp for myself."

"You what?" The look on her face was one of complete incredulity.

"You heard me. WisFirst has made me offers in the past and it seemed time to take them up on it. Moonlight Bay is going to remain a camp for kids." He ran his hands up her arms.

Lucy shook her head as though the words he was telling her would not take hold.

"Ian, I don't believe it. You told me there was absolutely no way that would happen. Why would you do this?" Her eyes were beginning to tear.

He and Colleen shared a brief smile. "Life has a way of pointing you in directions you never would have dreamed. So, believe it, Lucy. The camp will remain, and you're going to help me run it." He took her hands in his. "All those ideas you had for keeping it afloat were brilliant, and we're going to do it, you and I. We'll update the lodge and open it for dining and meetings all year round. We're going to winterize some of the cabins and open the place up to families and youth groups through the winter months. There will be skating on the lake and sledding and tubing on the south hill and cross-country skiing through the forest. We'll have bonfires at night and holiday parties in the lodge. Colleen, what do you say, you want to be our cook?" A knot the size of Balsam Lake was forming in his throat.

"Hey, I'm up for it. You know it."

Jonah joined in. "Ian says I could be a counselor some day. Just like you, Lucy. 'Course I don't want no naughty kids. Only the good ones."

They all laughed at that.

"I don't know what to say." He watched a tear spill over one cheek and bent to kiss it. The taste of her, the smell of her hair intoxicated him from the top of his head to the tips of his toes.

Ellie chimed in, "Say yes, Lucy. This is your dream. This is a dream for all of us."

Lucy remained speechless, staring up at him with

watery, grateful eyes.

"Are you sufficiently surprised?" he whispered against her skin.

"I'm shocked. Ian, I can't get over this." She wrapped her arms around him, plying his lips and cheeks with kisses. Until they lost their balance and tumbled onto the quilt in a heap.

Laughing, Ian cupped her face in his hands. "Well, hold on because there's more." He stood and pulled her up before him.

"More? Ian, I don't need anything more for the rest of my life. Truly, I don't."

"Well, I do." He swallowed the knot in his throat and took a deep breath to steady his nerves. "The most important part of the equation."

"What's that?"

He pulled a small box from his pants' pocket.

"Wow," Ellie gasped and covered her mouth with her hands.

"Oh my Lord," Colleen exclaimed and began to giggle and clap.

"Lucy." Gently he opened the box to reveal the largest diamond ring he could find. "Will you marry me?" He searched her eyes for a sign that he hadn't completely misread her feelings. "I love you and I want to make a life with you."

"No." She shook her head in fast, short clips. "No."

He felt his heart plummet and his knees weaken. Ellie and Colleen both echoed her "no" with a completely different meaning, and Shooter said, "Well, shit."

Lucy covered his hands with hers and closed the tiny box he held. "Ian, you couldn't possibly be happy stuck in a camp for kids away from the fast pace of the city and all your important deals."

"I wasn't happy there. I haven't known what happiness was, ever." He looked at the box in his hands. "Colleen and Katie have shown me what family means. I want family and I want you to be part of my family." Now he felt the tears threaten. "Do you believe it? I want the chance to teach a kid to fish and swim in a lake and paddle a canoe. I want to build on what is there, with respect for the past and look to preserve that for the future."

Lucy took his face in her hands. "I'm sorry, Ian. This is too drastic a step for you. I can't marry you until I know without a doubt that this is what you want and where you want to be." A tear trickled down her cheek. "I can't."

"I guess I didn't stop to consider that maybe you don't love me." He swallowed hard and tried to continue. "Just like me to charge ahead with my own agenda."

Lucy covered his hands and the tiny box in hers once again. "I do love you, Ian. I haven't been able to think about anyone else, but..." This time she was the one who struggled for clarity. "I want to be sure. I need to see for myself that the camp and those kids mean something to you. And I need to see that this isn't some momentary lapse in judgment, although I think that rarely happens for you." She smiled up at him through her tears. "Like I told you once before, this isn't over, Flynn—not by a long shot."

He wrapped his arms around her and said, "I'll hold you to that."

Epilogue

One year later:

A cooling breeze danced over the waves of Balsam Lake as the moon cast a milky shimmer upon the black, mirroring the stars above. Overhead the pines sighed and the birch rustled while ferns dressed the forest floor with a lacy spread. Campfire smoke wafted on the breath of evening and all was right in the world. Lucy Mitchell's world, that was.

She leaned against the stark white of a birch trunk and watched as Ian put the last screw into the new screen door on Willow cabin. A wisp of her hair touched the side of her face and she wiped it aside.

"This would have been a lot easier if we'd have remembered a flashlight." Ian worked with his nose as close to the new hinge as possible to see the small screws. Just then the screwdriver slipped and poked him in the cheek. "Damn it all to hell." His words echoed.

Lucy hurried forward and inspected his cheek in the moonlight. "Looks like you'll live, but"—she bit the inside of her mouth to keep from laughing—"that's going to leave a mark."

Ian rubbed his face and puffed out a weary sigh. "Why not. Now I've got something to go with the bruise on my ribs after falling off Beaver. Don't know why I thought I could shingle a roof."

Lucy let loose with a chuckle. He looked so cute, she couldn't resist. Rising on tiptoes, she dusted his lips with a kiss. "Hiring out is a good thing, isn't it?"

"Yeah." He chuckled. "A very good thing."

"This place is shaping up. I'm proud of you."

"It's been quite a year." With a look of pure satisfaction, he glanced at the new door.

"And it's not over yet. I didn't tell you I received the templates of the new menus for this fall." Her heart expanded in her chest as she visualized all that was to come. "Quite impressive, although there's one that stands out, making it an easy choice."

Ian gathered her in his arms. "I've come to appreciate those easy choices. And, darlin', you were the easiest of all."

He bent to kiss her deeply.

"I love you, Ian," she whispered against his ear.

A noise in the trees startled them.

"Hey." Jonah sauntered toward them. "Jule's got us all singin' by the fire again so I snuck away. I think I'll stay here with you guys if ya stop that kissin' crap. Promise?" He stared them down like a schoolmarm with her errant students.

Lucy giggled as she turned and leaned back into Ian's sturdy form. Ian reached out and ruffed the boy's hair.

"Right now, Jonah, all I can promise you is that life is full of surprises. All you have to do is open your heart and you get a life. It's as easy as that." Ian kissed her neck and she closed her eyes for a moment to drink in the warmth of him against her.

She leaned her head back and kissed his cheek. "Amen to that." She held out her hand and watched the glint of the moon upon her engagement ring.

"Remember when you told me to 'get a life'?" she asked, keeping her eyes on the bauble on her finger.

"Don't remind me." He chuckled again.

"Well, I've got one." She smiled up at him. "I feel like I've got the whole world right here with you."

"Aw geez, guess I'll go back and sing." Jonah disappeared into the trees, leaving them to each other.

And somewhere in the distance, two loons glided into the ribbon of moonlight and sang into the night.

A word about the author...

My love of reading began when my mother introduced me to *Black Beauty* followed by *Little Women* and my father recommended *Caddie Woodlawn*. My love of writing began when I read a book, can't remember the name anymore, and absolutely hated the ending. It bothered me so much, I rewrote the last chapter. Challenging myself to write that chapter opened a whole new world for me.

I was born and raised in the same community in northern Wisconsin that I reside now with my husband, four dogs and one vagabond cat. I spend my spare time tending the vegetable, strawberry, herb and flower gardens that surround our cottage in the woods. We have two grown sons, a beautiful daughter-in-law, and two grandchildren who fill our lives with fun. I am a member of Midwest Fiction Writers, Romance Writers of America, and a past member of WisRWA. The members of MFW have been my mentors, inspiration and friends. Dare to dream—you never know.

Thank you for purchasing
this Wild Rose Press publication.
For other wonderful stories of romance,
please visit our on-line bookstore at
www.thewildrosepress.com.

For questions or more information,
contact us at info@thewildrosepress.com.

The Wild Rose Press
www.TheWildRosePress.com

Printed in the United States
114020LV00001B/4/P

9 781601 540201